ABOUT THE AUTHOR

Roger Corke is a TV journalist who has travelled the world, producing and directing documentaries for series like ITV's *World in Action*, BBC's *Panorama* and Channel 4's *Dispatches*.

He lives with his wife, Lynn, in Oxfordshire.

Deadly Protocol is his debut novel.

Thanks to…

Many people have made this book possible and encouraged me along the way. Mandy Little has believed in it since she first read it. So have Joanna Frank and Simon Berthon.

Dr Jane Stevens is a former consultant haematologist whose ideas and improvements have been invaluable.

Diamond Crime author Paul Durston, who spent thirty years in the Met, advised me on how to manage police procedure.

I would also like to thank readers Lorna Abbott, Andrew and Edward Corke, Alasdair Glennie, the late Eddi Goodwin, Victoria Grebe, Julia Stevens and James and Sylvia Thomson for all their suggestions.

Huge thanks must also go to Steve Timmins, Jeff Dowson and Phil Rowlands at Diamond Crime for showing faith in me and Deadly Protocol. Their rigorous editing has made the book a much better read.

Cover photo:
Discord/Midjourney - AI

Book cover design:
jacksonbone.co.uk

For information about Diamond Crime authors
and their books, visit:
www.diamondbooks.co.uk

Dedicated to
Lynn and in memory of Joanie

DEADLY PROTOCOL

WHY MURDER A SCIENTIST SEARCHING FOR A CANCER CURE?

ROGER CORKE

CHAPTER ONE

The smell was faint but unmistakable. Ronnie had smelt it once before and never wanted to smell it again. Burning flesh.

She could taste it, too. Just like last time, when a father-of-three with ninety per cent burns was wheeled in on the last day of her ER rotation. He looked like a side of beef – and dripped like one. The guy never stood a chance.

Ronnie was desperate to run now but she knew she couldn't. Doctors don't turn tail.

On the far side of the gleaming designer kitchen was an open doorway, leading into a cavernous conservatory that housed a swimming pool. The smell was much stronger here and Ronnie breathed through her mouth to stay in control.

Then she saw the blood, splattered in flecks across the tiles by the shallow end. There must have been a hell of a fight; a dark red trail of it stretched from the poolside to a sauna.

A mop was pushed through the wooden handle on the sauna door and wedged up against an old-fashioned mechanical time switch on the wall, stopping the heater inside from switching off. The temperature gauge read 110 degrees Centigrade.

Ronnie pulled out the mop and the ratchet began counting down to zero – *tick-tick-tick-tick-tick.* Then she took a deep breath and forced herself to open the door.

A blast of heat smacked her in the face, followed by a wave of nausea. It started in her bowels but moved up through her stomach to reach her throat in seconds.

Inside, the brightest star in the world of cancer research was roasting on the electric heater that stood along one side of the sauna chamber. Professor Hasely Stone lay naked on his arched back, his head flopped down towards her, his salt-and-pepper hair singed. There was an intermittent fizzing sound, like bacon frying in a pan.

Stone had been dead for some time. The left side of his skull was caved in and congealed blood trailed from his nose across the cheek of his tanned face all the way to his ear. And the stench. The revolting, stomach-churning stench. It invaded every crevice of Ronnie's nose and mouth and palate.

The eyes that had seduced her a few short hours ago now stared straight at her, lifeless and wide open. It took all of her willpower to wrench her gaze away. Only then did she see the crude graffiti looming above her on the opposite wall. *B U P! B U P! B U P!* sprayed in white letters a foot high.

Ronnie ran out and collapsed by the pool, her hand over her mouth as she gagged and retched. Somehow, she stopped herself from throwing up and stumbled into the kitchen, where she grabbed a landline phone off the counter and dialled 911.

'The number you have dialled has not been recognised.'

Stupid. The Brits used 999, didn't they? She hung up and began to redial but stopped and put the handset down before the call connected.

She picked the phone up again and this time pressed the right keys, only to find herself disconnecting the call and dropping the handset once more. Now her brain wouldn't even let her fingers pick up the phone, let alone dial the number.

For a few seconds, Ronnie didn't know why. Then she understood. Completely. If she were found here, she'd be finished. It was that simple.

Dr Veronica Ackerman couldn't let that happen. She'd escaped a tough start in Boston, Massachusetts, to win a coveted post here in London at one of the world's top ten cancer research facilities. Now she was gripped by a growing certainty that she had to get out of here fast or she'd be saying goodbye to the Lipman Institute within a week.

Mrs Hasely Stone would see to that, as soon as she found out Ronnie had slept with her husband last night. The Lipman was based at St Agatha's University Hospital, where Angela Stone was a professor of neurosurgery and almost as significant a figure there as her husband. Ronnie's days at Aggies would be numbered, for sure.

A random image flashed into her brain. Stone pulling a condom out of its crinkled little packet after they'd stumbled onto the bed.

Another image. Angela Stone, with a piercing stare, walking towards Ronnie down a dark hospital corridor.

Then a third. Those eyes and the fizzing sound and the *tick-tick-tick-tick.*

The eyes shook her back to the here and now. There was nothing she could do for Stone, was there? Of course not. But there *was* something she could do for herself.

She had to work fast. In the kitchen, she found a packet of hand wipes and a box of bright green nitrile gloves; the brand used by the hospital. Ronnie put on two of the gloves, pulled out a wipe and ran upstairs to the bedroom. She cleaned anything she might have touched there and began to tidy her side of the bed.

She stopped short. A strand of her long, black hair lay across the pillow. Ronnie checked for others – none she could see – and took the hair into the bathroom. The condom packet was floating in the toilet bowl and its translucent rubber contents submerged below.

Ronnie dropped the hair into the bowl and pulled the handle. When the rush of water subsided, the condom and the hair were gone but the packet was still there. She fished it out, wrapped it in tissue and stuffed it in her pocket.

She wiped every surface in the bathroom. Not that she could recall coming in here, but there was a lot she couldn't remember about last night. Not even whether they'd had sex; alcohol made women so horny but men so useless.

Finally, she went back into the bedroom and finished tucking in the sheets so it looked like Stone had spent the night alone. Now she just had to go downstairs, remove any trace of her presence there and get the hell out.

The doorbell rang.

CHAPTER TWO

Daniel Plowright's eyes watered with the pain. It was that bad. Like someone had picked up a Black & Decker and drilled through the bare skin on his back and into the shoulder blade beneath.

But his skin wasn't bare. Far from it. He was wearing a light-weight stab vest under his shirt. Since a Star TV reporter was knifed last year, their news crews were made to wear them at any threat of violence.

Like today. Violence was a feature of almost every rally organised by the British Union of Patriots, the BUP.

Daniel wanted to scream but he couldn't. A black gloved hand smothered his mouth and nose. Brand-new leather, never worn before; he could smell it. But not for long; he was losing consciousness.

The grip relaxed and Daniel was kicked to the ground with such force that the small amount of oxygen left in his lungs was knocked out of him. He curled up in a foetal position to protect himself from further blows, but none came. Instead, he heard the sound of boots thudding away across the ground, solid as concrete after eight weeks with no rain.

Daniel couldn't turn his head fast enough to see his attacker but he knew he couldn't stay where he was. A full-scale riot was kicking off around him.

"What are you doing down there, mate?"

His camera operator, Jon Foote, stared down. Daniel told him about the attack.

"Christ, let's get you away from here," Jon said.

They stumbled back through an obstacle course of mayhem.

"Don't you need to be filming this?" Daniel shouted above the din.

"Don't you ever switch off? There are plenty of agency guys here and you look white as a sheet."

Daniel knew it could all go pear-shaped from the start. The BUP couldn't have chosen a more symbolic location for their rally – London Fields, an ancient area of parkland cutting right through a gentrified part of the East End.

Yesterday, he interviewed a one-hundred-year-old woman living nearby who remembered Sir Oswald Mosley's fascists strutting down her road in the 1930s. Today, the Blackshirts' political descendants – and their bitter opponents – were ready to fight the Battle of Cable Street all over again. The rally was supposed to be in protest at asylum seekers getting priority social housing in Hackney but neither side had that uppermost in their minds.

In the blue corner stood the BUP, all shaven heads, bomber jackets, steel-capped boots and tattoos. Every face white and screwed up with blind hatred.

In the red corner, a much larger – and more dishevelled – contingent of counter demonstrators from the Root Out Racism pressure group. An ageing Trot, sporting a dyed black ponytail and shouting through a megaphone, was whipping them into a frenzy.

As the midday start time approached, a thin line of riot police separating the two sides began to buckle. Then a copper slipped over and the line was breached. The BUP poured through the gap and their foot soldiers got what they'd really come for – a bloody good punch-up.

"This is nasty," said Jon, peeling back Daniel's shirt in the relative safety of the press area. "Your stab vest is punctured right through. You've already got a Technicolor bruise coming and this nice bit of schmutter is a write-off."

He poked his fingers through a two-inch gash in Daniel's Armani jacket.

"I'll fill in the expenses form when we get back."

"First things first, you need to be checked out at A&E."

"First things first, I'm doing a piece to camera and then I'll go to A&E. If we go to Aggies, we might even be able to make Stone's press conference as well. It's about time something went right today, after he stood me up this morning."

Jon picked up his camera.

"So what are you going to say in the PTC?"

"We can start with the fact a BUP supporter tried to kill me. That's a pretty good line."

"Except for one thing."

"What's that?"

"You can't be sure it *was* a BUP supporter."

CHAPTER THREE

Every ring on the doorbell was longer than the last.

Ronnie had been frozen at the top of the stairs for a couple of minutes but it felt like an age. The landing front window was ajar. She summoned up the courage to creep towards it.

A woman stood on the driveway, talking to a fresh-faced young policeman. Her head was turned away but Ronnie recognised the slight figure and shoulder-length blond hair, fading fast to grey. Hasely Stone's PA, Laura Sellars. She turned and squinted up at the house, the sun flattening the lines on her face. Laura's wrinkles were testament to the fact she could fret for England. Soon, she'd have plenty to worry about.

Ronnie crept close enough to the window to make out what they were saying.

"There's something wrong, I'm sure of it," she said. "Look at that window. Nobody leaves a window open, not here in St John's Wood. Not unless they're at home."

"I'm sorry, Miss Sellars," the policeman replied. "It's June, it's a heatwave and people are leaving their windows open all the time. We can't go breaking into a house because the owner hasn't been seen for a couple of hours. Especially, if you don't mind me saying so, houses like this."

"But this is a terribly important day for Professor Stone. He's been given a peerage in the King's Birthday Honours List and he's holding a press conference at two. That's in less than two hours and he's nowhere to be seen. You must break in. He might be lying inside, desperately ill or something."

"And he might not be in there at all, madam."

Ronnie's pulse beat so hard she could hear it throbbing through her temples. She knew what she should do – open the damn door – but an invisible hand gripped her by the scruff of the neck.

"It would be fine if Mrs Stone could give us the go-ahead," the policeman said, frowning.

"How many times do I have to tell you?" Laura snapped. "She's at a conference in Chicago."

He pondered for a few more seconds.

"How many hours in front of us is Chicago?"

"Six, and they're behind us, not in front."

"So … it's about six in the morning there now?"

"Just gone."

"And you've got Mrs Stone's mobile number?"

"I've already told you. It's back at the hospital."

"So if we went there, what with the traffic and that, it wouldn't be far off seven in the morning her time, would it? Now, that's a bit more of a civilised hour to wake someone up. If she's happy, we can break in with no comebacks. What do you say?"

"Then let's go now."

Ronnie felt her pulse slow down with every step they took down the drive.

Now there was no time to lose. She went downstairs, wiping the banister on her way. The open-plan dining area, next to the kitchen, was strewn with dirty dishes and three empty wine bottles. Ronnie washed and dried all the crockery, cutlery and glasses she had used. After a few minutes' frantic searching, she found the right cupboards and put them away.

She left everything Stone had used on the table, unwashed, along with the empty cartons from London's most upmarket take-out. So what if he'd ordered for two? Maybe he was a big eater.

In the living room, she nearly tripped over the bottle of Armagnac on the floor and the two brandy glasses next to it; his drained to the bottom, hers drunk down to the point where things ... got out of hand.

She shook out her cream linen jacket, dumped in a heap after he helped her take it off. Linen – a terrible choice. It creased to hell. It seemed so lucky yesterday; an unexpected dinner invitation from her boss and she happened to be wearing the most business-like garment in her wardrobe. The one least likely to give a guy with a bad reputation bad ideas. How wrong she was.

Ronnie wiped every surface she might have touched and picked up her brandy glass, leaving his in place. Back in the hall, she stopped short; the study across the way was a terrible mess. Someone had pulled out every drawer in the desk and dumped the contents on the top, where they were soaking up the remains of a half-drunk coffee cup lying on its side. There was no point her going in. She hadn't been in there last night.

Stone's cell phone in the lounge rang as she rinsed her glass under the kitchen tap. She dashed through and saw the name *Daniel Plowright* flashing up. When the ringing stopped, the screen was full of missed calls.

Ronnie put her glass back in the cocktail cabinet, fluffed up the couch and surveyed the scene. It looked like Hasley Stone had spent a quiet night in with a take-out and a bottle of Armagnac.

Her scrunchie! Yesterday, she'd pulled back her hair with the cream coloured scrunchie that matched her jacket. Where the hell was it? Her heart missed a couple of beats before she spotted it behind the sofa.

Should she go home and change or go straight to work? There was no choice. Her colleagues at the institute would already be wondering where Ronnie was but she had to be there when the press conference started. Everyone received the email yesterday, inviting them along to watch the great man perform. Better to call up, say she'd overslept and get there fast.

She picked up a landline handset lying on the top of the cocktail cabinet and dialled Laura's number; she wouldn't be there yet, so there was no chance of an awkward conversation.

'You have reached the office of Professor Hasely Stone—'

Ronnie slammed the handset down. The call would come up on Laura's phone, dammit.

She had to get out of here. But not yet. First, she must leave the murder scene exactly as she found it, with the body of Hasely Stone roasting inside the sauna.

At the open door, the stench repulsed her. And those eyes still stared back at her. Curious. Apart from the massive injury to his head, the rest of Stone's body seemed intact. The attack couldn't have gone on for long. Ronnie shuddered as she wiped the door free of prints. This kind of thing didn't happen to people like her.

And no amount of ER training could have prepared her for the next task. She had to turn the heater switch back up to sixty minutes and jam the mop against it, like she found it.

She couldn't do it. She knew she couldn't hurt Hasely Stone any more than he'd been hurt already but she couldn't do it. Instead, she pushed the mop through the door handle until it rested just below the switch, like it had slipped down. The ratchet continued its *tick-tick-tick-tick*.

She left.

CHAPTER FOUR

Gemma Chapman speed dialled the number as she vaped on the fumes of her favourite e-cigarette. Red chilli flavour.

'I'm afraid I can't answer my phone right now but if you leave your name and telephone number, I'll—'

The voicemail message cut out.

"Sorry. I couldn't pick up in time."

"Afternoon."

"Who's this?"

"Chapman."

"What the hell are you doing, ringing me here, you fuckwit? How did you get my home number?"

"Easy enough if you're in my line of business and—"

"Don't ever ring me here again. I gave you a mobile number to call."

"Tried that, but it went straight through to voicemail and your office said—"

"You phoned my fucking office as well? Are you mad?"

"Calm down."

"Don't tell me to 'calm down', Chapman."

"Look, I didn't leave my name and they can't trace the call. This mobile's a burner. One burner, one client."

"Which is why I use a clean mobile to talk to you."

"Then you'd better keep the battery charged up, hadn't you?"

"Shit. I'll stick it on charge now. But never ring my home or office numbers again. Got it?"

"Yeah, yeah, yeah."

"Anyway, what do you want?"

"Just thought I'd spread a bit of good news around on this beautiful summer's day, 'specially after Plowright slipped through Baz's fingers half an hour ago."

"What are you talking about?"

Baz tried to whack him at the BUP demo but the blade bounced off. Must've been wearing some sort of stab protection under his shirt."

"What's the cretin doing, going for Plowright in a public place?"

"Taking his chances, that's what. Baz follows him for three days with fuck all to show for it. Then Plowright falls over in this massive punch-up, so my boy gives it a go—"

"Fucking hell. What about the CCTV?"

"Baz is the last person they'll be looking for, isn't he? Wrong colour. Anyway, after that little ... disappointment, I thought you'd like to know everything went like clockwork at Stone's. Couldn't have gone better, in fact."

"Where ... where did you find him?"

"Having his swim – starkers – at half six, just like you said. Great places, swimming pools. They're so helpless when they're in the water."

"Was it ... quick?"

"Didn't feel a thing. Keeled over like a nine-pin. Bled a fair bit, mind."

"I don't need all the details. Did you find his laptop?"

"I'll have it with me tomorrow. No flash drives or SD cards, though. Funny, that. But it was easy-peasy, lemon squeezy, as my kid would say. By the way, I've laid on a little surprise which should keep the Old Bill busy for a while."

"What 'little surprise'?"

"Well, it wouldn't be a surprise if I told you, would it? See you tomorrow with the laptop. Eleven o'clock, Albert Memorial. Have a good one."

CHAPTER FIVE

Ronnie had a stroke of luck when she finally crept out of Stone's house. A large party of Chinese tourists were walking past the post box at the end of the street. She guessed where they were going – the pedestrian crossing on Abbey Road that featured on the Beatles' album cover.

She joined the middle of the throng, hoping it would offer some protection from the ever-present gaze of London's CCTV cameras. This city had more than any other in the western world and she hoped there were none nearby. A Caucasian woman standing at five-seven in flat shoes couldn't just disappear into a crowd like this, even with her sunglasses on and head down. She was taller than all the women and most of the men.

Ronnie felt like the eyes of every driver passing by were focused on her, burning through her linen jacket; her back even began to feel warm. She was braced for a shout from behind at any moment. What would she do? Turn around or run? She had no idea.

As she reached the famous crossing, she risked a glance up and could see only two CCTV cameras, both pointing the other way.

She veered off from the tourist party and kept walking. Finally, she stumbled into Regent's Park and sat down on a bench. Too late, she discovered she was sitting next to a full trashcan, its overflowing contents stinking in the midday sun. They'd been cooking for a couple of days, judging by the look of the putrid hamburger that had fallen off onto the tarmac, a feast now for a swarm of flies.

Ronnie's ER training may have stopped her throwing up in the house but not now. The moment a warm breeze wafted the smell of rotting food in her direction, she vomited until there was nothing left to bring up. She threw the condom wrapper on top of the bin, together with the bright green gloves she realised she was still wearing. Damn. Should've taken them off as soon as she left the house. She walked on.

The water from a nearby drinking fountain was warm and metallic but, right now, it tasted delicious. Ronnie leaned over it for what seemed like hours, her mouth rancid with bile and her body badly dehydrated from all the alcohol.

"Can I have a drink now?"

A small boy stood behind her.

"Sure. Sorry to have kept you waiting."

"No problem. Are you all right?"

"Yeah. A bit too much sun."

Who would have thought the first lie she would tell after running away from a murder scene would be to a small boy at a drinking fountain?

Ronnie walked on, her mind lurching a full one hundred and eighty degrees every few seconds, one moment convinced she'd been right to get out, the next that she'd been crazy to leave.

But what if she had stayed? The BUP thugs would have discovered she was a potential witness and police protection wouldn't guarantee her safety. Yesterday's tabloids led with the contract killing of a guy who gave evidence against a drugs gang. He lived under an assumed name but they still found him and cut his tongue out before slitting his throat. Ronnie clung on to the last grisly thought.

The image of Hasely Stone shot to the front of her mind, those eyes still staring at her. Was he dead when they put him in the sauna? At least unconscious? If he wasn't …

Near the Regent's Park Open Air Theatre, Ronnie found a public toilet. She washed her face, brushed her straggly hair and put on fresh make-up. She began to feel vaguely human again.

But how could anyone with an ounce of humanity have walked out like that? Especially a trained physician. Stone might have been dead but every medical student was taught a deceased patient isn't a piece of meat. That's exactly what Hasely Stone had become, spitting and sizzling on that heater. She left him there – to save her own skin. She looked at those jaded brown eyes in the cracked mirror of the public toilet and didn't like the person she saw.

And that's when Ronnie had her 'lightbulb' moment. In an instant, she realised how stupid she'd been, dammit. Not for drinking the town dry or ending up in bed with Stone last night. That was stupid, for sure, but what was really crass was leaving his house today.

Instead of wiping the place clean of prints, she could have ruffled up a bed in a spare room and told the cops she slept there. They'd have believed her. Angela Stone might have been suspicious, given her husband's reputation, but Ronnie had toughed out a lot worse in her life.

Too late. She'd made her bed – in more ways than one. Now she'd have to lie in it.

CHAPTER SIX

Daniel was bored and annoyed. No, he wasn't. He was very bored and very annoyed. Where the bloody hell was Hasely Stone?

He changed position yet again on the least uncomfortable chair he could find in the conference room of the Lipman Cancer Research Institute. His back was very sore but he refused to stay at A&E after he discovered he would have to wait six hours to see a doctor.

"I can get checked out later," he insisted, in the face of Jon's protests. "If Stone turns up, we can still grab the interview."

Yesterday, it had all seemed like plain sailing. Stone rang him in the afternoon. Off the record, he was getting a peerage in the Birthday Honours List. There would be a press conference today but he would give Daniel an exclusive interview beforehand. They could discuss it over dinner at La Bella Gioconda, the smartest restaurant in St John's Wood. With Stone paying the bill, it was a win-win.

It was also perfect timing. Daniel couldn't make the press conference because of the BUP demo but he would have an exclusive in the can by then. 'Nobel Prize-winner from the backstreets of Trinidad gets peerage' was a great story. What's more, it was Daniel's story.

Then Laura, Stone's PA, called. Sounded a bit put out. Dinner was off but he still wanted to do the interview in Aggies at 9a.m. today. Except that Stone never showed. Daniel and Jon hung around for as long as they could before they had to leave for London Fields.

Daniel's mobile warbled. No number displayed. He answered anyway.

"Hi, it's me."

Alice was the last person he could deal with right now.

"Can I call you later?"

"After you've told me how you are. I've just seen your report on the lunchtime news. Are you Okay?"

Daniel sighed. It was a bit late for Alice to worry about his fucking health. She should have thought about that when she walked out a year ago after he was diagnosed with cancer. But there was no point in taking it out on her; she was just feeling guilty, as usual. Why else did she still call him three times a week more than a year after she left? Anyway, he was trying to stop saying 'fuck' quite so much. Outsiders were always amazed that it was TV people's favourite word; they were in the communication business, after all.

"I'm fine, apart from my back, which is still throbbing like mad. I'm surprised you weren't there."

"I was but you wouldn't have seen me. I was in charge of the police snappers on the high-rise. We're still here, mopping up. Where are you?"

"I'm at Aggies for an interview with Hasely Stone."

"I thought he might have something to say about today's little fracas."

"I'm not here to talk to him about that, though a quick soundbite wouldn't do any harm, come to think of it. Stone's never short of an opinion on the BUP. I'm here because the old sod's getting a peerage."

"Good for him. But what about you? It sounds like it was pretty rough."

"You could say that, considering someone from the BUP tried to kill me."

"Shit. What happened?"

"One of their gorillas stabbed me in the back."

"You didn't say that in your report."

"My cameraman talked me out of it, and he was right. The bastard legged it too fast for me to see who it was. Easier all round for me to say I'd been assaulted. But I'd have bought it if I wasn't wearing one of those new stab vests. You remember how we all took the piss when Star Corp made us wear them?"

"Uh, huh."

"Well, today one saved my life."

"When can you come in and make a statement?"

"I don't think I'll bother."

"Why not, for fuck's sake?"

"I told you, I didn't see anything. The guy was wearing black gloves, that's all I remember. I felt this terrible pain and then he threw me to the ground. It was only later I discovered what he'd done."

"What about your cameraman?"

"Jon saw less than I did."

"But somebody else may have seen someth—"

"On top of which, my back hurts like hell and I'll have to spend half of tomorrow filling in insurance forms in bloody triplicate to get the money back for my ripped jacket. It was that rather nice one you bought me the Christmas before last, more's the pity."

"That's a shame. You look good in that. But I still think you should report this. Maybe—"

"No 'maybes' about it, Alice. There's no point."

"Have it your way – for now. But remember, I can be very persistent."

* * *

'Have it your way' was not an expression Detective Chief Inspector Alice Mahoney used very often in her scramble up the promotion ladder at Scotland Yard. More used to having it her own way, she stared down at the mobile, biting her bottom lip.

"Theo, have you got a second?"

The Met Police photographer on the other side of the street stopped packing his equipment away and looked up.

"Ma'am?"

Alice dug out a photograph on her phone and walked over.

"Is this guy familiar?"

Theo squinted at the screen, washed out in the bright sunlight.

"Maybe."

"Daniel Plowright? Reporter on Star News?"

"Of course. I never forget a face. It just takes longer for it to reach the top of the old filing cabinet these days."

"Someone tried to kill him here today. Stabbed from behind.

"Blimey. How is he?"

"He's fine, apart from being a bit sore. By the way, I don't want any of that spread around."

"My lips are sealed. Who did it?"

"I'm hoping you can help me answer that one. Can you and the other snappers comb through your photos to see if you can find the attacker or, better still, the actual attack? All Plowright knows is that the guy wore black leather gloves."

"Should narrow down the field a bit. It's a bit warm for them."

"I'll ping you this photo for reference. He's a lot shorter than he looks on TV, by the way. Less than five-six."

"Do you know what he was wearing?"

"A charcoal grey jacket." Theo frowned. "Sorry … that's not much to go on, I know. When do you think you can get back to me?"

"Tomorrow?"

"What about tonight? Doesn't matter how late."

"You're the boss."

CHAPTER SEVEN

"Fuck, fuck, fuck."

Daniel's coffee cup scattered its contents across the conference room floor as soon as it slipped from his hand. So much for his new resolution to stop swearing.

"You all right, mate?" Jon asked. "I said you should have gone to A&E straight away. I'll clear up this mess. You look terrible."

"I'm fine, honest."

Daniel wasn't fine. He was far from fine. His hands, especially, were not fine. They'd started to shake straight after he discovered how close he came to being killed today. They were still shaking now.

But he'd brushed close to death twice, so why react like this when it happened a third time?

Of course. Today was personal. The BUP moron didn't know he was attacking Daniel Plowright of Star News, of course. But the attacker still singled *him* out and plunged a knife blade straight towards his heart.

It hadn't been personal the first time, when an improvised explosive device blew up fifty yards in front of him on the Aleppo road four years ago. The poor bastards whose limbs were scattered across the tarmac never stood a chance, of course, but the militiaman who planted it didn't set out to kill anyone in particular. Daniel was just lucky that day.

It wasn't personal the second time, either, when lung cancer ripped through his body. Okay, it was in the sense that Professor Hasely Stone said he would fight like hell to save him, but that was all.

And talking of the old bastard, where was he?

The hospital press officers couldn't help. All four of them were off sick from the latest bout of norovirus ripping through Aggies. That's what happens if you cut the cleaning budget to the bone …

Daniel decided it was time to speak to Aggies' chief executive, Paul Eriksson. He was in charge of press today. He might know something.

The usual three-minute walk to the chief executive's office took twice that time because the place was a building site. The 1970s Brutalist monstrosity that previously housed the Lipman was being torn down and new state-of-the art facilities built in its place. Meanwhile, the institute's temporary home was a sprawling two-storey complex of Portakabins, planted in a corner of the hospital courtyard.

Daniel arrived to find the chief executive's outer office empty. The door beyond was slightly open and Eriksson was barking down the phone.

"No, Professor Stone is not available … I don't know … He's got a press conference at two … Well, if your deadline's that tight, perhaps you should have come along in person."

Daniel didn't like him one bit. Or what his company, Du Long and Freyer, was doing to this place. Since the country's most aggressive drugs giant won the franchise to run Aggies last year, the hospital's caring ethos had flown out of the window, along with its standards of cleanliness. Eriksson was certainly a chip off the company block.

"No, the entire press team are ill … Give me your number and Professor Stone will get back to you … Thank you … Goodbye."

Daniel knew the real source of the chief executive's irritation. Stone told him yesterday, with undisguised glee, how he had arranged the press conference without asking permission first.

Eriksson slammed down the phone. Daniel knocked and entered.

"Good afternoon, Daniel. About the only member of the press I can tolerate. The soon-to-be-ennobled one told me he was giving you an exclusive."

"He was, but he hasn't showed up and—"

"You want to know where he is. Well, join the club. I've done nothing but talk to bloody journalists since I foolishly agreed to the switchboard putting press calls through here and—"

The phone rang again.

"Here's another one."

Eriksson hit the speaker button this time.

"Paul Eriksson."

"Mr Eriksson, it's Laura Sellars here."

"Any sign of him?"

"Nothing at all, Mr Eriksson. There's no answer at the house. I asked the policeman to break in but he said he wouldn't until I telephoned Mrs Stone, who's at the Triple A-S convention in Chicago."

"Well, if he won't break in until you telephone Mrs Stone at the Triple A-S convention in Chicago, you'd better telephone Mrs Stone at the Triple A-S convention in Chicago, hadn't you?"

Why did people like Eriksson – six-figure bonus, seven-figure salary and an even bigger pension pot – always feel the need to put down the little people?

"At the moment, Mrs Stone's phone is switched off," said Laura. "I'll keep trying but please could you go across to the conference room at two and deal with the journalists and television people?"

Eriksson took off his metal-rimmed glasses and slammed them down on the desk.

"Isn't there someone from the institute capable of doing it? They've only got to hold these people's hands until Stone gets there."

"Well, several of the research staff are also at the Chicago conference and Dr Bright's on her way back from a funeral in Newcastle. There's the new American post-doc, Veronica Ackerman —"

"Then get her to hold their hands. They'll like that."

"I'm sorry, Mr Eriksson, but Dr Ackerman hasn't been seen all morning, either."

CHAPTER EIGHT

For most people battling it out in the white-hot competition of cancer research, the offer of a post-doctoral contract at the Lipman Institute would be the chance of a lifetime. For Dr Veronica Ackerman, it was a chance to get away from the train wreck her life in Boston had become since Michael walked out.

Ronnie could cope with the loneliness every night without him. She couldn't deal with the bitterness, eating her up day after desolate day. The bastard. The wimpy, shitty bastard.

Michael left it two weeks – two weeks, dammit – after he got back from Dallas before telling her he'd taken a job there. Then he dumped her twelve hours after she saw him off at Logan Airport with a four-line text.

And the fact that her soul-mate, Todd, was no longer two minutes down her corridor in Harvard Medical School made it so much worse. She'd always relied on him whenever the days were dark. But he moved to the Cobbett Cancer Institute in Colorado three months after Michael dumped her. The last straw.

So when the email from London flashed up on her screen, offering her the job, she breathed a huge sigh of relief. But the Lipman would always have been her top pick anyway, thanks to its two Unique Selling Points.

Number one – the way it concentrated its efforts on the biggest killer in the world of oncology. Lung cancer. The cancer that killed Pop.

Number two – Hasely Stone. He was head and shoulders the world's greatest living lung cancer expert. He'd come from humble beginnings, like her. Nothing less than a Nobel Prize had been good enough for Professor Hasely Stone. There was no reason for her to settle for anything less.

But on her first evening in London she found out life at the Lipman wasn't going to be easy.

"There was a lot of fall-out when you were appointed," said Nikki, the hospital resident from whom she sublet a room off the Fulham Road. "Three PhDs had to leave when they missed out on your post-doc contract. And there's still a lot of competition because there's a fellowship up for grabs next year."

Ronnie's eyes lit up.

"A fellowship? You're kidding me."

With the research world offering ever-shorter contracts, a permanent fellowship at Aggie's would be like winning the Mega Millions in the Massachusetts State Lottery.

"They didn't mention that when they offered me the job."

"And your colleagues won't volunteer it, either," said Nikki. "They'll know you're bloody good or you wouldn't be here. Just don't expect them to do you any favours."

"Thanks for the heads-up."

"And watch Stone's deputy, Stephanie Bright. She's got this annoying nervous tic, so you think she must have a brain the size of a planet, but she hasn't. Sorry, that sounded cruel, didn't it? It wasn't meant to, but the woman's published hardly anything. Her appointment was pushed through by Paul Eriksson, so Bright and Stone don't get on. You're his choice, so don't expect her to be your best mate."

Ronnie didn't. But she wasn't expecting the wall of resentment that confronted her on a drizzly January morning when she walked into the Lipman Institute for the first time.

"So you're the whizz-kid from Boston," said an overweight man in his late twenties, sent to collect her from reception. Dr Jason MacGregor introduced himself without a trace of warmth in his face or his tone. He took her upstairs to meet the other two post-docs, who were different in shape but not in gender or demeanour. The three – all internal appointments – eyed her up and down.

"Great to meet you guys," Ronnie said, trying to break the ice. "I'm really pleased we're working together."

They weren't. Over the next few weeks they did their best to freeze her out, holding furtive conversations on the other side of the large open-plan office they shared with Stephanie Bright. All four post-docs were taking part in the same research project, to study the speed at which a cocktail of cutting-edge drugs reduced patients' secondary tumours. But the trio contrived to leave Ronnie with all the most complicated cases to follow up.

That meant she was left with virtually no time for her own research, into how diet affected tumour growth in non-smoking lung cancer patients. The success of the post docs' personal projects would play a big part in deciding who would land the precious fellowship at the end of the year but Ronnie had hardly started hers. Just what MacGregor and his buddies wanted.

Ronnie couldn't complain to the man who appointed her. The day after she flew across the pond to London, Hasely Stone flew in the opposite direction to his native Trinidad for a last-minute sabbatical to set up a cancer clinic in a poor part of Port of Spain. He wouldn't be back for months.

Within four weeks, she hated the place.

After four months, she *really* hated it. She hated the warm beer, the lousy service, the fast drivers, the feeble water pressure in the shower, the lack of air conditioning during the hottest and driest spring in living memory. She hated the disgusting coffee at the institute. She even hated the Englishisms she used to think were real cute, like calling a woman's purse a 'handbag'. Most of all, she hated Aggies.

* * *

The two o'clock press conference!

Ronnie had been moping in the Regent's Park toilet for so long that she'd forgotten about it. She stuffed her make-up bag back into her purse, ran out the door and started to sprint across the park towards the hospital.

Then she stopped. Better to be cool, calm and five minutes late, than hot, sweaty and punctual.

She was a lot more composed by the time she strode past a TV crew in the hospital quadrangle just before 2pm but still cursed herself for running away from Stone's house. Stupid, stupid, stupid. And how should she play it now? Admit she had dinner with Stone last night, or lie and bluff it out?

"Veronica, I've been looking for you everywhere."

Apart from Stone, only one person in Aggies called her that. Laura Sellars advanced towards her. Ronnie did her best to fix a smile. From now on, she must concentrate. Everything had to fit together.

"I'm sorry Laura. I was on my way in, so I didn't bother to call."

"You don't look very well." Laura's tone sounded almost aggressive. "Are you alright?"

"I've been awake most of the night with a migraine."

The lie popped out of Ronnie's mouth without a second thought.

"I know how you feel," said Laura, sounding slightly more sympathetic. "I get them. Are you feeling better now?"

"A little, thanks."

Dumb. If she was feeling better, why did she look so terrible? If she was still ill, why come into work? Laura didn't notice.

"Look, Veronica, I've got a small favour to ask. The press conference is supposed to be starting any minute and I can't find Professor Stone anywhere. Do you feel up to helping me look after the journalists? It will only be until Mr Eriksson arrives."

Glad-handing a bunch of reporters was the last thing Ronnie felt like doing but she was too hung-over to think of an excuse. She followed Laura across the courtyard and into the conference room.

The tall figure of Stephanie Bright stood at the far end, chatting with Jason MacGregor. He nodded away with enthusiasm. Ronnie thought she was ambitious till she met that odious man.

"Good afternoon, Ronnie, glad you could make it in at long last," he sniggered.

"Now Jason, please treat Veronica gently," said Laura. "She's had a migraine."

No point in wondering what story to tell now.

"The bloody train from Newcastle was three hours late, I've got a pile of work to do and now this is dumped on us," Bright said, blinking faster than ever. "Where has Stone got to, and what are we supposed to say to these people until he turns up?"

"Nothing. I'll do it," said a weary voice behind them.

Paul Eriksson had arrived.

"Wearing black is a bit premature, isn't it, Dr Bright? Professor Stone's only been missing for a morning."

"I've just come back from a patient's funeral."

"I thought you people never went to patients' funerals. Bit of a sign of failure, aren't they?"

"This patient wasn't a failure. She'd been cancer-free a year. It was a car crash."

Eriksson told the news crews that Stone had been 'unavoidably' delayed but couldn't explain why. Most of them went off to an Italian restaurant round the corner, vowing to return in an hour.

"Never keep a good journalist from his lunch," whispered Bright to Ronnie, after they'd shooed most of the newshounds out of the room. "You still don't look well."

"I could murder a coffee," Ronnie replied. "Sorry. I didn't mean that. I mean, I'd love one."

"You sure you're all right with coffee? With your migraine, I mean?"

"Yeah, fine … Cheese sets it off with me."

Bright went to get the coffee and Ronnie gazed round the room, desperate to take her mind off the image swirling around in her head of Stone's body and those lifeless eyes.

She focused her attention on the man in his early thirties chatting to Paul Eriksson. He was the best-dressed guy here, for a start. His black linen blazer, which matched the colour of his well-cut, wavy hair, clearly cost a bundle and it was obvious from the chief executive's body language that this guy was worth cultivating. The other thing that struck her was the man's height. Eriksson loomed above him.

Stephanie Bright returned with the coffee. For once, Ronnie thought it tasted fine.

"Who's the guy talking to Mr Eriksson?"

"Daniel Plowright. He's a TV reporter on Star News. He's a patient here, as a matter of fact. Non-small-cell lung carcinoma. Doing very well. Twelve months clear."

Ronnie left the room as soon as possible. Coming into work was crazy; far better to have taken a sickie.

But now she was here, it would look strange if she didn't do anything. She went to her desk and began to examine a scan on a patient that had just come in.

Not for long. Her brain couldn't function. After twenty minutes, she logged off and picked up the cycle helmet she'd left on her desk yesterday. Time to go home.

Downstairs in reception, the guy from the TV was talking to Laura.

"… and her name's Susie. I took her for a spin down to Mum and Dad's at the weekend."

He looked up and smiled. Ronnie didn't return the gesture; she wasn't in the mood for details of this man's love life.

"Laura, I'm sorry to interrupt but I'm still feeling terrible. I'm going home."

"Very wise, Veronica. Take care on that bike of yours if you're still feeling fragile. There's still no sign of Professor Stone but I've finally managed to speak to Mrs Stone in Chicago. She's given permission for the police to break into the house. I hope everything's all right."

Ronnie began to walk out the door.

"Before you go Veronica, meet Daniel Plowright. He's our star patient, aren't you Daniel?"

"I'm not sure about that but I am one of your success stories, I'm pleased to say."

"Good to meet you."

Ronnie knew it didn't sound as though she meant it but she didn't care. She regretted coming into work today so much. Another regret to add to a very long list from the last twenty-four hours.

* * *

Daniel didn't want to stick around in A&E. The waiting time had grown to seven hours. Neither was he in the mood for a convivial *spaghetti alle vongole* in the *ristorante* round the corner. But he couldn't go back to Star News, at least not until the rest of the press pack called it a day.

Popping round to Stone's house seemed like a good idea in the circumstances, especially as Daniel was the only journalist who knew the police were breaking in. Not much of an edge, compared with what he'd promised the news desk, but worth checking out.

Jon agreed to drive him, on condition he came back to A&E to be checked out afterwards. As they reached Abbey Road, Daniel peeled the Star News sticker off the windscreen.

"What are you doing?" Jon asked.

"We won't get very far as a film crew, will we? I'm a friend of Stone's and that's the way I'll approach the cops."

He eased himself out of Jon's car and walked up to a police sergeant who was looking over the front of the house. Daniel already had his spiel worked out. He was due to meet his friend, Hasely, this morning and was concerned when he failed to show, so he thought he would pop round to see if there was anything wrong.

A constable clambered over a gate from the back garden.

"Nothing open round there, sarge," he said, wiping algae off his hands. "I reckon we're best breaking in through the front. You sure it'll be all right?"

"According to the professor's missus. His PA rang her in America somewhere."

The sergeant went to the boot of his patrol car, returned with a heavy crowbar and prised the front door open. He looked at Daniel.

"Please stay outside, sir."

Daniel couldn't push his luck and went back to chat to Jon. Then he heard the sound of feet running across the gravel and turned around just in time to see the sergeant part company with his lunch in a flower bed.

"Don't go in," he said, choking.

Daniel moved to do exactly that.

"I said, don't go in. He's dead. Someone's fucking cooked him."

CHAPTER NINE

"Look where you're going, asshole!"

The wing mirror of the minivan almost clips her as it turns out of Stone's driveway. 'Fine Dining at Home from La Bella Gioconda' is emblazoned across the back.

Fine Dining at Home? Aren't we going out to eat there?

"That was the plan," says Stone, after greeting her on the doorstep of his imposing Victorian villa. "But Luigi rang and said a big party had just booked in, so he suggested their private dining service cater."

Maybe. Maybe not. There seemed to be plenty of tables available when she checked the place out online this afternoon. Better watch this guy.

"Thanks so much for inviting me, Professor—"

"Hasely. Please call me Hasely."

He smiles. By the look of those teeth, he spends a pile on orthodontics. And his monogrammed shirt, covering a pretty fit frame for his age, can't have been cheap, either.

They walk through to a patio in the back garden. He picks a bottle of Champagne out of an ice bucket.

"Heidsieck Monopole Gold Top 2012?"

"Sounds great." Let's start with the small talk. "This is a beautiful house."

"Thank you. Bought it for the pool. A mile of freestyle every morning. Breaststroke is for wimps."

The vintage Champagne, which he pours out in liberal quantities, is golden, nutty and delicious. When they move through to the dining area next to the kitchen, the corner of the table is already laid with two place settings and three wine glasses each. Three?

Stone picks a bottle of white wine out of a cooler and uncorks it.

"This is a 2014 Puligny Montrachet. The best year for white Burgundy this century."

In front of them are silver domes covering two large plates. He removes them with a flourish to reveal large, plump oysters nestling in their shells on crab foam.

"Luigi did offer to provide waiting staff but I said we'd be fine."

Sure you did. Time to talk business.

"How was your sabbatical in Trinidad?"

"Very … productive, but I had to come back early."

"Why?"

"There are a few things happening over the next day or two that'll keep me busy. The peerage, for a start. You got the email about the press conference?"

She nods. A real Lord. Who wouldn't be impressed?

His knee touches hers for a moment too long. She can cope. Hasely Stone isn't in the Harvey Weinstein or Donald Trump league. Not yet, anyhow.

The main course is a dressed lobster salad, with yet another wine, a red. The alcohol is starting to have an effect. On both of them.

"You wouldn't think a red would go with shellfish, would you?" he says, with a slight slur. "Unless you drink it slightly chilled, like the French do with this Chinon down in the Loire. But enough about the wine. What do you think of your colleagues at St Agatha's?"

"Actually—"

"I'll tell you what I think. I don't trust any of them. Not since Paul Eriksson and those bastards from Du Long and Freyer took over. I'd never have gone along with this franchise business if I'd thought DLF were in the frame for it. You can't trust anyone in this hospital since they arrived. The only person I trust there is you."

So dull. Why does every married man have to use the 'you're different' line?

"And they're terrified of the Big Idea, terrified. I've spent my whole life trying to find the Big Idea."

She isn't sure what to make of these ramblings from a man with too much wine inside him.

"So what's your Big Idea?"

He winks.

"Maybe I'll tell you later. Let's see how things go."

He brings over two magnificent domes of spun sugar, with crème brûlées beneath. There's also a bottle of a golden dessert wine.

"Comes from the foothills of the Pyrenees. Their best kept secret."

"I think I've had enough."

"Come, come, Veronica. You're not going to be a party pooper, are you?"

It's the dessert wine that makes her flip. One moment, she's a little tipsy. The next, she's very drunk. So when he tells her that he and his wife live separate lives, she knows what that's code for. But does she call a cab to go home? Does she hell. Instead, she finds herself being led through to the living room, where he pours her a glass of Armagnac to go with coffee.

And when he begins to kiss her and kiss her again, it's as though it's all happening to someone else…

* * *

Ronnie woke with a start, disturbed by the strident chords heralding Sky's Nine O'Clock News. She'd been asleep on the couch in her apartment for four hours.

Her cell phone vibrated. A voicemail from Todd. She pressed 'play' and up popped his friendly face – all sun-bleached hair and bronze complexion, apart from the ski goggle line around his green eyes.

'Hi, darling. It's shaping up to be a great day. Not a cloud in the sky. Enstone is so beautiful right now. What a place to build a research facility, eh? I can't believe I'm still boarding on the tops this late in the season. Gerard's been out from Connecticut and I finally got him on skis after all these years. We had a ball!

'In fact, I've got some very exciting news. Gerard's moving out here and we're getting married! How wonderful is that? And we've both decided we want you to be our bridesmaid! Give me a call when you get this, darling. Stay fabulous.'

Ronnie couldn't face Todd right now; she had too much to tell but nothing she could say. Her mouth tasted like the bottom of a chipmunk's cage and her clothes felt stuck to her skin. God, she needed a shower.

The hot water dribbled out at its usual pathetic rate but even an American-strength jet couldn't have washed away the mistakes of the past twenty-four hours.

Afterwards, Ronnie fixed herself a green tea and began to hop through the TV channels, news websites and social media. The big news was still the latest 'Me Too' scandal – a former Cabinet minister facing multiple allegations of using his powerful position to persuade interns to sleep with him. There were a few posts about a possible murder in St John's Wood.

Hasely Stone was named as the victim in the lead report on ITV's Star News at Ten bulletin. Daniel Plowright, the reporter she met earlier, was pictured outside the house, appearing a lot taller on screen. He looked desolate as the news anchor quizzed him.

'Daniel, you knew Professor Stone well because you were a patient of his, weren't you?'

'Yes. I'm now clear of lung cancer, thanks to him. His death is an absolute tragedy, not only for those who knew him but for the world of cancer research. He won the Nobel Prize five years ago, when he was just forty-four, for developing the blockbuster drug, Tamoxadrene. It's doubled the average life expectancy of many late-stage lung cancer patients.'

'He wasn't only a high-flying scientist, was he? He was also influential politically.'

'Yes. He is ... was ... a white Trinidadian but very much aware of the problems faced by people of colour and a former chair of the Root Out Racism campaign. He was also an advisor to Prime Minister Stephen Truman's government on health policy. That stems from his close friendship with the Deputy Prime Minister, Dr Gerry Crewton. They met as undergraduates at Imperial College here in London and later studied together at Cambridge University. Hasely Stone was a standard-bearer for Dr Crewton's controversial health franchising policy, bringing in pharmaceutical companies to run our teaching hospitals and pay for the ever-growing demands on the NHS. Hasely Stone lobbied for his own hospital, St Agatha's, to be the first in the country to be franchised out.'

'And accolades from the world of politics are already coming in, aren't they?'

'First and foremost, from the Prime Minister and his deputy. I managed to contact Dr Crewton and he's very upset, as you can imagine. In a moving tribute, he said that he'd lost a brother and both this country and Trinidad had lost a son.'

'Any ideas about motive?'

'Police have made no official statement yet, but theft is a possibility. Thanks to Tamoxadrene, Professor Stone was a wealthy man and lived in this very exclusive part of London. In the past, he also received threats from both far-right and animal rights groups.'

'When can we expect an update?'

'The head of Scotland Yard's Homicide and Serious Crime Command has scheduled a press conference for ten o'clock tomorrow morning. Commander Adam Gough will be anxious to pinpoint Professor Stone's movements over the past twenty-four hours and speak to anyone who saw him.'

Ronnie switched off the TV and made another cup of tea. She needed to talk to someone. Right now, before she dug herself in any deeper. There was only one person. From the moment she signed up for Dr Todd Hogan's cellular biology class, they'd clicked, helped by the fact that there could never be any sexual side to their relationship. He answered in three rings.

"Hello, my darling. I'm so pleased you got my message."

"Toddy, I've got some terrible news. Hasely Stone's been killed. Murdered."

"Jesus, you're kidding me."

"I wish I was."

"What happened?"

Ronnie could usually tell Todd anything. Not now. Tonight, she lost her nerve. Completely. She told him nothing about dinner with Stone. Nothing about discovering his body. Nothing about where she slept last night.

If she couldn't tell the man who was she was closest to in the whole world, how the hell could she tell the police?

CHAPTER TEN

Alice Mahoney pulled her car over the moment she saw who was on the line. If Commander Tom Edwards was ringing at this time of night, the call needed her full attention.

"Sorry to ring you so late, Alice."

"No problem, sir. How can I help?"

"I've just had the Commissioner on the phone. He needs someone from Racist Crime to help Adam Gough out with the Hasely Stone murder investigation."

"May I ask why, sir?"

"Because there's evidence the BUP were involved."

"Such as?"

"BUP graffiti was daubed on the wall at the murder scene."

"Shit … sorry, sir. It's just that the BUP dish out plenty of violence to the anti-racist lot at their rallies but I've never heard them going beyond that."

"Well, the Commissioner thinks he needs the experience of the finest DCI in the Yard's Racist Crime Command on this one. That would be you."

"Thank you, sir."

"Gough won't like it, so don't expect him to welcome you with open arms. And make sure you let me know if you turn up anything. I don't want his lot taking all the glory for nailing this if you get a breakthrough. He's holding the first team briefing at 7am and he's expecting you to be there. Before then, have a gander at our files. Stone's been receiving death threats recently and Racist Crime knew all about it, apparently."

"That didn't come across my desk, sir. I'll check it out."

"Good. This could come back to bite us. And keep me in the loop, whatever you find out."

Alice couldn't resist a triumphant 'yes!' after Edwards rang off. With the superintendents' selection board on Tuesday, the timing couldn't be better. Then it dawned on her. Hasely Stone hadn't been the only person on the BUP's hit list today.

* * *

Daniel took an unopened bottle of Bushmills Malt from the top of his sideboard and poured a generous slug over the ice in his glass. His back hurt a lot less after taking a couple of painkillers powerful enough to stop a horse, but his mood still needed plenty of TLC.

The police were tight as a duck's arse with information, apart from the poor sergeant who'd found the body and opened up to Daniel whilst he was still in shock. Then the Star News editor-in-chief, Francesca Cross, and all her counterparts, got a call from Downing Street. No one should be contacted for a reaction until Stone's name was released by the police.

That's what happens if you have friends in high places, thought Daniel … had friends in high places.

His only slice of luck came when Stone was named a few minutes before *Star News at Ten* went on air. At least he could announce that, plus the gruesome details he prised out of the copper at the scene. The tabloid hacks, who had arrived much later, were all over him the moment he finished his live two-way.

"Some exclusive," he said, as Jon dropped him off at his flat. "Thank God this bloody day's over."

Daniel hadn't gone back to A&E. Too tired, but not too tired to be angry. Very angry. How could you kill someone who'd done such good in the world? Okay, Hasely Stone was no saint – his wife would vouch for that – and the breakneck speed at which he won the Nobel Prize infuriated many of his rivals. But late-stage lung cancer patients had few options before Tamoxadrene came along. Stone's wonder drug gave them the chance of life.

Daniel swirled the melting ice round his glass. This job could be really shitty sometimes. How often had he said that in the last two years? He'd been on the point of resigning twice in that time, ever since the American Star Corporation bought ITV's main news provider.

The first thing the Star Corp suits on the seventh floor did when they took over was to poach Justin Hillman, the news editor from the country's most aggressive Sunday tabloid, to 'shake up' the newsroom, as they put it. Stories 'in the public interest' soon made way for soft-focused items that were 'interesting to the public' and everyone in the newsroom feared there was worse to come. Daniel's investigative journalism didn't get a look-in; he and Hillman hated each other. Francesca Cross was still editor-in-chief only because Star had promised she would be safe for three years. She would be out the door then.

His mobile warbled; no number displayed but he still answered out of instinct.

"Daniel, it's me."

Alice's late-night call was even more unwelcome than her earlier one.

"Didn't you get any of my bloody messages?" he snapped.

"All of them, but I'd have been bollocked if I'd breathed a word to you."

Even when Daniel lived with Alice, she was always very circumspect about anything to do with 'the Job', as coppers call it. She had set herself on track to become the youngest Commissioner for two hundred years and was determined nothing would stop her.

"So why are you ringing this late?"

"Because my commander has appointed me Racist Crime Command liaison with Homicide on the Stone murder investigation."

"Why are your lot getting involved?"

"Because the BUP killed him."

"Jesus. Are you sure?"

"There's BUP graffiti over the murder scene."

"Fuck. The sergeant who found him didn't tell me that."

"Probably had other things on his mind. What's more – and you can't use this – Racist Crime are in deep doo-doo over this. Stone's had a load of death threats recently. Five letters, all sent by snail mail, each

58

posted in a different part of London on consecutive days. He called us in but we didn't make the right noises."

"Why not?"

"Fuck knows. Would've done if it had come across my desk but I was away at the first round of supers' boards. My DI sent the letters away for forensic analysis. Proved negative, of course, so he just filed Stone's complaint away. He's in for a bollocking."

"Alice, if you won't let me use any of this, I can't see why you're telling me."

"Here's why. The 'billets doux' to Stone weren't the usual stuff from nut jobs. They were all marked 'to be opened by addressee only'. Not a spelling mistake in sight. Even the odd semicolon here and there. Which means two things. One, there's at least one member of the BUP with GCSE English. Two, we now know the BUP have tried to whack two people in the last twenty-four hours – Hasely Stone and you. So I need your statement ASAP."

Daniel sighed.

"I keep telling you, I didn't see the bastard. There's no point in me making a statement."

"Yes, there is, because there's one more extraordinary coincidence between the two attacks."

"What's that?"

"You and Hasely Stone knew each other."

* * *

Alice wasn't surprised. Daniel could be an obstinate little fucker when he liked. The link between the two attacks was just the sort of new line she would love to bring to Adam Gough to show him she meant business. But she couldn't talk about it, not without Daniel's say-so. She rang Theo.

"Hello, ma'am."

"Got anything, Theo?"

"I was just about to ring. We haven't got a clear shot of Daniel Plowright's attacker but one of our guys snapped him in the corner of another photo. The assailant's face is turned away from camera but you can see him holding Plowright as he's forced onto the ground. And there's one other thing you can make out crystal clear, ma'am."

"Go on."

"The attacker's not your typical white, Anglo-Saxon Protestant racist, ma'am. He's black."

* * *

"You stupid twat, Chapman. You were supposed to kill Stone, not torture him."

"Take it easy, mate. Like I told you, he was out cold with the first blow. Didn't feel a thing."

"I'm not your fucking mate. What the hell happened?"

"I'll tell all when I see you."

"I want to know right now. And how the hell did you drag him into the sauna?"

"Take another look at the CV they sent you. I was Combined Services women's middleweight boxing champion three years in a row, and a member of the

British team. Still keep fit. Wish I could stop the vaping, though. Anyway, how do you know all this stuff?"

"Turn the bloody TV on. It's all over BBC News24. So, let's get back to the point, shall we? Why the fuck did you barbecue him?"

"I used to be a Red Cap, remember? I know the way coppers think. They draw up a profile and then they hunt for the suspects to fit it. So, what happens when they draw up a profile for this one? Half the 'MO' fits the profile of the BUP because there's graffiti all over the sauna. The other half doesn't, 'cos Stone's given a roasting into the bargain and that's a bit psychotic even for them arseholes. By the time the Old Bill have untangled that little lot, the trail will be as cold as yesterday's barbecue."

Chapman laughed.

Her client didn't.

CHAPTER ELEVEN

Ronnie knew something was different the moment she woke up the following morning but, for a split second, couldn't work it out. Then she heard the ticking of that time switch once more, smelt that stench and saw those eyes staring at her out of the gloom.

Nikki's bedroom door was ajar and the curtains open; she must have stayed over with her boyfriend. Thank God.

Ronnie switched on Star TV's 7a.m. bulletin. The murder of Hasely Stone wasn't the main item, it was pretty much the only item. There were tributes from everyone – all the party leaders, the Trinidadian High Commissioner, even the Prince of Wales; Hasely Stone was on the board of some charity connected with him.

The smart-suited leader of the British Union of Patriots was interviewed and denied any involvement in the murder. Since he also rejected the idea that the BUP used any violence at all, he got a rough ride.

The tabloids' banner headlines were splashed across the TV screen in the review of the Saturday papers. 'FRIED ALIVE!' screamed The Sun. 'BRIT BOFFIN's BBQ DEATH' splashed the Daily Star. 'PROF LORD's SAUNA TORTURE' bellowed The Mirror.

The broadsheets were more sober. 'NOBEL PRIZE-WINNER MURDERED' was the front-page headline in The Guardian, while The Times went for 'GOVERNMENT CANCER EXPERT MURDERED ON EVE OF PEERAGE'.

Social media was buzzing, too. #HasleyStoneRIP was the number one hashtag trending, followed by #bantheBUP.

Ronnie summoned up the resolve to cycle into work. Since Du Long and Freyer took over at Aggies, Saturdays were as busy as any other day of the week because the place was packed out with private patients. Not this morning. Many had heeded calls in the media to stay away.

Outside the main gates, a sea of flowers stretched for twenty yards in each direction and anti-racists were staging a silent vigil, holding up placards calling for the BUP to be banned. Inside, journalists and TV crews wandered all over the courtyard but two hospital security guards stopped them from entering the Lipman's Portakabins. Ronnie flashed her ID and walked in.

She half expected all eyes to be on her, like she felt yesterday near the Abbey Road crossing. In fact, a collective daze had settled over the place. People were standing around reception, muttering in twos and threes; there was only one topic of conversation, of course.

Ronnie didn't want to talk to anyone and walked straight ahead, avoiding everyone's gaze. As she passed Laura's office, she glimpsed her sobbing in the arms of Stephanie Bright.

She was about to start analysing the scan she was working on yesterday when she realised how strange that would appear, getting straight down to work the morning after your boss was murdered. Instead, she got herself a coffee and wandered back to reception to chat to a couple of nurses who were standing by the front window. Ronnie was surprised how easy she found it to make the right noises, maybe because she was still in a state of shock.

Shortly after nine thirty, Paul Eriksson walked into reception with Sir Desmond Harris, the Chairman of Du Long and Freyer. The two men began working the room, fortunately on the opposite side from Ronnie.

A dark grey Range Rover swept into the quadrangle. Eriksson and Harris hurried outside. A tall man, dressed in a sober suit with a black tie, stepped out and shook hands with them.

Ronnie recognised him from the TV news. It was the Deputy Prime Minister, Dr Crewton. He didn't look as though he'd slept a wink. His face was drained of colour, apart from the broken veins on florid patches in the centre of his cheeks. The cameras whirred, and one or two less sensitive reporters called out questions, but most of the press pack were polite and subdued. Dr Crewton and a red-haired aide came inside and stood in reception with Eriksson and Harris for a few minutes, talking in low voices.

The nurses moved off to talk to someone else. Ronnie didn't mind in the slightest.

"Hello," said a voice behind her.

She turned around.

"Daniel Plowright. We met yesterday."

"Hi. I saw your report on *News at Ten*. It must have been a terrible shock."

"Just a bit. I've been awake half the night and feel like shit, if you'll pardon my French. In fact, you don't look so good yourself."

"I … had a migraine yesterday."

"Are you better now?"

"Yes, thanks. Sorry, but how did you get in? I thought journalists were being kept outside."

"There aren't many advantages to having non-small-cell lung cancer, but this is one of them. Paul Eriksson let me in."

They stood in silence for a while, both looking at the floor.

"Dr Crewton looks in a bad way," Ronnie said, eventually.

"He is. I spoke to him last night. Quentin Plover doesn't look as though he's faring much better."

"Sorry?"

"The guy with the ginger mop next to him. He's the Prime Minister's Chief of Staff."

Dr Crewton looked up, spotted Daniel and walked over.

"Good morning, Deputy Prime Minister."

"Morning, Daniel. Dreadful business. Dreadful."

He turned to Ronnie.

"I don't think we've met."

"Ronnie Ackerman, sir. I'm a post-doc here. I'm sorry for your loss. I understand you and Professor Stone were close friends."

"Thank you. It's Angela and the boys we must all think of at this time. When I picked her up at Heathrow this morning—"

"I'm sorry to interrupt, Deputy Prime Minister, but it's almost ten and the news channels want to run you live on the hour."

Paul Eriksson had crept up unnoticed. The two of them left to talk to the cameras. Eriksson spoke of his shock and vowed to continue Hasely Stone's work. The Deputy Prime Minister talked about his love and friendship for Stone, his brilliance as a scientist and his wise counsel. He ended with a vow to make sure his killers were hunted down.

The media circus, including Daniel Plowright, departed not long after the Deputy Prime Minister. Then Paul Eriksson called the institute's staff together.

"I know you're all very upset, but it's in everyone's interests for this place to get back up and running. There's work to be done."

Laura burst into tears. Eriksson ignored her.

"Over the next few days, it will be impossible to get these wretched reporters off our backs, but I've given Security standing instructions to escort any member of the press off the premises if they're found anywhere beyond main reception.

"Finally, a brief update on the police operation. I spoke to the Senior Investigating Officer first thing this morning and he said detectives will want to interview all of you about your movements on Thursday night and yesterday morning."

CHAPTER TWELVE

Alice picked her way through a dozen white-suited scene-of-crime officers examining and photographing every inch of Hasely Stone's conservatory.

She was shocked to see Adam Gough there; commanders never attended crime scenes. But here he was, suited and booted and talking on his mobile by the sauna door.

"A very good idea of yours, sir. DCI Mahoney is Racist Crime's lead on the BUP, after all."

Alice knew who must be on the line. Gough looked up and nodded.

"In fact, she's just arrived … No problem, sir." He hung up. "Good afternoon, Alice. This one's got so much political shit flying around it, I'll never get the bloody commissioner off my back. What have you found out so far?"

"Well, sir, you won't be happy with this. All our sources inside the BUP – and there's no shortage of them after the work we've put in over the past couple of years – are stumped. They hadn't heard so much as a whisper about anyone being totalled. Quite the contrary, in fact. Would you believe it's a disciplinary offence for their boys to kill someone?"

"You're joking."

"I'm not, sir. 'Beatings create soldiers for us, killings create martyrs for them.' That's the way the BUP directorate puts it. Cute, eh?"

"So what the hell happened here?"

"Must've been a rogue BUP element who killed Stone because I'm as certain as I can be that the leadership didn't know anything about it. They're panicking like mad today, putting in place contingency plans in case they're slapped with a ban."

Alice and Gough shuffled into the sauna in their plastic overshoes. She took one look at the graffiti and froze.

"This wasn't the BUP, sir."

"How do you know?"

"Because of this." She pointed at the letters daubed on the wall. "There's no arrow on the graffiti. The BUP symbol has an arrow at the bottom of the P. No self-respecting supporter would ever think about leaving it off. It's like a trademark to them."

"Couldn't they have just forgotten?"

"Not a chance. Take a look at the BUP graffiti sprayed round the East End. Every bit of it has an arrow on the P. I bet you a pound to a penny Hasely Stone's murder wasn't the work of the BUP. Someone is trying to frame them."

* * *

"What have you got for me, Alice?" Tom Edwards asked.

"Rather more than I expected at this stage of the investigation, sir."

She told Edwards about the graffiti in the sauna and the photograph of the man who attacked Daniel. Alice described him as a 'contact'. Her private life was nobody else's business.

Edwards thought for a moment.

"Okay. Unless the BUP has recruited its first-ever black supporter, it's no more responsible for the attempted murder of Daniel Plowright than for the killing of Stone. Yet someone is trying to dob it in for both. On top of that, the two victims knew each other. The attacks must be linked."

"Absolutely, sir. And, if that's the case, we must assume the attempted murder of Daniel Plowright wasn't just random, any more than the murder of Hasely Stone was."

"So?"

"So it means they might try again. By the way, sir, Daniel still refuses to make a statement about the stabbing, so I haven't mentioned anything about it to Commander Gough."

"And I think you should keep it that way. For now. But you'd better tell Plowright to be careful."

"Can I tell him we've got a picture of his assailant, sir?"

"Absolutely not. That information's far too sensitive. If you haven't told Adam Gough, you can't very well tell Plowright. Have your snappers got any more photographs of the attacker?

"No, sir, but I think I know where I might be able to get some."

* * *

Daniel logged on to a terminal in a quiet corner of the Star News basement and started viewing the footage from the London Fields demo, frame by frame. It was tedious and gruelling work. After only ten minutes, he was seeing double. He picked up his phone and grinned as he read Alice's message for the fifth time.

'Hi Daniel. I'm so sorry for getting on your case about the statement. Won't mention it again. But could I have a sneaky copy of the stuff your cameraman shot the other day at London Fields? Completely between ourselves, of course. Ax'.

He couldn't recall Alice ever being 'so sorry' about anything. Even when she walked out of their relationship because of her bloody phobia about illness and hospitals, her apology was half-hearted. Something was up.

Daniel couldn't give her news footage that hadn't been broadcast. He could create screengrabs instead – still pictures of the moving images Jon shot – but he wasn't going to do it without something in return.

He rubbed his eyes and got back to the task in hand; it would take hours to screengrab all this stuff. As each image flashed up, he took his time to examine it. One of the faces in front of him could belong to the man who tried to kill him.

His mobile burst into life.

"Hi, it's me. Did you get my message?"

"Of course I did, Alice."

"And can you get me the footage?"

"No chance. Star News never releases rushes without a court order, you know that."

"I was rather hoping we wouldn't have to go to the trouble."

"You will if you want the rushes. But I might be able to get you screengrabs – if you can return the favour."

"Like how?"

"Come on, Alice. You're working on the biggest murder of the year."

"And you want a bloody exclusive."

"Let's call it a fair exchange of information."

"Fucking hell, Daniel. That should be the last thing on your mind, considering the danger you may be in."

"What are you talking about?"

"Look, this is all off the record, Okay?"

"Okay."

"You thought the attack on you was random, didn't you?"

"Of course."

"Well, there's a chance it might not have been."

"What are you saying? The guy was trying to kill me? Me personally?"

"Possibly."

"Jesus. How do you know?"

"I don't know. But as soon as I went to Stone's house today, I realised his murder's a damn sight more complicated than it seemed at first sight."

"What's that got to do with what happened to me at London Fields?"

"Look, Daniel, I can't say any more on the phone but watch your back, all right?"

"Hang on a second. First, you warn me to watch my back. Then you tell me the attack on me wasn't random—"

"Might not be random."

"Okay, might not be. Then you won't tell me why, apart from dark mutterings about what you found at Stone's place. Is my life in danger or not?"

"Possibly. Are you free for a drink at the D&T at six on Monday?"

"I'm on early shift. Should be finished by then."

"Good, because I'm at a supers' selection board on Tuesday."

"So it's Superintendent Mahoney next, is it?"

"We'll see. And bring those screen grabs with you."

"So that's what this is all about, is it?"

"No, it bloody isn't, Daniel. It's about protecting your back. And stay in one piece till we meet on Monday, all right?"

CHAPTER THIRTEEN

Ronnie cycled the long way home from Aggies, hoping it might clarify her thoughts. She had a choice to make – 'fess up to the police or keep quiet.

She pedalled through the chic streets of Chelsea in the hot evening sun, her head so full of conflicting thoughts that she felt it could burst open at any moment. The road ahead was a blur and she flew through a red light at one intersection, avoiding an oncoming garbage truck by inches.

She got home, no nearer making up her mind, and turned on the TV news. The story was already moving on and the British Union of Patriots was the focus of attention now. A bunch of tough-looking cops in riot gear were pictured, raiding the BUP's headquarters in east London.

'And now we're going straight over to Number Ten where Stephen Truman is about to make a statement.'

The Prime Minister walked through the Union flags festooning the stage of the Downing Street media centre and up to the lectern.

'I have just come from a COBRA meeting at the Cabinet Office. From midnight tonight, the British Union of Patriots will be a proscribed organisation under the

Terrorism Act. Membership will carry a maximum sentence of ten years' imprisonment.

'I have also asked the Commissioner of the Metropolitan Police to keep the Deputy Prime Minister informed on a daily basis of all developments in the hunt for Hasely Stone's killer or killers. We will fight the scourge of racism in this country until it's extinguished. The people responsible for this outrage will be brought to justice.'

Ronnie switched off. Time to make a plan. She was only in this mess because she'd panicked; now she had to think things through. She grabbed a pen and paper and wrote down all the pros and cons of each course of action. That often helped if she had a tricky decision to make.

The list of reasons for keeping quiet was persuasive. She hadn't seen anything, so what use could she be to the police? The horrific murder of the guy in Witness Protection showed coming forward might not be such a smart move. And the cops would be really pissed with her if she went to them now and admitted she was not only at the murder scene but wiped it clean of prints. Then there was the little problem of her career being in shreds the moment she did that.

The list of reasons to come clean was equally compelling. If she didn't tell the cops, she would be in even more trouble if they found out anyway. They might; one of the neighbours could have seen her leaving Stone's house yesterday morning. And who was she kidding, thinking she cleaned up everything? There could easily be a fragment of her DNA somewhere. How would she explain that away?

She still wondered whether she could tell the police part of the story – that she had dinner with him, maybe? No way. Telling Laura about the migraine had put paid to that. People with migraines don't go out for fancy dinners.

Ronnie spent a fitful night and the whole of Sunday wondering what to do. By the time she got to work on Monday morning, lack of sleep made her decision even more difficult.

Everyone at the institute was due to be interviewed today. Ronnie's game plan was to find out what she could about the line of questioning from those interviewed first. It didn't work out that way. She got an early call. Conference Room A at ten o'clock.

As she walked towards its dark doors, Laura came out and flashed an almost hostile look as they passed each other. Weird.

It was make-your-mind-up time. Ronnie opted for what seemed like the least suspicious course of action. She would play the shocked little woman. At least she might have time to think if the police caught her out with a difficult question. It wouldn't be easy, of course. Todd always said she was the world's worst poker player.

Ronnie set her face rigid and knocked.

"Come."

The owner of the voice turned out to be a big man – mid-forties, maybe – with a lived-in face and a shock of wiry hair too uniformly brown to be natural at his age. He sat behind a solid mahogany table with a green leather top.

Next to him sat a female detective, younger than Ronnie. Her fingers hovered over a laptop, ready to take notes. In the corner sat another, much smaller, woman with blond hair who was a little older. No one was wearing uniform.

The man beckoned Ronnie to take a seat on a straight-backed chair placed several feet away from the table. She felt like a witness giving evidence to a hostile congressional committee. That was clearly the idea.

"It's Dr Ackerman, isn't it?"

"Yes, sir."

"My name is Commander Adam Gough. This is Detective Sergeant Melanie Booth and over there is Detective Chief Inspector Alice Mahoney. As you know, we're investigating the murder of Professor Hasely Stone and I am the Senior Investigating Officer. SIOs aren't normally tasked with carrying out interviews like this but this is not a normal murder investigation. You might have noticed how much interest our political masters are taking in this case, so we all have to do our bit. I hope you can do yours by answering a few questions."

"Of course," Ronnie said, in a quiet voice. "We're in real shock here but if I can help in any way."

"Yes, I'm sorry for the distress this must cause you all."

"Actually, I'm not sure I can be much help because I didn't know Professor Stone too well. I've only been here at the Lipman since January and he was away in the Caribbean until a week or so ago."

Gough's eyes looked straight into hers then down at her hands. They were starting to shake.

"We'll see, Dr Ackerman. Now, you say you didn't know Professor Stone very well."

"I'm sorry, no."

"But you knew Mrs Stone was away in Chicago when the murder took place?"

"That's what they said on TV."

"Including Thursday evening and Friday?"

"I guess so. Chicago's where the Triple A-S convention was happening … sorry, American Association for the Advancement of Science. Everyone in the institute knows that. It's the biggest meeting of the year."

"Would you mind telling me what you were doing on Thursday evening?"

"I was … at home."

"Ah yes. We've spoken to Laura Sellars and she mentioned you were ill on Thursday with … a migraine."

As Gough emphasised the final word, he stared out of the window. Ronnie glanced down at her hands, trying to keep them still.

"Now, from what you said, I take it you wouldn't regard yourself as a friend of Professor Stone."

"No, sir. As I said, he was away when I—"

"Quite. You hardly knew him. But everyone at the institute knew he had a reputation for close … friendships with female colleagues, didn't they?"

That knocked Ronnie right off balance. On every cop show she'd ever watched, the first question was always 'Where were you on the night of the murder?'

She gave a slight nod.

"I'll take that as a 'yes', shall I?" Gough's tone was sharper. "So, if Mrs Stone was in America and you were at home with your migraine, you wouldn't know who Professor Stone was entertaining on Thursday evening, would you? We know he was with someone because he used his American Express card to pay for dinner for two. Delivered to his home from a rather expensive restaurant in St John's Wood called La Bella Gioconda. A bit out of my price range, La Bella Gioconda. How about yours?"

Ronnie didn't need to give the impression of being in shock now; she was in shock.

"He was supposed to be having dinner there but changed the booking at the last minute to a home delivery for two. Very cosy."

She stared at the floor.

"Anyway, Dr Ackerman. We will find out who Professor Stone was with – and sooner rather than later. Your whereabouts on Thursday evening. Can anyone verify that?"

"I … don't think so. The girl I share my apartment with was working all night. She's a resident here. Then she went straight off for a long weekend with her boyfriend."

"That's a pity, Dr Ackerman, because Professor Stone wasn't the only member of staff not to turn up on Friday morning." He looked at her, straight between the eyes. "I understand you weren't in work, either. Migraine still playing up, was it?"

Ronnie felt as if someone had just picked up a baseball bat and smashed it in her face. She nodded and looked down to her hands, trying to keep them under control.

"I'd also like to find out who phoned Laura Sellars's office around midday on Friday lunchtime from Professor Stone's landline. I can't understand why a murderer would do that. Can you?"

Ronnie looked up and gulped. Gough was looking straight at her again.

"Thank you, Dr Ackerman. That's all. For now."

"Sure. Thank you."

Ronnie walked out, cursing herself. That lie about the migraine seemed so trivial at the time. But little lies turn into big lies. And big lies turn into whoppers.

CHAPTER FOURTEEN

Daniel didn't often drink Bud Lite. It was gnat's piss, as far as he was concerned. But he made quite a few changes to his routine after Alice's call three nights ago. He varied his journey to work; he put the chain on his door at night; he drank a little less alcohol, too. Bud Lite might be gnat's but it helped him keep his wits about him.

He stared round at his fellow drinkers in the Dog and Trumpet, glad most of them were coppers. Daniel felt that little bit safer with them around.

Coppers always suggested a pub full of Old Bill, and Alice was no different. She might have a First in archaeology and anthropology from Cambridge University, but she liked her pubs full of Old Bill.

She walked through the door, her frame so tiny Daniel was amazed the Met ever accepted her, even if there were no height restrictions any more. So were her colleagues. They nicknamed her 'Minnie Mouse' from the start.

"Hi Daniel. I haven't got long. What are you drinking?"

"Bud Lite."

"Turning over a new leaf?"

"Something like that."

Alice returned with a bottle of lager for Daniel and her usual, a large Scotch and ice.

"All right," Daniel said. "What's all this about?"

"This is completely off the record, agreed? No 'anonymous sources at the Yard' bollocks. Clear?"

"I've got the message."

"The BUP didn't kill Hasely Stone."

"You're not serious."

"Don't I sound serious?"

"How do you know?"

"Let's put it this way. Someone went to elaborate lengths to blame the BUP and, if they hadn't been too clever by half, they'd almost certainly have got away with it."

"Clever like how?"

"The graffiti, for a start. It's not genuine."

"Are you sure?"

"Yup. The moment I saw it, I knew it wasn't sprayed by anyone close to the BUP. Can't tell you why."

"Of course you can."

"No I fucking can't, Daniel. We've already had the first weirdos ring up to claim responsibility. Keeping crucial facts out of the public domain means we can eliminate them straight away. Exactly how the graffiti was sprayed on the wall of Stone's sauna is one of them. And we've found out another key piece of evidence which also confirms that someone's trying to frame the BUP for Stone's murder. I can't tell you about that, either."

"Fair enough."

"Anyway, we're getting off the point slightly. This is supposed to be about you."

"All right."

She took a sip from her glass.

"We've received information that makes us think your attacker was no more a BUP supporter than the animals who totalled Stone."

"Shit. What information?"

"I can't tell you but—"

"You must be able to tell me something, for fuck's sake. I could have been killed last week."

Daniel banged his beer bottle on the table and several customers looked up. Alice glowered at him.

"How do you think I got clearance from my commander to speak to you? Now do yourself a favour and shut up."

"Sorry."

"We don't know your attacker's identity but we're sure as we can be that he wasn't BUP. Don't ask me why again. If that's the case, it turns everything on its head. Instead of the attacks on you and Stone being linked because they were both carried out by the BUP, they're linked because neither of them were. But in each case, someone tried to blame them. With Stone's murder, they did it by spraying BUP graffiti at the scene. In yours, by whacking you at a BUP rally. Now you know why I need your rushes or stills or whatever."

"I was wondering when you would get round to them."

"Did you bring them?"

"I haven't done them all yet. It takes forever. I might have them by the end of the week, depending on how much grief I get from the news desk over the next few days." Daniel took a swig from his beer bottle. "So what's in this for me, Alice? If Star News found out I'd given anything to you, I'd be in deep shit. So, come on, what can you offer in return?"

"I can't make any promises and—"

"Well, if you can't, neither can I."

"It really is in your interests, Daniel."

"What you mean is, it's in the interests of Detective Chief Inspector Alice Mahoney of Scotland fucking Yard. I'll have to think about whether it's in mine."

"No need to be tetchy, Daniel. The one thing we know about these people is that they're determined. They've killed Stone. They tried to kill you. Who's to say they won't have another go?"

CHAPTER FIFTEEN

Ronnie felt the familiar stickiness from the tears around her eyes before she forced them open. She was used to it. Almost every night for the past six wretched months in London, she'd endured the same terrible dream, reliving that terrible day Pop died. The day she turned eleven.

Waking up used to bring her relief. Not anymore. Now she was in the middle of a real-life nightmare of her own making. What the hell was she going to do?

Sleep was out of the question. She got up, made a cup of green tea and sat outside in her pyjamas, watching a robin breakfasting on a coconut shell hanging from the bird table. The patio was still warm from the day before. It was going to be another scorcher.

Her mood began to lighten. Everything seemed more positive in the milky light of dawn. Yes, she should have rung the police when she found Stone's body. She should certainly have come clean with Gough yesterday. But now she should sit tight and do nothing, because she couldn't find out what the police had discovered.

Then, in a flash, Ronnie realised. Maybe, just maybe, she could.

* * *

For years, the Familiarisation Tour had been compulsory for every new member of staff at Aggies. After the 9/11 attacks in 2001, the hospital ran a full-scale exercise in case the same thing happened in London. It was chaos. Too many staff were hampered by not knowing their way round. The FT was introduced, and it worked. Aggies had run like clockwork every time terrorists had attacked since then. Nevertheless, most people, Ronnie included, still regarded the FT as a chore.

Not now. She picked up the phone the minute she got to her desk; she couldn't hang around till people read emails. Within an hour, most of her tour was in place for the following day.

It started at 10a.m. sharp and, as it progressed, Ronnie began to realise how little she knew about the hospital layout. There were some departments she'd never been inside, even though they were vital to her work. Patient Records was one. The man in charge, Maurice Sutcliffe, taught her how to access data on patients much faster using its shiny new IT system.

"This is about the only thing we can thank Paul Eriksson and Du Long and Freyer for, if you ask me," he said. "It's based on the system they use to coordinate their clinical trials."

Nevertheless, Ronnie's real reason for taking the tour was not to explore the finer points of Aggie's computer records. It was to visit the department she arranged to be her last stop – pathology.

"Most medics try to avoid this place," said Professor Rhodri Davies. "You all regard sending your deceased patients here as a sign of failure … Don't shake your head, there's no need to be polite."

Ronnie knew what he meant. Pathology had a crucial role to play in treating cancer when the patient was still alive, analysing tumours and giving the oncologist vital information about how they might respond to treatment. But a lot of pathology still consisted of post-mortem examinations. Prof Davies had carried out the autopsy on Hasely Stone. If anyone would know what the police had discovered at the murder scene, it was this bubbly little Welshman.

She spent an inordinate amount of time asking polite questions about his work before picking her moment.

"Professor, I'm really enjoying our chat. As it's the end of the day, do you have time for me to buy you a drink so we can go on talking?"

Alcohol had been her downfall in this so far. Now was the time to turn it to her advantage. Laura had confided that Davies was rather lonely since his wife left him – God, was there anything the woman didn't know? – so Ronnie would have felt a bit insulted if he declined. He didn't.

The Marquis of Granby was packed, but a couple vacated an outside table just as they arrived.

"What can I get you?" he asked.

"No, no. Let me get the drinks. I insist. I asked you, don't forget. What would you like?"

Ronnie kept her fingers well and truly crossed. A pint of beer would be fine; no one would notice a shot or two of vodka in that. Hard liquor and a mixer would be perfect.

"If you're sure. I'll get the next one. I'll have a gin and tonic, I think."

"I'll have the same."

Well, not exactly the same. She ordered two double gin and tonics but poured the spirit from her glass into his before filling them both up with tonic. In the next round, Davies bought them each a single G and T. By the time Ronnie pulled the same trick again, the alcohol was having the desired effect on her companion. He couldn't wait to tell her about the most high-profile autopsy he had ever carried out.

"It wasn't the BUP who killed Stone, you know," he said in a low voice, becoming less distinct by the minute.

"But haven't those guys been banned?"

"That's politics for you, but the police are certain it wasn't them. Virtually certain, anyway."

Davies told Ronnie about the missing arrow on the graffiti at the murder scene.

"And that was only the first mistake."

"No way."

"Promise not to say anything?"

"Promise."

"Well, when I opened up Hasely Stone's right hand, what should I find inside but a BUP badge, ripped off in the struggle. At least, that's what we were supposed to think. But this badge had never been sewn onto anything. There were no needle holes or stray strands of cotton. Someone tried to blame the BUP, but made too much effort. I was rather proud of that little discovery. Another drink?"

She nodded. This was going far better than she could have imagined.

He tottered back ten minutes later with two more glasses after a long wait at the bar.

"I've gone on to tonic. The gin was going to my head."

"Must be the heat. Anyway, you were saying … The killer wasn't a member of the BUP?"

"Killers, not killer. There were definitely two people."

"How do they know that?"

"Because they found two sets of footprints in the blood at the scene. One set was a size seven Dr Marten's boot, quite small for a man. The other was a woman's shoe, size five. She must have come on the scene later because her footprints scuffed up the blood after it had started drying."

Shit. How could she have forgotten the damn floor?

"This woman must have let the murderer in and – get this – the police think Stone had dinner with her the previous evening."

"Why?"

"Because he'd booked a table for two at a rather smart place called La Bella Gioconda, around the corner from his house. Then he cancelled the booking at the last minute and asked the restaurant to deliver instead.

"He ordered a very nice meal for two. Oysters, lobster, crème brûlées. I found remains of it in his stomach, plus a lot of alcohol. There were cartons left on the kitchen table, plus a receipt, but ..." Davies chewed an ice cube for what seemed like an age "... there was only one set of dirty plates. The lady having dinner with him must have washed hers up."

"Couldn't Stone have eaten it all on his own?"

"No chance. I'd have found a lot more food inside him if he had. No, he had a cosy dinner with this woman and she cleared up to give the impression she wasn't there. And all must have been very cosy by the end of the evening, because they ended up in bed."

Ronnie gasped, sending a mouthful of gin and tonic down the wrong way.

"Are you sure?" she said when she had recovered.

"Oh yes, no question about it. Wiped her fingerprints off everything and made her side of the bed. But she didn't tuck the sheet in properly. They're very particular about hospital corners in the Stone household, it seems. Then she must have gone downstairs to join her partner in crime."

Ronnie wanted to scream, 'It didn't happen that way!'

"Her accomplice was short – about five foot six, judging by his shoe size – but with a lot of strength for his height. He picked up Stone's body out of the pool, dragged it across the floor and lifted it onto the heater in the sauna. Not being funny, but this is the point where the pathology gets particularly interesting. I'm not boring you, am I?"

'Bored' was the last word Ronnie would use.

"No, no, professor. I'm fascinated."

"Well, this is the strangest post-mortem I've carried out in a very long time. The prof was killed by just one powerful blow to the upper left temple. A domestic claw hammer, probably. He would have died more or less instantly."

"So he wasn't tortured before he died?"

"Good grief, no. Dead as a doornail by the time he was dumped in the sauna. The lethal blow was the only one struck."

Another sigh of relief. Davies didn't notice.

"How do you know?"

"If you're attacked, what do you do? You try to protect yourself with your hands. You lash out. You scratch. But there were no injuries to Stone's hands or fingers, no human tissue from the attacker under his fingernails. The prof keeled over straight away."

"So why put his body on the heater?"

'I've been asking myself the same question. It could be that this couple are Hindley and Brady mark two.'

'Sorry?'

'Myra Hindley and Ian Brady. Just about the most notorious killers in British history. Both got life way back in the sixties for torturing and killing children on the Yorkshire Moors. Missed the end of capital punishment by a whisker, more's the pity. Died in jail. Hasely Stone's killers could be like that. A couple killing for kicks, but, somehow, I don't think so. I think these two were playing a very clever game."

"Why do you think that?"

"Because when he was a student, Hasely Stone was involved in a serious car accident and ended up with the left-hand side of his skull so badly fractured he was in a coma for two weeks. He keeled straight over in the pool because the blow to his head landed in exactly the same place, where the bone was still fragile. I know it sounds a bit 'Agatha Christie' – the victim had a thin skull and all that – but, in the prof's case, it was true. I know what you're thinking. The killers struck lucky, if you'll pardon the expression. But I don't think luck came into it.

"The Christmas before last, Stone was involved in another car crash – very near here, just outside Lord's Cricket Ground. Nothing like as serious as the first … pissed as a newt but not seriously injured. No one else was involved, so an ambulance whisked him back to ours before he could be breathalysed. The police were furious. Phone lines between the nick and Aggie's were zinging for days."

Ronnie wasn't sure where this story was leading.

"Anyway, when they got him back here, they gave him a CT scan. Not strictly necessary but perfect if the patient is one of your own and you want to keep the police off his back until he's sobered up a bit. The scan showed damage to his left temporal bone from the previous accident. It was the only thing of significance in his medical notes". Davies chewed another ice cube. Ronnie could see he was enjoying the attention. "And I think whoever killed the prof may have known all about it."

Ronnie's pulse quickened.

"Why?"

"Just before he died, Hasely Stone got Laura Sellars to print off a hard copy of his notes."

"A hard copy? I can't remember the last time I printed off a hard copy of anything."

"Well, that's what Stone got Laura to do. Good job I talked to her in the coffee queue or I'd never have got hold of them."

"Why didn't you just log on to the system to get them?"

"That was the first thing I tried to do, of course. But someone got there first. Every word of Hasely Stone's medical history, apart from his name and hospital number, had been wiped from his hospital file."

CHAPTER SIXTEEN

The first thing Ronnie did when she returned from the Marquis of Granby was to wash the sandals that had scuffed the blood at the murder scene in a strong solution of bleach. Then she laundered all the clothing she'd worn on that fateful day, even her underwear, and put everything in the clothes bank round the corner from her apartment.

Next, she needed to prepare for Stone's funeral. The Lipman would be closed as a mark of respect, so she had to attend. But so might his neighbours. What if one of them saw a woman wearing a cream-coloured jacket and conspicuous green gloves walk down the street that day? Ronnie had to look as different as possible from then, so she spent a small fortune in Harvey Nicholls on a very formal navy suit. She put temporary blond highlights in her hair and pushed it up into a loose knot. Perfect.

When she woke up on the day itself, she felt better than she expected; the constant gut-wrenching she first experienced after finding Stone's body two weeks ago was now only coming in waves. Ronnie started every day since by scouring social and broadcast media, to make sure there were no nasty surprises.

This morning, breakfast TV ran an item about the funeral, but only as part of another story.

'Britain's biggest drug company, Du Long and Freyer, has reached an out-of-court settlement in the so-called Frankenstein drug trial case. Our legal correspondent, Chris Glazier, is at the High Court and can tell us more.'

The camera cut to a bespectacled reporter outside an imposing grey gothic building.

'Yes, this is the pharmaceutical test that went so horribly wrong seven years ago. DLF were testing a new arthritis drug, codenamed N7241. But not in Britain. Instead, they trialled it in Bihar, one of India's poorest states, and the guinea pigs were a thousand landless farm labourers. Seventy-five of them died and the injuries the others sustained were shocking. Most lost hands, feet, arms or legs.

'No one's confirming any figures, but it's thought the victims will get no more than ten million pounds compensation between them, or ten thousand pounds each.'

Footage appeared on screen of anti-capitalist demonstrators throwing bags of red paint over the marble façade of a building.

'This was the scene yesterday outside DLF's Warren Street headquarters. These activists want executive Paul

Eriksson to resign. He's the man behind the company's tough stance over compensation.'

'Will he go, Chris?'

'Unlikely. There's a lot of sympathy in the City for Eriksson at the moment. He's now running St Agatha's University Hospital for DLF under the government's franchising programme. It's been in real turmoil since the murder of cancer expert Professor Hasely Stone a fortnight ago. St Agatha is the patron saint of nursing and Aggie's needs all the help it can get to nurse it back to health, so Eriksson is safe.'

Ronnie switched off. What a great day to announce bad news.

* * *

The funeral service was held in the Georgian splendour of St John's Wood Church. Everyone was astonished at the speed at which it was arranged but Rhodri Davies reminded anyone who would listen that every fragment of forensic evidence had been taken from the body. There was no issue about cause of death and Stone could be exhumed if necessary as the family had opted for a burial rather than cremation.

Still, friends in high places must have smoothed the way to release his body so fast and a lot of them turned up to pay their respects. The Prince of Wales was there and Prime Minister Stephen Truman. His deputy, Dr Gerry Crewton, accompanied an ashen-faced Angela Stone and her three sons. Trinidad's high commissioner represented the country of her husband's birth.

A gospel choir sang a spiritual as Stone's coffin was brought in, covered in the red, white and black Trinidadian flag, with his framed Nobel Laureate citation on top. The service was relayed to hundreds of silent mourners outside who turned up to show their solidarity. Many more watched online. In eight days, Hasely Stone had become an anti-racist icon.

Ronnie got through the service with only a few wrenches of her well-exercised gut, but the next hour or so would be different. The Stone family had invited all the Lipman-staff, along with VIPs and close friends, back to the house in St John's Wood for refreshments.

She would soon come face to face with the woman whose husband she shared so recently. And in the very place where she found his body.

But there was no choice. Ronnie had to go.

CHAPTER SEVENTEEN

Daniel spotted Alice lurking in a corner the moment he walked onto the patio.

"I didn't expect to see you at the wake, Chief Inspector Mahoney."

"There speaks a member of the Protestant landed gentry. If you had a thimbleful of Irish blood in your veins, you'd know a wake is held before a funeral, not after it."

"Whatever. I'm amazed it's being held here."

"It's Angela Stone's idea. She told Adam Gough she didn't want her home to become a no-go area. Said it was part of the grieving process."

"And why are you here?"

"Someone had to hold Gough's hand."

"Plus the fact that you knew I'd be here and I haven't come back to you about those screengrabs yet."

She grinned.

"Well, you haven't, have you?"

"That's because it takes forever. I finished them at three this morning. Just one tiny wrinkle. You still haven't explained what's in it for me if I hand over such valuable material."

"I can't make any promises. It's not down to me."

"Who would it be down to? Gough? Let's go and ask him."

"No. Not here." She put a firm hand on Daniel's arm as he made to walk over. "I said no."

Daniel smiled.

"Now I get it. You haven't told Gough about the attack on me, have you?"

Alice looked down at the crazy paving.

"We've got no real evidence for anything right at the moment and Tom Edwards thought—"

"So he knows, then. But have you told him the attack on me and the murder of Stone are linked?" She didn't shift her gaze. "Of course you have. And Edwards wants to make sure his lot get the credit if you crack the case, doesn't he?"

"It's not like that."

"Yes it is. If I went over to Gough now and—"

"I don't think that's a good idea."

Alice looked so anxious that Daniel found it hard to repress a laugh.

"I'll see what I can do about getting you some sort of story in return for the stills," she said.

"Now you're talking."

* * *

Ronnie slipped her arm through Laura's as they walked up to the front door of the Stone residence.

"That's kind," said Laura, not realising her companion needed to steady her nerves more than she did.

A security guard crossed them off a list. Ronnie noticed the names of two late additions to the party handwritten on top – Commander Gough and one of the women detectives who'd sat in on her interview. She swallowed hard and took deep breaths, but couldn't look Angela Stone in the eye when they shook hands.

She took Laura into the garden, where most people were sipping glasses of wine. Jason MacGregor, sparkling mineral water in hand, was busy ingratiating himself with Eriksson. Ronnie despised him more by the minute.

"Look who's here," Laura said. She nodded towards Daniel Plowright, deep in conversation with the Deputy Prime Minister and his aide. "He asked me about you the other day. I think he rather likes you."

"Come on, Laura. He doesn't even know me. Anyway, he's got to be three inches shorter than me."

"What he lacks in height, he more than makes up for in charisma. He'll be over here in a flash. Yes, here he comes. I'll say hello, then I'm off."

True to her word, Laura made a swift exit. Ronnie and Daniel were left on their own.

"I almost didn't recognise you, with the highlights," he said.

"Just an experiment."

This guy sure knew how to dress. An expensive midnight blue suit, white shirt with double cuffs and a subdued maroon tie. In fact, she couldn't help thinking he was quite cute. Well, sort of.

"Where do you come from?" he asked.

"Boston. Been here since January."

"My favourite American city. I've got a good friend from Uni who lives in Back Bay. We go to Fenway Park whenever I make it over there in the summer."

"So you're a Red Sox fan."

"Absolutely. I love baseball."

"A little different from your cricket, I think. Don't they play for, like, days at a time?"

"Can be five if it's a test match."

"Wow. I don't think I could sit around for that long."

"You don't have to. These days, you can watch shorter versions of the game, like Twenty-Twenty cricket. It takes about the same time as a baseball match."

Angela Stone walked onto the patio and over to speak to the Deputy Prime Minister. Daniel nodded in her direction.

"She's lucky having Gerry Crewton around at a time like this," he said.

"I guess she knows him very well."

"Been friends for years. She was at Cambridge when he and Hasely went there to do their PhDs. He's almost as devastated as she is."

A waitress refilled his glass with a very large Scotch.

"Dr Crewton seems to be drinking a lot," Ronnie said.

"It's about the only thing he and the PM disagree about. Stephen Truman's strictly a Perrier man. Gerry Crewton's the biggest drinker in the Cabinet. Still, he's got Quentin Plover to look after him today … the guy with the ginger hair? He was with him at the institute last week, remember?"

Remember? How could Ronnie ever forget?

"Why does this country have such a thing about gingers?" she asked. "I read somewhere that even Prince Harry was bullied when he was a kid."

"Maybe, but don't worry about Quentin. He can look after himself. He's one of the sharpest operators in Whitehall and more powerful than most Cabinet ministers. He's looking for a safe seat, so he might even be a Cabinet minister himself after the next election. That's assuming the government wins the next election, of course."

"And will it? Win the next election?"

"That'll be down to how our much-maligned NHS performs. It's top of voters' concerns in every poll. But our rapidly ageing population and a drugs bill going through the roof have put it on life support."

"No different from the States, then. So go on… you cover this stuff. What's your solution?"

"If I knew how to fix it, I'd be standing for Parliament myself. I hate Gerry Crewton's franchise system and the way sharks like Du Long and Freyer are ripping the heart out of our great teaching hospitals but the money's got to come from somewhere. If you've got any bright ideas, Number Ten will be only too pleased to consider them. Sorry for going on. I could talk about the crisis in the NHS all bloody day."

But she didn't mind this man 'going on'. In fact, she rather liked it. She could see why he was a reporter. He was a natural communicator. And he was certainly making this occasion much more bearable for her.

He went off to refill their wine glasses and she glanced around. To her left stood Gough and his female colleague, scrutinising people's faces. Ronnie looked down in case she caught their eye and watched a white butterfly drinking the nectar from a cluster of pinks. It flitted off.

By now, Dr Crewton and his aide were talking to a man who looked about sixty. He was painfully thin, with fragile, light brown skin stretched over gaunt features. Ronnie had noticed him earlier, taking time out to talk to a young black waitress.

He cut a curious figure. Heavy gold wrist chain, chunky rings on his lean fingers and a diamond encased in his top front tooth. In the part of Boston where Ronnie came from, guys who patronised that kind of jeweller usually had a history. When Daniel returned, she asked about him.

"That's Hasely Stone's half-brother, Leon. Hasely told me all about him once. They had the same mother but different fathers, both absent. Brought up in one of Port of Spain's toughest areas. A place called Laventille. Both boys were very bright but mum could only scrape enough money together to send one of them to the high school. Hasely was older, so he got the gig."

"Leon is younger than Professor Stone? He doesn't look it."

"Been very ill recently. Cancer, I think."

"That figures."

"Anyway, Hasely got a scholarship to come to university here, whilst Leon stayed back home. He's now worth a lot of money. Where he got his wealth from is a bit … questionable, shall we say? He's had some unsavoury business associates over the years, quite a few in the narcotics trade. Jamaica may have the reputation for drugs and violence but parts of TnT aren't far behind these days."

"TnT?"

"Trinidad and Tobago. Not that Leon was mixed up in the violent end of the drugs business. His speciality was money laundering. Last year the Home Office stopped him from coming into this country for medical treatment, even though people from Trinidad don't need a visa for the UK."

"You seem very well informed."

"All part of the job. A Scotland Yard contact told me the Met even wanted to prevent him coming for the funeral. Then the word came down from on high and Leon was given permission to stay for a week. It was the last thing Gerry Crewton could do for his old friend."

Daniel's phone vibrated with a message. He apologised for reading it.

"Hey, look, they want me to prepare a piece for the six thirty news. Hasely's funeral will be wrapped up with the court settlement of the Indian drug trial. DLF are behaving appallingly over that."

"You bet. Anyway, it was good to meet you. Maybe next time it will be in happier circumstances."

"I hope so. I'd better get going."

But he didn't get going. Instead, he looked down and fiddled with a signet ring on the little finger of his right hand.

"Look, er … look, this is pretty poor timing, given where we are, but if you fancy seeing how we Brits stage a big ball game, there's a T20 match at Lord's tomorrow and I've got a spare ticket. I suppose you wouldn't be free?"

Ronnie heard herself accepting with barely a moment's hesitation. Daniel handed her his phone.

"Great. Here ... punch your number into my mobile and I'll call you later."

He smiled and said goodbye.

She stood for a while, waiting for Laura to reappear. Apart from Commander Gough and his colleague, the only other person she could see not making small talk was Stephanie Bright. She stood alone, deep in thought, her eyes blinking faster than ever. Stone's death had hit her hard.

"It's Dr Ackerman, isn't it?"

Ronnie turned to see the man with the diamond in his tooth proffering his hand.

"I'm Leon Stone, Hasely's kid brother. You are Dr Veronica Ackerman?"

"Yes."

"I overheard you talking earlier. Hasely told me there was only one American working at the Institute right now."

"I'm sorry for your loss."

"Thank you, ma'am."

"Were you close?"

"We were as kids and we got close again when he started coming back home to see Mom before she died. He stayed with me recently while he was on ... what do you call it? Sabbatical."

"I wish I'd had the chance to know him better."

"Well, he seemed to know a lot about you. He told me you joining the team here was very good news. In fact, he said you were the only person at the institute he trusted."

Ronnie had heard those words before – from Stone's own lips over dinner at his home. She thought it was a chat-up line.

"But we hardly knew each other."

"Maybe that's the point, Dr Ackerman. You're an outsider, you're not part of the furniture. Hasely fought hard to get you appointed because you're from another hospital – another continent, even. He mentioned you to me two days before he was killed. He called to tell me about the peerage and asked me how I was. I haven't been too well, recently. And he said you and I should keep in touch if anything happened to him. He had big plans and he wanted you to be part of 'em."

"What plans?"

"He didn't say no more, ma'am. Two days later, he was dead."

He fished in his pocket and pulled out a crocodile-skin wallet.

"Here's my card with my cell phone number. My home number is on the back. I realise you millennials don't bother much with landlines but I still kinda like 'em. I remember how hard our mom scrimped and saved to get one."

"There's still a landline in my apartment."

"Do you have a card, by any chance?"

"Sorry, no."

"You can write your numbers on the back of one of mine."

How could she refuse?

CHAPTER EIGHTEEN

"So Ronnie, you're not that keen on this guy, then," Nikki said, grinning at her flatmate.

"Absolutely not."

"Then why have you brought him up in conversation every five minutes since breakfast?"

"I haven't. I've—"

"You have so!"

Ronnie felt herself starting to blush and retreated into her bedroom to fix her hair and make-up.

Daniel rang the doorbell ten minutes later.

"What happened to the highlights?" he asked, as they walked down the street.

"I washed them out this morning. Didn't work for me."

"I'm no expert but I think your hair is great as it is. Come and meet Susie."

"Sorry. I didn't realise anyone else was coming."

"Oh, you'll love Susie. Here she is."

He stopped in front of a gleaming motorbike.

"Ronnie – Susie, Susie – Ronnie." He smiled. "Isn't she beautiful? I've just bought her."

"You can't call a motorbike Susie," Ronnie said, laughing.

"Of course I can. She's a Royal Enfield Bullet. A 1950s British design that's been made in India for the last fifty years. So much cooler than a Harley, don't you think?"

"Why Susie?"

"I'll tell you later. Hop on."

It took them less than thirty minutes to reach Lord's.

"Right. If I'm a Red Sox fan when I'm in your hometown, you have to support my team here," Daniel said.

"It's a deal."

Ronnie discovered T20 cricket had just as much razzamatazz as baseball. The players were dressed in bright colours and a skydiver opened proceedings by landing on the pitch with the match ball. She soon found herself very relaxed in this man's presence – much more than she had expected. He seemed very comfortable with her.

"Ackerman's Jewish, isn't it?" he asked, during the interval.

"Comes from my grandfather. He married out. A very big deal back then."

"What about your parents?"

"Mom was born in Tallahassee, Florida, but her parents high-tailed it out of there when she was in third grade and chose the most liberal state in the union, the good ol' Commonwealth of Massachusetts, where she met Pop. He was Boston through and through. They set up home in Dorchester."

"Sounds pretty."

"It sure wasn't when I was growing up. Just about the poorest zip code in Boston. Changed a little since the oatmeal macchiato folks started to move in."

"Brothers and sisters?"

"Nope. I'm an only child. Mom couldn't have any more kids after me. She died last year. We were never close, to be honest. Not real close. Not like Pop and me.

"Pop was always a smoker. Died of lung cancer when I was a kid. The saddest day of my life. Everything I've done since stems from that moment. That was when I decided to become a doctor so I could cure the cancer that killed him."

"So where did you study medicine?"

"Harvard."

"Impressive."

"Let's say I ticked all the right boxes, which helped get me a full scholarship. And I guess it helps that I've always been a superfast reader."

"Wish I could say the same."

"But I still had to work tables in a little Italian place four nights a week to make it through school, while the preppie kids who fill up most of the colleges round there hung loose and spent their trust funds in joints like mine. Then I went home to Mom's and started on my books while those guys ordered another round of beers."

"And I bet you beat all those preppie kids in class, didn't you? Top of your year?"

"Something like that, but I still despised the prepperonis for—"

"The what?"

Ronnie felt herself blushing.

"Prepperonis. That's what I used to call 'em, the preppie kids who spent all their time living the high life instead of studying. They'd order pitcher after pitcher and soak it up with pepperoni pizzas. Okay, sometimes it was a Four Seasons or a Margherita but I had to call them something and 'prepperonis' kinda stuck."

"I always order an American Hot with plenty of pepperoni. I'll never be able to think of it in the same way again."

He flashed her a smile, not so much with his mouth but his eyes. They focused just behind hers for an instant. It gave her goose bumps. Only one man had ever generated that reaction in her – Michael, on the night they first slept together.

"So how come you went into research?"

She took a deep breath.

"During my first clinical rotation, a patient was wheeled in. His heart stopped. The attending physician finally had to call it. But I realised I couldn't do that. I couldn't spend my working life telling people what I'd been told when I was eleven – that the person they loved most in the whole wide world was dead. Stupid, eh? Pop dying … that's what got me into medicine in the first place and that's what stopped me practising it."

"But you didn't drop out of medical school?"

"Hell, no. I couldn't let Mom down. Seeing her kid graduate from Harvard was the proudest day of her life. But I went straight into research after that and did my PhD there. I'm still trying to cure cancer but without the tough stuff, if you know what I mean. Then last year

I got dumped by a guy and came over here in January. That's it. The story so far."

The home team won with a boundary in the last over of the match and the crowd erupted.

"I could get hooked on T20," Ronnie said, as they walked out.

"Great, a convert. Now, I can drop you back home straight away, unless you've got time for a quick bite. If so, there's a great place I know not far away. Do you like Lebanese food?"

"I'd love to give it a try."

"You're in for a treat."

* * *

Gemma Chapman was curious. Normally she phoned the client, not the other way round. But here were three missed calls from him, one straight after another. No voicemail messages. She called back anyway.

"You stupid bitch, Chapman."

"What the fuck are you talking about?"

"Stone had a woman upstairs in his bed."

"Christ. Who?"

"No idea. The police don't even know who she is yet. But she may have seen you, which could be why she's keeping her fucking head down. Why didn't you check out the rest of the house, you twat?"

"Because I didn't want to hang around. I assumed Stone was there on his own."

"Well, he wasn't, was he? Where are you now?"

"Bounds Green."

"Where?"

"Top of the Piccadilly Line. Plowright's here with a girl. They've stopped outside some scuzzy kebab place. God knows why he's brought her here but no chance of … an accident while she's on the back of the bike."

"Get the job done soon. And no more fuck-ups."

CHAPTER NINETEEN

"Bounds Green really is one of the least cool places to hang out in north London," Daniel said, as he locked up the bike.

"Then I'll be right at home," replied Ronnie, smiling. "I come from one of Boston's least cool neighbourhoods."

They walked past a line of people queuing out onto the pavement for takeaways and into a kebab shop. The heat from the charcoal grill, sizzling with skewers of lamb and beef, hit them as they passed.

'This place does the best Lebanese food this side of Beirut,' Daniel said.

He led the way through a door at the back of the shop into a large restaurant.

'Hey, it's like the Tardis,' Ronnie said.

'I wouldn't have put you down as a Doctor Who fan.'

'There are a lot of things you don't know about me,' she said, with a wink.

The restaurant was a further assault on the senses. Bright lights reflected off gold, brass and red Arabic fittings, whilst the competing aromas of fresh bread, cumin and the sweet smell of honey, dripping from baklava on a trolley, wafted across the warm evening air. The place was almost full, even though it was early.

"Marhaba," Daniel said to the maître d', who greeted him like an old friend.

"Ahlan wa sahlan," replied the waiter.

"Shukran."

They were shown to a table by a window. A faint breeze found its way through. A godsend on an evening like this.

"I booked ahead for this spot," Daniel said.

"I'm glad you did," Ronnie replied, looking around at the other diners. "The food must be good for all these guys to be eating it in this temperature."

"It is."

"What did you say to the maître d'?"

"I said 'hello'. He wished us 'welcome' in return and I said 'shukran' – 'thank you'. That's about my limit on conversational Arabic, I'm afraid."

The waiter handed them each a menu.

"It all looks great, but I wouldn't know where to start," Ronnie said, eyeing up what her fellow diners were eating.

"I never have a main course in a place like this, just lots of small dishes in a mezze. I could suggest a few things."

"Better still, why don't you order for us?"

The waiter brought them hot puffed-up Arabic breads and Daniel ordered what seemed like a never-ending selection of little dishes, plus a bottle of red Chateau Musar.

"I love this wine," he said. "It's from the Bekaa Valley in Lebanon. And I love this place. No one recognises me here."

"Isn't it part of the job, being recognised?"

"I suppose so, but it's a pain. People have a horrible habit of sucking up to you because your face is on the telly. That's why I was intrigued by you."

"How come?"

"Well, the first time we met, you didn't exactly sign up for membership of the Daniel Plowright fan club, did you?"

She laughed.

"I was having a bad day."

"You were just being direct. Makes a change from the air-heads who swear they're your biggest fan."

"If you don't like being recognised, why do you work in TV?"

"Because I love it. I don't really think of it as a job. My definition of a job is something that's so dull, you only do it because someone pays you. I'd probably do this anyway. At least, I would have said that until a couple of years ago, when Star Corp took over. It's been downhill since then and I'll definitely be jumping ship if their impartiality campaign is successful."

"What's that about?"

"By law, broadcast news in Britain has to be balanced, fair, impartial. It used to be that way in the States but you guys changed the rules way back. Now you've got shock jocks and Fox News. Star Corp is pushing for the same thing here when the new Broadcasting Bill goes through the Commons. The suits on the Seventh Floor spend half their time lobbying for it in Whitehall."

"The world sure doesn't need another Fox News," Ronnie mumbled, through a mouthful of falafel.

"The job still has its compensations, though. My life's full of fascinating people. Like you, for instance. More wine?"

"You bet. It's delicious. I'm a convert to Lebanese cuisine after just one meal. We must do this again."

He smiled.

"Any time."

"Now it's your turn," Ronnie said. "What's your story?"

"Brought up in Berkshire. Dad's a merchant banker. Mum does charity work. They still don't think I do a proper job, not like my two big brothers. Ben's in the City, Jasper's at the Foreign Office."

"Where did you go to school?"

He paused.

"Near Windsor."

She thought for a moment, then smiled.

"If your father works in the City and your folks live in well-to-do Berkshire, I bet you went to Eton College, didn't you?"

"You've discovered my guilty secret."

She smiled again.

"There's no need for it to be a secret. Windsor Castle and Eton were the first places I visited as a tourist when I came here. It's beautiful there – and so old. They said Eton was founded almost 50 years before Columbus set sail for the Americas. Unreal. And after that, you went to Oxford, didn't you? All Old Etonians go there."

"I didn't go to Ukksforrd," Daniel said, in his best Bostonian.

"Cambridge?"

"I didn't go to either. Didn't even apply. They're both full of Old Etonians, for a start."

"Would that have been so bad?"

"Eton was pretty awful. I can't believe such institutions still exist in the twenty-first century."

"So you're not really a prepperoni, even though you went to a swanky school."

"I certainly hope not." He laughed.

"So where did you go?"

"I went backpacking round Australia on a gap year. Mum and Dad were furious. Ended up getting work experience on the West Australian newspaper in Perth. Then a Brit disappeared in the Outback for three weeks. It was a massive story because he came from my old alma mater and was a friend of the Prince of Wales."

"Hey, I remember that. It was big news in the States, too, because of the royal thing."

"I got the only interview with him, plus pictures. A world exclusive on my first big story. I was hooked. Came back here and applied to all the Unis with the best student newspapers and TV stations. Did politics at Leeds but spent most of my time there as a student hack, building up a cuttings file and a showreel. Went into TV news straight from there … There. That's me. Now it's my turn again."

"Not so fast. You haven't told me yet why you call your bike Susie."

Daniel took a deep breath.

"A couple of years ago, I was running up Primrose Hill and I collapsed, coughing up blood. They took me to Aggies. It was non-small-cell lung cancer. I couldn't believe it. I was only thirty and hadn't smoked so much as a spliff since Leeds."

She touched his hand.

"Telling my parents was bad enough. Mum was a wreck for weeks. But Alice couldn't cope at all."

"Alice?"

"We lived together for two years. She's a copper. Bit of a high flier. We were due to get married."

Ronnie looked away for a moment.

"You don't have to talk about this if you don't want to."

"No, it's fine. Anyway, it didn't take very long to discover my chances were terrible. After pancreatic and liver cancer, lung cancer's got just about the worst prognosis going, right?"

"It's not great."

"Then Alice said she wanted to end it. There wasn't anyone else. She's just one of those people who can't stand illness and hospitals and stuff."

Ronnie touched his hand again; left it there. Daniel didn't attempt to move it.

"What happened then?" she asked.

"An operation was out of the question. The tumour was too advanced. Instead, they used chemotherapy to shrink it and give me more time. But it grew to a stage four within a couple of months."

Ronnie took her hand away.

"You all right?" he asked.

"Er, sure."

"Then this new nurse started on the ward. From the first day, the effect she had on me was extraordinary. There was no sympathy. She just told me I would only get through this if I got off my arse and fought the bloody thing. 'Life is not a dress rehearsal'. That was her favourite phrase. For about a week I was madly in love with her – on the rebound, I suppose – but she was always professional. Then Hasely Stone came to see me. She'd recommended me for a clinical trial he was starting. It was just a Phase 0 trial, on a small group of patients to check how toxic a new drug regimen was. But what had I got to lose?"

"Are you sure your tumour was a stage four?"

"It was by the time I went on the trial. But I had a scan in the third week of treatment and it had already shrunk by half. By the end of the following month, it had disappeared completely. And it has not come back, touch wood."

"That's … quite a result. What did Stone say?"

"Just told me I was lucky. But the person I had to thank most was that nurse. I wouldn't have been on the trial if it hadn't been for her. She taught me that life wasn't a dress rehearsal, something I've said to myself every day since. And I live by it. I bought myself something I'd always wanted – an Enfield Bullet motorbike. And named it after her.

"The nurse's name was Susie."

* * *

Ronnie was confused. No she wasn't. She was furious. Fifteen minutes ago, she was having a wonderful evening with a lovely man. The chemistry with Daniel was special. She knew it, he knew it. So why did he ruin it all by spinning her a yarn?

If his tumour had been that advanced, he should be dead by now. Lung cancer patients like Daniel had one of the lowest five-year survival rates. Anyway, tumours didn't just disappear like that, so how dare he give her that load of baloney?

She walked back to the table from the ladies room.

"Something the matter?" Daniel asked.

She looked away.

"Tired. Been a long day."

"Same here. I'll get the bill. I'm off to Belfast tomorrow on the first plane."

"What are you doing there?"

"Bobby Strachan, the leader of the BUP, is giving evidence in the trial of an Ulster loyalist charged with kicking a Catholic's head in during a riot. Not that it was Bobby's argument. He was just there for the punch-up."

Ronnie made a decision. Enough of the small talk. She's never going to see this chancer again, so she might as well smoke him out.

"Hey, look, I'd be really interested in following up on your case. Would you mind if I looked up your file sometime?"

He agreed.

"I know what you're thinking. How the hell can anyone with a stage four lung cancer tumour still be alive and kicking?"

Ronnie felt the blood rush to her cheeks.

"No, no. But I think your case may be a little more … complicated than you realise."

"Well, take a look at the file by all means. I'd love a second opinion. There's a hard copy in my flat and we can pick it on the way back."

"A hard copy?"

"Laura sent it to me by snail mail last month. Hasely Stone asked her to. Weird, eh? Who the hell prints out hard copies of anything these days unless it's a wedding invitation? I asked him about it the last time he called me. He just said he felt safer – that was the word he used – knowing there was a hard copy of my file out there. Twenty-four hours later he was dead."

CHAPTER TWENTY

Daniel noticed the square headlights of the Lexus flash on as they walked out of the restaurant. The car had been parked in the same place two hours ago.

He pulled the Bullet away, with Ronnie riding pillion. Square Headlights followed. Daniel turned left along Alexandra Park Road towards Muswell Hill. So did the Lexus.

Time to shake this guy off. Daniel veered onto Grove Road and over the speed bumps. The car didn't follow and he relaxed.

Not for long. Half a mile ahead, Square Headlights was waiting for them at the top of Muswell Hill Broadway. This guy knew his way round north London, then.

Daniel stopped a hundred yards further up. The Lexus flashed past as he got off before walking over to an ATM. He took £300 out.

"Everything all right?" Ronnie asked, when he returned. "You seem a little jumpy."

"Er, fine. A car got a bit close back there, that's all. I never forget that you're more vulnerable on a bike than in the flimsiest of cars."

He rode on, only to see the Lexus lurking in a side turning at the end of the Broadway. It pulled out behind them once again.

Daniel decided it was time to shake this joker off once and for all. The road on the edge of Hampstead Heath, between the old tollgate and the Spaniards Inn opposite, was so narrow that only one vehicle at a time could get through. Traffic jams built up at all hours. Just what he needed.

He arrived at the tailback and glanced in his mirrors. The Lexus was right behind. The deepening twilight, contrasting with the car's strong headlights, made it impossible to identify the occupants.

Daniel reached the front of the queue. A convoy of cars was coming through in the other direction. Then he saw his chance. A slight gap between two of the oncoming vehicles appeared and he roared away, leaving his shadow stranded.

* * *

By the time Daniel and Ronnie arrived back at his flat in Primrose Hill, he'd made up his mind. He wasn't staying there tonight. 'Watch your back,' was Alice's advice. Now was the time to do that.

"I've decided to stay with Mum and Dad in Marlow tonight," he said. "It's a much better journey to Heathrow."

Daniel left Ronnie by the bike and dashed across the road into his flat. He filled a bag with enough clothes for a couple of days, plus passport, laptop and his medical file. He also packed a stab vest. Once bitten, twice shy. His pursuers could go hang.

Maybe not. As Daniel stepped back onto the road, he sensed movement to his right. Instinct made him turn towards it.

The wing mirror of the Lexus smashed into his left elbow, spinning him round and throwing him onto the tarmac. The back tyre missed his right foot by an inch as the car sped past without stopping.

First reaction – memorise the number plate. GS72 was all he could make out. Second reaction – you bloody idiot! And that was what he was shouting to himself as Ronnie ran across.

"Don't get up.", she said. Daniel began to pick himself up off the ground. "I said don't get up"

"I'm Okay, honest," he said. "Nothing broken. If you're hit by a car, make sure you're wearing brand-new Enfield leathers. Not so brand new anymore, mind."

"What was that guy playing at?"

"I don't know. Maybe I cut him up and he took the hump."

"We'd better ring the cops. And you need to get yourself checked out at the ER."

"No, I'm all right … Really. Let's get you home. Here's my file. Let me know what you think."

There were no further signs of the Lexus as they rode back to Fulham. Ronnie offered him coffee, but he declined. They parted with a peck on the cheek and he rode off.

Daniel turned the corner, pulled the bike into the kerb, and took out his mobile.

"Alice? You were right. They tried to kill me again tonight. Hit and run this time."

"Christ."

"Don't worry. I'm still in one piece."

"What happened?"

"It was outside my flat. The wing mirror of this red Lexus clipped me and I ended up in the road. But I was fucking lucky. If they'd hit me full on, it would have been curtains."

"Blimey. You didn't get the number, I suppose?"

"Only the first four digits. GS72."

"Good boy."

"And I think you'd better have those screen grabs right now. I'll send them to your phone."

CHAPTER TWENTY-ONE

Ronnie was pleased that her flat mate, Nikki, was working nights right now. She couldn't face a third-degree interrogation tonight about her day with Daniel, especially not the way he'd try to bullshit her about his illness.

But she was still intrigued about what she was going to find in his file. She made herself a cup of green tea, sat down in the still-warm yard and opened it.

Daniel was admitted to St Agatha's ER a little over two years ago. Chest x-ray and MRI scan ordered on day of admission. Stage three non-small-cell carcinoma. Wow. This tumour was big.

Path lab analysis showed it to be so unfavourable that chemo would have marginal benefits at best … Combretastatin and Tamoxadrene prescribed for palliative care only … cancer reclassified as stage four two months later.

Then there was an entry with Stone's initials next to it. 'Patient put on AI-Protocol Phase 0 trial'.

AI-Protocol? Strange. Ronnie had never heard of that. More curious still, there was no indication about the drug regimen used, just references to a series of injections.

Even more curious. Stephanie Bright had carried out all of them. Her initials were there each time. Clinicians of her rank never administered chemo.

Ronnie read faster. Eight injections over four weeks. An MRI scan in week three. Tumour shrunk by 55%. Another MRI five weeks later. No sign of any disease. Regular follow-up appointments and MRI scans. No recurrence of tumours. Jesus.

There must be a clue to why this patient made such an extraordinary recovery. Could she have missed something? But there was nothing, not even the name of the drugs Stone and Bright used in this AI-Protocol, let alone what 'AI' stood for.

Ronnie had a reputation for speaking her mind, even putting her foot in it sometimes. She was never lost for words. But on this balmy June night in the middle of a London heatwave, Veronica Ackerman, BSc, MD, PhD was speechless. Daniel Plowright wasn't making it up at all.

* * *

Daniel sat next to a couple of snoozing backpackers in Heathrow's Terminal Two, waiting for the 6.50a.m. Belfast flight to be called.

Foremost on his mind should have been the hit and run, of course. He knew it was only a matter of time before those bastards tried again. But all he could think about was why Ronnie went so cool on him last night.

Up to that point, it was a magical evening. No one had ever prised so much information out of him so fast. Some of the memories were painful but it seemed perfectly normal to talk about them to her, even though they hardly knew each other. Maybe it was because they talked about death, the ultimate taboo. Perhaps he was ready for another relationship; it was more than a year since Alice walked out. Or was it just because this woman was so captivating?

Sod the psychology. Daniel preferred the third option. Ronnie wasn't a classic beauty but she was very attractive. Feisty, too. He loved that. And she was bloody good at getting under his skin. She didn't even seem to mind that he was three inches shorter than her; a lot of women did. Then her demeanour changed completely.

His mobile rang. It was her. The lady herself.

"Daniel? I hope I'm not calling too early."

"No. it's fine. I'm about to board the flight. How are you today?"

"I'm… Okay. How about you?"

"Never felt better, considering I was smacked by a car a few hours ago. No big bruises or swelling, though. I'll live."

"That's good to hear."

"Aer Lingus flight EI930 to Belfast City is now ready for boarding at gate nineteen."

"Sorry. They've just called my flight."

"Look, Daniel … Before you go, I have to tell you something. It's the reason I'm ringing so early. You need to know I read your file and … I'm sorry for ever doubting you."

He breathed a sigh of relief and immediately hoped she hadn't heard it.

"There did seem to be a bit of a transformation towards the end of dinner," he said.

"I guess I may have thought—"

"That I was making it all up?"

"No, no. I knew you'd been ill, but I've never heard of anyone recovering so fast from stage four non-small-cell lung carcinoma. You're a medical miracle, Daniel Plowright."

"Nice of you to say." He was doing his best not to sound jubilant. "Look, forget it. Let's talk when I get back. Can I give you a ring?"

"I'd like that. A lot. Take care of yourself."

Daniel felt like punching the air.

CHAPTER TWENTY-TWO

A small contingent of anti-capitalist demonstrators was already camped outside St Agatha's by the time Ronnie got to work. They were waiting for Paul Eriksson, who had become their *bête noire* since the Indian drug trial settlement was announced.

Six burly security men linked arms to stop them scratching the immaculate paintwork of his black Tesla as it swept through the gates. Ronnie thought he deserved everything he got.

She sat down at her desk just as Stephanie Bright appeared.

"Good morning, Stephanie. You're in early."

Bright didn't reply as she walked across the room, head down, eyes blinking as usual.

"Stephanie, I wonder if you can help me here. Last night I had dinner with Daniel Plowright. You treated him, right?"

"What about it?" she snapped.

"Well, he lent me his hospital file and—"

"What are you doing with that?"

She walked over and snatched the file off Ronnie's desk.

"You have no right to be reading this, do you hear? No right."

"Excuse me, Stephanie, but Daniel's entitled to a copy of his own medical notes and he lent them to me. I'd like to know more about this AI-Protocol you put him on, because—"

"We've stopped it. We've stopped the protocol. The protocol did more harm than good. Forget you ever heard about it, understand? Understand?"

Bright stalked out of the room with the file, shaking with fear or rage. Ronnie wasn't sure.

There was no way she would give Daniel's notes back anytime soon. But it didn't matter. She just needed to call up his clinical record.

But when Ronnie logged on, she found nothing. His file was there, all right, together with his hospital number and the initials 'AIP' in the right-hand column, but nothing else. No scans, no details of injections, no reports. Not a thing. Daniel's notes had been wiped. Just like Hasely Stone's.

If anyone could help, it was Maurice Sutcliffe in Patient Records. Pretty soon, she was drinking coffee by his side whilst he tried in vain to locate the information removed from Daniel's file. Then he combed Aggies' backup files, held by Du Long and Freyer at its data centre in Leicester. The details were missing there, too. Maurice's face grew more tense by the minute.

"This material was deliberately removed," he said, his fingers flying across the keyboard in a desperate search for it. "The same thing happened with Professor Stone's medical file the week before last, but I only heard about it yesterday."

"Why on earth would anyone want to wipe the professor's notes?" Ronnie asked, trying to sound like it was news to her.

"God knows. I was here till one this morning trying to figure it out. I needed to rule out everything else apart from ..." he trailed off, still staring at the screen "... the fact we've been hacked, well and truly.

"Last night I didn't want to admit it to myself because the Information Commissioner's Office will be swarming all over this place when I tell them. Been that way ever since the first big NHS cyber-attack in 2017. But now I've got no choice. God knows what Paul Eriksson will say. I just can't see why anyone would want to wipe these files."

"The one thing left on Daniel's is that reference to AIP," Ronnie said. "Do you know what it stands for? AI, anyhow. I'm guessing the P stands for 'Protocol'."

"No idea. Let's search to see if there are any other AIP files." Sutcliffe's fingers danced across the keyboard. "Yes, three ... Maria Grigorenko, Heather Spink and Harry Kings. None of them contains any data, either. Look at the tiny file sizes. Although ... hang on ... I can find out when they were wiped. The Leicester centre contains details of all the incremental updates to the hospital database on a minute-by-minute basis." He typed away even faster. "Look. The four AIP files and Professor Stone's file were all accessed between eleven and eleven fifteen on the morning of Monday, June the fourteenth. That's when they must have been wiped. Now we're cooking with gas because ..." He pulled up a calendar on the screen. "... That's the morning when the DLF cyber security team came to do a spot check. At least that's who they said they were."

"Did they have ID?"

"Of course. And I got an email from DLF's head of cyber security giving me an hour's notice of their visit. No reason to doubt them. But they must have been our hackers"

"What did they look like?"

"A man and a woman. Worked for a contractor called Computercom … got her card somewhere … There you go. Siobhan Anderson. Thirties, short, mousy hair, a bit butch. He was taller and younger with glasses. Can't remember his name." Then Sutcliffe's eyes lit up. "Wait a sec. We should be able to pick them up on CCTV." He typed away for another thirty seconds. "Blimey. There's nothing there, either. God, these people are good."

"The CCTV files must be backed up, surely."

"Of course, but in Leicester again. I bet you a pound to a penny they've been wiped, too."

He was right.

* * *

By the time Ronnie got back to her office, the other three post-docs were in, gossiping over coffee. She sat down at her desk, cursing herself for not taking a copy of Daniel's file when she had the chance. But why would anybody want to wipe it and why was this damn protocol such a secret? Hell would freeze over before Bright gave Daniel's file back. She'd stormed out without even logging onto her laptop.

Her laptop! If you wanted to keep something confidential, where would you store it? Not on the hospital IT system. Anyone could access that. So you'd store it offline. And Bright's laptop was the logical place to start looking.

Everyone in the institute was handed their personal laptop when they arrived, a gift from a grateful billionaire still alive and kicking after a stage two tumour in his left lung was whacked by Tamoxodrene a couple of years back. They weren't the fastest machines in the world but they did the job. All were alarmed to prevent them being taken out of the hospital, so most people left them on their desks, Bright included. And they still used good, old-fashioned passwords.

Ronnie began to think fast. It wouldn't be easy getting Bright's password. Following fingers over a keyboard was difficult at the best of times. You really needed to video it. Of course…

Ronnie flicked on her phone's video camera and held it up to her ear. Then she wandered round the office, continuing an imaginary call. Standing at the noticeboard right next to Bright's desk, she leaned over so the phone would point in the direction of the keyboard and kept her head absolutely still

There was no time to check if she had the alignment right. Bright was back – without the file – and was sitting down at her desk. Ronnie ignored her and continued her imaginary phone call whilst her target logged on.

In the ladies' room she checked her 'rushes'. Phew – the keyboard was plumb in the middle of the picture. After five attempts to analyse Bright's lightning keystrokes, she made out the password, 'Brightorwrong'. Not very funny. Not very secure, either. Not even a number in it.

* * *

Chapman wasn't stupid. The last thing she needed was a speed camera clocking the red Lexus over the limit as it purred across the Severn Bridge, out of Wales and back into England. She set the speed limiter at 69mph.

The dashboard console lit up with a call. The client.

"So what happened last night?" he snapped. "Just how difficult can it be to deal with one man?"

"I did say we only clipped him," Chapman replied.

"You barely did that. He's been on the lunchtime news from Belfast and looks right as rain."

"Don't sweat. We'll get him. In the meantime, you'll be glad to know I should have everything mopped up at the Lipman by tonight. RIP AIP, you might say."

"I suppose you've got a good line in Holocaust jokes as well, have you?"

"Since you ask, have you heard—"

"Shut it, Chapman."

CHAPTER TWENTY-THREE

Ronnie waited till late before logging on to Bright's laptop. It was only three days after Midsummer's Day, so twilight would extend well into the evening.

At seven, she moved her bike from its usual place outside the institute's Portakabins to a rack on the other side of the quadrangle. It would look like she'd gone home already. Too nervous to eat, she went to the hospital gym to while away an hour or so.

By ten it was dark enough to go back to the Lipman. Ronnie locked the office door behind her but didn't switch on the lights. There was just enough twilight for her to see what she was doing.

She logged onto Bright's laptop and saw what she was looking for straight away. The folder, named "AIP", contained about twenty files.

Ronnie glanced down at the file names. Plowright, Grigorenko, Spink and Kings were all there but none of the other files seemed to refer to individual patients. There was no time to read them now. She slid an SD card into the slot and was about to copy the files when she heard the echo of footsteps down the corridor. And raised voices.

Something about their tone made her glad she'd left the lights off. One voice belonged to Stephanie Bright.

She sounded very scared. The other was lower, less educated – and menacing.

Ronnie whipped the card out of the laptop, closed it and sprinted across to her desk. There was just time to duck behind it before Bright opened the door and came in with a man. She didn't turn on the lights, either. The man was short, with tightly cropped hair and wearing a hoodie over a muscular frame.

Sweat ran into Ronnie's eyes but she didn't dare move to wipe it away. Her heart beat so hard she was amazed the others couldn't hear it. Then Bright's companion spoke. 'He' was a 'she'.

"For a scientist you're thick as shit, aren't you, Stephanie? You still don't know what you've got yourself into."

"I know you're a bloody animal, Chapman. Why did you have to kill Stone?"

"That's for someone way above my pay grade. I just carry out the orders. So I need your laptop and anything else you've got on this bloody protocol. Then I'm off."

"This is all I've got," Bright said, handing over a file. "The rest are on this laptop but you can't take that. An alarm will sound immediately you walk off site."

"That won't be a problem."

There was a muffled yelp, followed by a short struggle and a choking, gurgling sound. Then a crunch, like someone treading on a pack of potato chips. Ronnie knew what that was. Necks only break with a clean snap in the movies. Finally, Bright's body hit the floor. Chapman tucked the laptop and file of papers under her arm and left the office.

Ronnie kept herself well-hidden and waited for the sound of her footsteps to recede before scrambling out. She knew what she would find but checked Bright's prostrate body all the same. No pulse.

It occurred to her that a woman capable of doing so much damage with her bare hands must be very strong, but she didn't have time to think about it. The footsteps were returning. She dived under Bright's desk and slid up close to her body. A stench infiltrated her nostrils; Bright had opened her bowels in her last panic-stricken seconds.

Soon she smelt another. The fumes from the gasoline wafted in her direction as soon as Chapman began sloshing it round the room. She gave Bright's body a particularly generous soaking, even knocking Ronnie's foot in the process.

There was a crash. Chapman had smashed open the office door across the corridor and was pouring gasoline around there, too.

Ronnie waited until she was sure the killer had moved to the far end of the room opposite before she scampered out into the corridor. Bright's computer and Daniel's file lay on the floor but she was too frightened to stop for them. She ran out into the shadows and across the courtyard. At least her bike in the rack would give her some cover. Unless the killer came her way.

Chapman walked across the other side of the quadrangle, thank God, pulling her hoodie over her head. Then she flung a large pile of papers into the air. Seconds later, an explosion shattered the windows and flames roared out.

The institute was matchwood within minutes.

CHAPTER TWENTY-FOUR

Daniel was dozing off as the chimes of Big Ben rang out on the hotel radio.

> 'This is the BBC News at Midnight. Hundreds of patients were evacuated from St Agatha's University Hospital in central London tonight after an explosion and fire. The blast took place in the hospital's world-famous Lipman Cancer Research Institute and there are fears the blaze could spread to the rest of the complex.'

Daniel grabbed the TV remote and turned on the BBC news channel. Footage of flames licking around the charred remains of the institute led the bulletin. A rather breathless reporter held up a piece of paper up to the camera.

> 'On the ground are dozens of leaflets like this, purporting to come from the anti-vivisection group, Animals First. Over the past three years, it's staged a campaign against the drug company now running St Agatha's, Du Long and Freyer. It claims DLF inflicts unnecessary cruelty on animals at a laboratory it operates in Hertfordshire but the group has already denied responsibility for this attack.'

Daniel picked up his mobile and dialled.

"I thought you might call when you heard the news," Ronnie said.

"How are you?"

"I'm fine but I'm all in. I've got to get some sleep. Let me call you when I wake up."

"If you insist. My phone'll be on silent from nine thirty because I'm in court. With luck, I'll be on the three o'clock from Belfast City to Heathrow. Call me ... promise?"

"I promise. Now goodnight."

"Sleep tight."

* * *

Ronnie needed to talk to someone but not Daniel. They hardly knew each other. She picked up her cell phone.

"Hi darling," Todd said, after four rings. "How are things?"

This time, she told him everything. About the AI-Protocol and the fire and Stephanie Bright and Daniel Plowright. She told him about finding Stone's body and lying about it to the police. And – hell, he had to know – she told him how she landed up drunk in bed with Stone.

"That's ... quite a tale."

"I thought you needed to know all of it, Toddy. I don't think we had sex in the end but I still feel so stupid for sleeping with him."

"Stupid? You're not stupid. You're a victim, for Christ's sake. Haven't you heard of 'Me Too'?"

"Yes, but—"

"No 'buts', my darling. A powerful man gets a less powerful woman he works with so drunk that he gets her into bed. Just how does that end up being your fault?"

"When you put it like that."

"I do put it like that. But answer me one thing. Why didn't you call the cops when you found Stone's body and tell them you'd spent the night on the couch or something?"

"I thought about that the minute I got out of the damn place. It must have a gazillion spare rooms. If I said I'd slept in one of 'em, I wouldn't be in this dumb-ass mess right now."

"Well, you are. Look, let me think about this. I'll call you in a while."

He was back on the line twenty minutes later.

"Right, darling, you need to go to the cops. You know that, don't you?"

"I guess."

"Ronnie, you've got to. You're a key witness in two murders."

"I'll go tomorrow. I promise."

"No, no. That wouldn't be smart, my darling."

"Why?"

"Come on, think about it. What evidence have you got to show you're not involved in all this?"

"I don't get you."

"You're gonna tell them this Chapman woman killed both Stephanie Bright and Hasely Stone because they ran a mysterious drug trial called the AI-Protocol."

"That's the truth."

"But what evidence have you got this protocol even exists? You've got no patient files. They've been wiped. No corroboration. No nothing. Hell, you don't even know what 'AI' stands for. What you've got barely scratches the surface right now. And what have the cops got? Two murders and, hey, you've been at both crime scenes. If you're lucky, you'll get an obstruction of justice rap. If not, you could be facing two counts of murder one."

She'd never thought of that but Todd was dead right.

"So what should I do?" Ronnie asked.

"Go to the police, for sure, but first you need evidence this drug protocol is for real. If you can get it."

"How the hell do I do that?"

"Look, Stone sent this friend of yours, Daniel, a hard copy of his file, right?"

"But Stephanie Bright gave it to Chapman," snapped Ronnie.

"Don't be tetchy, darling. I'm only trying to help."

"Sorry."

"Well, maybe Stone sent the other patients on the protocol a copy of their files, too. Have you got their names?"

"Kings, Spink, and some Eastern European name."

"Can you get their addresses?"

"Laura – Stone's PA – she'll have them, for sure. She mailed Daniel's file to him."

"Great. If you can get their files, you can go to the cops with proof the protocol exists. They'll show how powerful this thing is. Powerful enough for someone to kill twice over."

"I guess."

"Those files won't answer the two big questions, of course."

"Which are?"

"Who the hell would want to kill Stone and Bright in the first place. And why?"

CHAPTER TWENTY-FIVE

"Morning, Daniel."

"Hi, Alice."

"You've heard the news, I suppose?"

"Of course. Anything new? The Beeb said last night that Animals First is in the frame for burning down the Lipman."

"Fat chance. We've got a briefing here at the Yard in half an hour, so I'll know more then. But the fluffy bunny brigade'll be as likely to have done this as the BUP was to have murdered Stone. Both killings have the same watermark, if you ask me."

"Killings?"

"Sorry. I should've explained. They found a body in the early hours. A woman. Burnt beyond recognition but her neck was broken."

"Christ. And you think it's linked to Stone's murder?"

"Two people murdered from the same department in the same hospital? Both killed within a fortnight of each other and at both crime scenes dodgy evidence connecting the murders to violent extremists? I'd stake my pension on them being linked, wouldn't you? It won't stop us pulling in the usual suspects Animals First, of course, but it'll be a waste of time."

"So who did do it, then?"

"How the hell do I know? Maybe one of the guys from your London Fields piccies. And very good they are, too. That cameraman you work with?"

"Jon."

"Yeah, him. The boy done good. We put his piccies through a couple of digital enhancement programmes, then we applied face recognition software. I assumed the people we're looking for are not connected to either the BUP or their opponents. So we excluded everyone in our existing rogues' gallery, plus coppers, and any members of the media accredited with the Met. When did you last update your press card photo, by the way?"

"I don't think I ever have."

"Time you did. You look about twelve."

"I'll stick it on my 'to do' list."

"Anyway, out of all the piccies you sent, we were left with only five people we knew nothing about. Four men and a woman."

"That's not many."

"You have to get lucky sometime. I'll send the enhanced picture files to your phone in a minute. See if they ring any bells, especially the black guy."

"Why him?"

"Because there's no way he can be BUP and we don't think the guy who attacked you was a member, either."

"You still haven't told me why."

"And I still can't. No luck on the Lexus that tried to run you down, by the way. The plates were stolen three nights ago."

"Always a long shot."

"Worth a try, though," said Alice. "Look, I've got to go. I need a strong black coffee to get my brain in gear before the briefing gets going. But I've been thinking. This outfit has murdered two people and tried to kill you a twice into the bargain. I might be able to arrange a bit of police protection, at least for a while. What do you think?"

"What's the point? You can't protect me for ever. I'm better off keeping my eyes open, aren't I?"

"I thought you'd say that."

"Thanks for the offer, though."

"All part of the service. By the way, I got the promotion."

"Congratulations, Superintendent Mahoney."

"Only 'temporary superintendent' for now."

"Well done, anyway. Do I have to be nice to you from now on?"

"You've always been nice to me. A lot nicer than I've been to you."

Alice ended the call.

Daniel's phone vibrated a few seconds later with the picture files. He flicked through them but none of the faces looked any more familiar now than when he first created them from Jon's rushes. He decided to give them names to jog his memory.

Daniel wouldn't forget Pic 1 in a hurry. Bald, overweight and with a scar on his right cheek. It looked like someone had split his face apart with a can opener. Pic 1 was *Scarface*.

Pic 2 was the black guy Alice mentioned. Mid-thirties and well built, with a diamond earring in his left ear. Easy – *Black Diamond.* Despite her hunch, Daniel didn't recognise him.

Pic 3's mum might love him but nobody else would, on account of the swastika-like symbol tattooed on his neck. Easy. *Stormtrooper.*

Pic 4 was more difficult. The only woman. Very short, light brown hair and no stand-out features you could put your finger on. A friend of Daniel's mother got a lot of work as a TV extra because she looked so bland. This woman could be her daughter. Pic 4 – *Ms Bland.*

Pic 5 was in his thirties with long black hair and a beard. Perfect for the lead in a Passion play. *Son of God.*

He flicked through them again. If one of them was the killer, he would be better prepared when he met them next time.

And Daniel was certain. There would be a next time.

* * *

Alice waited until everyone left the room after the briefing before she rang Tom Edwards.

"I think it's time to talk to Commander Gough, sir. I'm worried about Daniel."

"And how will telling Gough help? He's got enough on his plate with Number Ten ringing him every bloody day. Besides, you offered your man police protection and he refused it. I wouldn't say anything to Gough yet. Wait until you've got something concrete."

"But what possible explanation can I give for not telling him?"

"Simple. You say his boys and girls were so busy following up concrete leads you didn't want to burden them with half-chances until you'd firmed them up a bit."

"All right, sir. I just hope this doesn't come back to bite us."

CHAPTER TWENTY-SIX

The warble from Ronnie's mobile woke her for a few seconds but she dozed off again immediately. She'd had a fitful night. Every time she began to drift off, she could hear the crunch of Stephanie Bright's neck breaking.

When her pesky iPhone disturbed her again after a couple of minutes, she forced herself to read the text.

'This is a message to all members of staff at the Lipman Institute ... We regret to announce that a fire has badly damaged the institute's temporary buildings overnight. Please do NOT come into work until 2p.m. When you arrive, please assemble in the library on the first floor of the main building. Thank you for your co-operation at this difficult time.'

Ronnie cycled down Marylebone Road towards the hospital four hours later. She could taste something foul – and familiar – in the air.

Last spring, Michael took her to the Dominican Republic for a vacation after Mom died. They went across the border into Haiti for a day and passed a garbage tip. Hundreds of people eked out a living there by scouring the rotting rubbish, their lives shortened by the acrid smoke that clung to the place like a blanket.

This morning, the air round Aggie's smelt just the same.

Ronnie locked up her bike in the same rack as last night, walked round the police tape that cordoned off the institute's blackened remains and up to the library.

Laura was standing by the door, the colour drained from her face.

"They've found someone dead in there," she whispered.

Ronnie tried her best to look surprised.

"I thought they said on the news no one was hurt."

"They did. But I play badminton with the head of security's wife. He told me they've found a body."

"Who is it?"

"No idea. There'll be an announcement at quarter past."

At two fifteen sharp, Paul Eriksson walked in with a three-strong retinue. His demeanour was almost genial by his brittle standards.

"I've got several things to say at this very difficult time. First, I'm afraid the reports you may have heard about no one being hurt in the fire are not accurate. Emergency crews discovered the body of a woman in the early hours."

People began to talk amongst themselves. Eriksson held his finger up like a teacher telling off an unruly kindergarten.

"Second, no one will be allowed to retrieve any items from the institute for at least two days. Not that there's much left to recover. We can only assume these animal rights people are responsible. Shocking, truly shocking."

There was a general murmur of agreement.

"Third, you should know that the hospital's IT system has been hacked. So has the Du Long and Freyer data centre in Leicester, where our backups are held. This occurred two weeks ago but only came to light yesterday. At this stage, the police have no reason to believe it's linked to last night's terrible events but we informed the Information Commissioner yesterday and an announcement has just been made to the City, because this is price-sensitive information.

"Finally, we have an accommodation problem. Your colleagues at Planning and Resources will have to find somewhere off site for you all."

Ronnie nudged Laura.

"How like Eriksson to focus on office space and the DLF share price at a time like this."

"Commander Gough will be coming in to talk to everyone shortly," Eriksson continued. "Afterwards, please go home and do not return to work until you hear from P&R. There's nothing more you can do here."

Eriksson and his flunkies left. The hubbub resumed. Ronnie went over to the drinks machine, filled two cups with coffee and gave one to Laura.

"You look as though you could do with this."

"Thank you, Veronica."

"No problem."

"I wonder who the poor woman in the fire was. There's one person who isn't here, you know – Stephanie. I hope to God she's all right."

"I'm sure … she's fine. Er, Laura, I had dinner with Daniel Plowright the other night."

Her face broke into a half smile.

"See, I knew he liked you. How did it go?"

"Fine. Look, he mentioned that you sent him a hard copy of his medical file a week or so back."

"Yes, Professor Stone asked me to do it. He got me to print out quite a lot of documents shortly before he died. Quite why, I don't know, and… Well, we can't ask him now, can we?"

"Did you send out files to any other patients?"

"Oh, yes. I sent them to all four patients who were part of a small study the professor was conducting. You probably don't know anything about it. I don't, either. All a bit hush-hush."

"Laura… Those files you sent to the patients. I guess you wouldn't have copies, would you?"

"My goodness, no. That would be most improper."

"It's just that Maurice Sutcliffe told me yesterday their files have also been wiped from the hospital's records, for some reason."

Laura frowned.

"Maybe it's something to do with this hacking of the IT system. I'll contact them and see if they can send their copies back."

"Look, why don't I do that? You'll be frantic over the next few days. We've all got to pull together at times like this."

"That's really kind. Thank you."

Laura picked up her tablet and tapped the screen for a few seconds.

"There you go. There are their contact details. I wonder where Stephanie is. It's not like her to be late."

Ronnie's iPad bleeped with Laura's message as Commander Gough walked in.

"Ladies and gentlemen. I'm sorry for keeping you cooped up here on this hot afternoon. May I also say how sorry I am about the turn of events overnight. I think you already know a body of a female has been found. We don't know her identity yet, but we are treating the death as suspicious.

"Regarding the killing of Professor Stone, my officers have been very busy over the past fortnight. We now have a considerable amount of forensic evidence we believe could link a person or persons to his murder."

Ronnie swallowed hard.

"As a number of you will have been to his home in the weeks before he died, we need to eliminate you from our inquiries. The easiest way to do that would be to take a DNA sample from every member of the institute's staff, subject to your consent, of course. It would save a lot of police time if we could do that now, whilst you're all here together. Everyone happy with that?"

Gough stared round the room, daring someone to dissent. Ronnie found herself nodding in agreement with everyone else.

"Good. My team have DNA sample kits ready and waiting downstairs. I propose we take people in alphabetical order, so please could we start with ... Stephen Abbott, Tony Able and Veronica Ackerman. Thank you very much for your co-operation."

Five minutes later, Ronnie sat in front of a civilian member of the Metropolitan Police staff. He ripped open a DNA testing pack with an air of resigned boredom.

"How long will it take for the results to come back?" Ronnie asked.

"Three or four days. They could do it faster but this'll be low priority stuff for the lab. It's all a waste of time if you ask me. It's those BUP bastards they should be going after."

Just three or four days. More than thirty years to build a reputation. Less than a week to save it.

CHAPTER TWENTY-SEVEN

Ronnie went straight round the corner to her favourite coffee shop for a proper cappuccino and rang the first patient. Heather Spink lived in Newcastle.

"Matthew Spink speaking."

"Hi, Mr Spink. My name is Dr Veronica Ackerman from the Lipman Institute at St Agatha's."

"Hello. I've just heard about the fire. I'm so sorry. Those animal rights people are … Well what can I say?"

"In fact, Mr Spink, that's why I'm phoning. A lot of records were destroyed in the fire. But I understand Professor Stone sent your wife a copy of her file a couple of weeks ago."

"I came across it only yesterday, as a matter of fact."

"Well, I wondered whether Mrs Spink could let us have a copy. Ours perished in the fire. Is she available to talk to right now?"

Silence.

"You don't know?" he said.

"I don't think so, Mr Spink."

"Heather was killed in a car crash on the A1 three weeks ago."

"Oh my God. Look, Mr Spink, I had no idea. I do apologise for disturbing you at this terrible time."

"Don't worry. I'm getting used to conversations like this. I've tried to make sure everyone knows but there are still a few who don't. I assumed you would know because Dr Bright was kind enough to come to her funeral. Would you like me to post Heather's file to you?"

Ronnie had no time for that.

"No, no. There's no need. It looks like I might have to travel up to Scotland in the next couple of days. I could collect it from you on the way. Would that be Okay?"

"Of course. Give me a ring. I'm keeping this mobile of Heather's on for now."

"Thank you. I'll call you. And, once again, I am so, so sorry for your loss and for calling at this time."

After taking a deep breath, she rang Maria Grigorenko in Cardiff. The call was answered by her daughter, Natalia. Her mother was in intensive care after being overcome by fumes from a faulty gas boiler two days ago.

Ronnie felt an uneasy sense of foreboding.

"The doctors say, even if my mother comes out of the coma, she has terrible damage to the brain," the tearful young woman sobbed. "But why did she turn on her heating? The weather is so hot here now."

Ronnie dialled the last patient, Harry Kings, in Warwick.

'This is Rosanna Kings. Please leave a message. For those of you who haven't heard, I am sorry to say that Harry tragically took his own life last Saturday. The boys and I would like to thank everyone for all their support and prayers at this time. The funeral is taking place on ...'

Ronnie flung a ten-pound note onto the counter and fled.

CHAPTER TWENTY-EIGHT

Daniel switched on his mobile as soon as his plane landed at Heathrow. Twelve missed calls – eleven of them from Ronnie, plus a message.

> 'Daniel. Where ARE you? They are trying to KILL you! The cancer treatment Stone gave you, they're trying to KILL all the patients on it! ALL THE PATIENTS!!! Please please call me. Rxxx'

He did.

"Ronnie, it's me."

"Oh my God. I thought you were dead. I thought you were dead ..."

Her voice dissolved into sobs.

"Hey. Come on, come on. I'm fine."

"I've been trying to get you for hours."

"Sorry. I forgot to plug in my phone last night, so it was dead as a doornail this morning. I bought a battery pack to charge it up when I landed a few minutes ago."

"Listen, Daniel. They're trying to kill you. Do you get this? They are trying to kill you."

"I know."

"What do you mean, you know. How do you know?"

"Long story. I've known for a while. I'll tell you later."

"And the same people who are trying to kill you murdered Stephanie Bright and Hasely Stone."

"Hang on. Stephanie died in the fire? How do you know?"

"I was in the office last night when this woman – Stephanie called her Chapman – broke her neck. Then she set light to the place. I was hiding behind my desk. Daniel, there was nothing I could do."

"Jesus."

"I got out before the fire started. But Daniel, you're next. They've killed two of the four patients who were part of the drug trial you were on and the other's so brain damaged she'll never recover. You're the only one left. Daniel, please be careful."

"I will. Where are you now?"

"At my apartment."

"Stay there. I've got Susie here. I'll be with you as soon as I can."

"Please watch out."

Daniel didn't need any encouragement on that score. On the other hand, how could he watch his back in an airport terminal? Any one of ten thousand people could be following him. He checked over every inch of the Bullet in the car park. Even searched for a tracking device. Not that he knew what one looked like.

He pulled up at one of the exit barriers next to a black BMW and made his way onto the M4 towards London. Ultra-cautious, not riding too fast, staying in the middle lane and leaving plenty of room between him and other vehicles. He started to feel more comfortable.

Maybe too comfortable. The black BMW must have been doing seventy when it came up the outside, whipped across and clipped his front wheel.

Then everything went into slow motion. The Bullet keeled and screamed down the carriageway, sparks flying from the crash bars as it spun round two revolutions. Daniel was thrown clear, only for a white van to hurtle towards him as he lay across the tarmac.

For once White Van Man didn't live up to his reputation of driving too fast, or too close, and his front wheels stopped a couple of feet in front of Daniel's prostrate body. Drivers behind didn't react so fast; he could hear the sound of vehicles shunting into each other as the motorway ground to a halt.

A young man in an Arsenal shirt jumped out of the van.

"You all right, mate? That guy in the black Beamer … Christ, what a nutter … Don't get up yet. My mate's calling an ambulance."

A sea of faces surrounded Daniel. And then he saw her, standing at the back. She was only there for a few seconds but it was her all right.

Ms Bland.

Then she was gone. By the time Daniel was helped back on his feet, the black BMW and the woman were nowhere to be seen.

"You were really lucky there," said the young man, pulling Susie up onto the hard shoulder. "Your bike's not too bad either, considering."

He was right. Daniel only had the crash bars fitted because they looked the part. Now they'd saved his life.

An ambulance siren wailing in the distance kicked his brain into gear. If he was a sitting duck here, he'd be even more vulnerable in A&E. He shook the young man's hand and stood astride the Bullet.

"Thanks for not running over me but I've got to go now."

"Here, you shouldn't be riding that thing till you've been to hosp—"

But Daniel was off, the bemused shouts of drivers on the M4 ringing in his ears and a question swirling around his head that he couldn't begin to answer. How the hell did Ms Bland know he was flying into Heathrow's Terminal Two this afternoon?

* * *

Ronnie held Daniel so, so tight.

"You didn't call," she sobbed. "I thought I'd lost you. I really … I really thought I'd lost you. You've just come into my life, you bastard, and I thought you were gone."

"And you're the best thing that's happened to me in a very long time, Veronica Ackerman, so I'm not going anywhere." He stroked her forehead. "But it was close today. Somebody knocked me off the bike on the way here."

"What?"

He told her about his brush with death on the M4.

"And get this. I've got a picture of the woman who did it."

"How?"

"Long story. In fact, I think we've both got long stories to tell. You first."

Ronnie decided she wouldn't leave anything out, any more than she had with Todd. When she told him about Stone asking her round for a cosy dinner at home, Daniel laughed.

"The cheeky bastard. He was supposed to be taking me out to La Bella Gioconda that night. I got stood up for you."

"I wish you hadn't. Then I wouldn't have ended up drunk in his bed."

"Shit."

"He was in an even worse state, thank God. Nothing happened."

Daniel didn't say another word until it was his turn to tell his side of the story.

"Why didn't you tell me they were trying to kill you when they ran you down outside your apartment?" Ronnie asked.

"Because you'd gone all cold on me in the restaurant."

"I am so sorry. I couldn't see how all the stuff about a stage four tumour just disappearing could be true. Will you forgive me?"

He kissed her. "What do you think?" He dug out his phone. "This a photo of the woman who tried to run me down this afternoon. She's so nondescript, I call her Ms Bland. It's from footage my cameraman shot at the

BUP's London Fields demo. Could she be the woman who killed Stephanie Bright?"

Ronnie gazed at the image for fully ten seconds.

"Maybe. It was dark. The shape of the head looks about right but it was her voice I remember most. Her accent."

"Where's it from?"

"Not sure. Definitely British, not too educated. London maybe?"

"I think it's time to make a plan," Daniel said. "Todd's right. You do need to go to the police. But first we need proof the protocol exists. Can you call the daughter of the Cardiff patient to see if she's found her mum's file? We can go down to Wales tomorrow and pick it up."

"You're coming too?"

"I think we're in this together now, don't you?"

She nodded and snuggled closer.

"That makes me feel much better."

"We'll take Susie," he said. "If they get back on our tail, we'll have a much better chance of losing them on a motorbike. Then we can go to Warwick to see the poor woman whose husband jumped under a train. Not that he did, of course. We might even make Newcastle for the other file by tomorrow night."

"Sounds good to me."

He stroked her hair.

"Just one thing. I can't go back to the flat. It's the first place they'll look for me. Can I stay here? The sofa's fine."

"I think I might need a little more personal protection   than   that."

CHAPTER TWENTY-NINE

Daniel woke early.

Ronnie lay next to him, her face bathed in the light from the sun streaming through a gap in the curtains. She opened her eyes and smiled.

"Hi."

He kissed her.

"Good morning. Sleep well?"

"You bet. You?"

"Great, but I've been awake for a while. I've been thinking … You know Maurice Sutcliffe told you about those two computer people who wiped the files. Well, I've been wondering whether—"

Ronnie gave his chest a playful poke with a finger.

"I've just spent a wonderful night with this lovely man and all he wants to talk about is the hospital computer."

He kissed her again.

"Listen for a second. Maybe Ms Bland and the woman who wiped the files are one and the same. "

"There's an easy way to find out," Ronnie said. "Send Maurice Sutcliffe the screengrab of her. I'll call him."

Sutcliffe told her he already knew Siobhan Anderson's details didn't check out because no company called Computercom was registered in Britain. Ronnie sent him Ms Bland's photo. It was the same woman.

* * *

Daniel pulled the Bullet into Chieveley Services on the way down to Cardiff. A ravenous Ronnie volunteered to get bacon sandwiches while he took out his mobile and sat down at a lonely table by the window. No one could eavesdrop on this call.

"Alice Mahoney speaking."

"Hiya. I thought you'd like to know a black BMW tried to run me down on the M4 yesterday."

"Fuck. Are you alright?"

"Bike and rider aren't too bad, considering. But I can't go on being this lucky. More important, guess who tried to kill me? Ms Bland."

"Who?"

"Pic 4. I've christened her Ms Bland because she looks so boring."

"How can you be sure it was her?"

"She got out of the car to see how much damage she'd done before doing a runner. You might want to dig out the CCTV for yesterday afternoon near junction 3 on the eastbound carriageway. Around 4.30. Before she legged it, her black Beamer must have been parked on the hard shoulder beyond the traffic jam."

"I'll do it now."

"I decided I might be a bit of a sitting duck in hospital, so I didn't wait for the ambulance. Ms Bland calls herself Siobhan Anderson, by the way. And says she works for an outfit called Computercom. She's the one who hacked into Aggie's computer system. She also uses the name Chapman. No first name."

"Where have you got all this from?"

"It's a long story. I'll give you everything, but there are a couple of things I need to check out first. At which point, I might need that police protection you offered."

"I'll start setting it up. Looked online recently?"

"Not since I left an hour ago."

"Then you won't have heard the latest. The woman who died in the fire is Hasely Stone's deputy, Stephanie Bright."

"I wondered when that would come out."

"How the hell do you know about that? What the fuck are you up to, Daniel?"

"Keep your hair on. You'll have it all very soon. And you'll want it."

"Do you realise what an idiot I'll look if this goes tits up, and it comes out my ex was withholding information?"

"It won't. I promise."

"It'd better not. And I suppose you haven't heard the other piece of Aggies news."

"What's that?"

"Du Long and Freyer are scrapping plans for a shiny new building to house the Lipman Institute. Instead, they're moving the whole shooting match up to Birmingham and merging it with their cancer research labs there. And guess what they're going to do with the land in London? Redevelop it into luxury apartments."

"The bastards. They can't have just decided that. DLF must have been planning it all along. It'll be Eriksson's doing."

"I'm sure it won't do his pension pot any harm."

"Every cloud has a silver lining for some bastard or other, Superintendent Mahoney. I'll call you soon."

Ronnie was returning with breakfast as he finished the call.

"That Superintendent Mahoney you were talking to. That wouldn't be Alice, by any chance?"

* * *

Natalia Grigorenko opened the door of her mother's small, terraced house in the down-at-heel Cardiff suburb of Adamsdown and gave Ronnie a feeble smile.

"After you phoned, the hospital called. My mother died at six o'clock this morning."

Ronnie hugged her. Daniel made tea.

"The police have arrested the man who put in the boiler, but he says he did his work properly. He is very upset."

Ronnie spied a familiar buff-coloured folder on a bookshelf.

"Are those your mother's medical notes, Natalia?"

"Yes."

"Would you mind if I take a look?"

"Please do." She stood up to fetch it. "How could this happen now? My mother had everything to live for, now she is cured from the leukaemia."

"I'm sorry, I didn't realise your mother had leukaemia as well as lung cancer," Ronnie said.

"Lung cancer? She did not have lung cancer. She had leukaemia. Acute myeloid leukaemia. The worst kind, yes?"

Ronnie's teacup crashed to the floor.

CHAPTER THIRTY

Daniel mopped up and Natalia showed them out.

"What the hell was all that about, Ron?" he asked, when they were back out on the street. "First, you throw tea all over the poor girl's carpet and then you leave me to mop it up and apologise. I'm amazed she let you borrow the file."

"Don't you see?" Ronnie said.

"Don't think so."

"Maria Grigorenko had acute myeloid leukaemia. She didn't have lung cancer, she had leukaemia. The AI-Protocol worked for her too."

"So?"

"So, it's not just a drug regimen for lung cancer. It also treats one of the most serious blood cancers there is. God knows what other cancers it can treat."

Daniel was thinking.

"Shit. If that's true, this could be the biggest fucking story—"

"Will you stop acting the TV reporter for a second? This could be the biggest fucking breakthrough in the history of medicine, more like."

"On the other hand ..." Daniel began to frown. "Let's not forget the first rule of journalism. The better the story, the less likely it is to be true."

"But what if it is? Think about it. Every medical advance seems impossible until it happens. Tuberculosis struck as much terror into people as cancer before penicillin came along, and Alexander Fleming only found out about that because he messed up a petri dish."

"But why would anyone kill to stop a discovery like this getting out. Especially with only four patients on the trial. You can't tell much from them, can you?"

But Ronnie's eyes were wide open with excitement.

"We only know about four. There may be others. And stopping the protocol is a very good reason to kill … Think about it Daniel. Who runs the hospital where these patients were treated? At the same time earning gazillions in profits from chemotherapy drugs?

"Du Long and Freyer."

"And all this could wipe billions off their stock price."

"Would they be that ruthless?"

"Du Long and Freyer? The corporation that cares so little about human life they ran a drugs trial, maiming and killing hundreds of Indian labourers and then forces them to accept peanuts in compensation?"

"Fair point, but I still think we're making a lot of assumptions here."

"Tell you what… Let's call Harry Kings' wife in Warwick. See what kind of cancer he had."

This time Rosanna Kings was in to answer the phone. Her husband had been diagnosed with stage four osteosarcoma, a rare form of bone cancer that had spread to his pancreas.

"She'll look for the file and can meet us tomorrow," Ronnie told Daniel, after hanging up.

"Okay, you win," he replied. "What a gobsmacker."

* * *

They set off for Newcastle but the traffic slowed them down. They would never make it tonight. Instead, Daniel booked a double room at an ancient stone pub in the Yorkshire Dales he remembered from his days at uni.

"Which side of the bed?"

Ronnie looked away.

"Something wrong?"

"It's just... Look, last night was special. But I'm not sure it's a great idea for us to quite so involved while this is happening."

"Sorry. I shouldn't have made assumptions, booking a room with a double."

She put her arms round his neck and kissed it.

"You weren't to know, especially after last night. I mean what's uppermost in anyone's mind at the start of a new relationship?"

"Sex?"

"And what should we be thinking about right now?"

"Staying alive?"

She kissed him again, on the lips this time.

"Daniel Plowright, I want to make love to you right now but let's ease up a little on the physical stuff for a while. We've got a lot to think about."

He smiled and kissed her back.

"I hate to admit it, but you have a point."

* * *

Matthew Spink was packing for a holiday away with his children when Ronnie knocked on his door.

"The car was such a mess after it exploded that they still haven't worked out why she hit the bridge," he said. "Thank God she'd just dropped Imogen and Charlotta off at nursery."

Heather Spink had a stage four adenocarcinoma in her stomach. She was given two months to live but her specialist at Newcastle's Royal Victoria Infirmary used to work with Hasely Stone. He sent her to Aggie's.

They arrived at Warwick to see Rosanna Kings in the late afternoon. She hadn't found her husband's file so far but confirmed his cancer disappeared within weeks of starting treatment at the Lipman.

"Do you know what's eating me up?" she said, picking up a photograph of her husband from the mantlepiece. "How much I hate him for it. We went through hell together, only for him to throw himself under a bloody train. Why would he do that?"

As soon as they left, Ronnie switched on her phone. It warbled with a voicemail – from Trinidad. It was Hasely Stone's brother, Leon. It was urgent.

'I'll call your landline in case you're at home. If I can't reach you there, I'll leave a longer message.'

Ronnie called the flat and interrogated the answerphone.

'Hi Veronica. I've just got back from London and there's a letter here from my brother. By the postmark, he

171

mailed it the day he died. It contains an SD card that he insists I must not open. I have to hand it to you – in person. He says it contains everything you need to know about the Adoptive Immunotherapy Protocol. Do you know what that is?'

CHAPTER THIRTY-ONE

Gemma Chapman stared at her burner. There had to better ways of earning a living than this, just waiting for it to ring. Every time she answered it either she got an earful from the client or the identity of someone else to deal with.

The phone burst into life.

"Chapman? I've got a name."

"That was quick."

"She's an American at the Lipman, called Dr Veronica Ackerman. Lives in Fulham. I'll send you the address. The Yard won't get her DNA results for a couple of days, so there's plenty of time."

"Okay. No point in pissing about. I'll get onto it straight away."

* * *

Ronnie was losing patience with Daniel. For a bright guy paid to investigate stuff, he was being so stupid. She'd explained it to him twice but he still didn't get it.

"Let's try it again. This drug regimen is called the Adoptive Immunotherapy Protocol, right? With immunotherapy, you use a patient's own immune system to fight the tumour."

"I asked about that when I was first diagnosed but my oncologist said it was too late for me."

"Then you might know it doesn't fight the cancer itself but the cells and structures surrounding the cancer … what we call the tumour microenvironment. Somehow, Stone seems to have found a way of harnessing the immune system by using tumour antigen to upregulate surrounding cells, causing the tumour cells to spontaneously apoptose."

"Apoptose?"

"Self-destruct."

"I tell you what. Why don't I try to put it in words I can understand, and you tell me if I've got it right?"

"Let's try it."

"Okay, what you're saying is the AI-Protocol stimulated my own immune system and that's what killed off the cancer cells in my body."

"Yup. Think about what a tumour is. It's a group of cells that has lost the ability to die. Those tumours then attract blood vessels, hormones and proteins, all of which help the cancer grow even faster. We have three very blunt ways of dealing with it – surgery, chemotherapy and radiotherapy.

"But now we also have personalised gene therapy, where you engineer an individual drug based on the genetic make-up of the patient and the tumour. So far, it hasn't quite been the Holy Grail everyone was predicting a few years ago and, boy, is it expensive. My guess is that Stone's AI drug regimen works in a similar way but without going through the time and expense of creating a personalised drug for every patient."

"Now you're talking 'human being'. I understood all that."

"Good. We've been knocking on the door of adoptive immunotherapy becoming a mainstream treatment for years. In 2014, researchers in Australia used it to develop the best treatment we've found so far for malignant melanoma. Then an American company produced a similar drug for the most common form of childhood leukaemia. Maybe Hasely Stone hit a home run, because his protocol looks like it works on a whole range of cancers."

"But how can it work so quickly?"

"You've heard of the Elephant Man drug trial at Northwick Park Hospital a few years back?"

"Of course. They were talking about it at the weekend. How much the victims were paid out, compared to the tiny amounts DLF will pay those poor bastards in India."

"Right. The drug in that trial was TGN1412. No one in my business will ever forget that code name. It was developed for use on arthritis, leukaemia and multiple sclerosis and designed to harness patients' immune systems. But it produced a catastrophic reaction instead. And it happened fast. In minutes. Patients lost fingers and toes, like those guys in India.

"Hasely Stone seems to have found a way to hyperactivate the immune system like that, but in a way that cures rather than kills. I'll need to see what's on the SD card his brother has before I know exactly how he did it. Right, class is over for today. Time to call him."

Leon Stone answered straight away.

"I don't know what was bugging Hasely to make him so cautious," he said.

"I'm getting a good idea," Ronnie replied. "I'll be on a plane real soon. And I may bring a friend with me."

CHAPTER THIRTY-TWO

Ronnie knew something was wrong the minute she walked through her front door. The place smelt weird.

"I can't smell anything," Daniel said.

"That's because it's not your apartment. I can. When you come home to a place that's been shut up, especially in this heat, it smells different. Sort-of musty, if you know what I mean."

"Kind of."

"Nikki's been in Spain all week, so how come this place smells like someone's opened the doors and windows recently?"

She glanced around. The dishes were still on the drainer, the magazines scattered over the coffee table, the note Nikki left with her address in Granada still by the phone.

"The phone," Ronnie said.

"What about it?"

"The voicemail light's not flashing."

"Why should it?"

"Because I listened to Leon's message remotely. The light continues to flash until you come home and clear the voicemail."

She pressed the replay button.

'You have no new messages and no saved messages.'

"It's been wiped. How did they get in?"

"I noticed that you didn't undo the mortice lock," Daniel said.

"We never bother with it."

"That's your answer, then. Any self-respecting burglar can get through a front door if it's not double-locked. Look, I'm phoning the police. It's one thing for these bastards to have a go at me but I'm not having you involved."

"I'm already involved, stupid. And you're not phoning the police. You're coming with me to see Leon Stone in Trinidad. When we've got the card from him, we can go to the police together. And I'd better warn him. Ms Bland and her friends must've listened to his message before they wiped it. They could even be ahead of us. On a plane right now to pay him a visit."

She called Leon again. He didn't turn a hair.

"I didn't survive in this town to forty-six years of age without having plenty of friends to call on," he said.

Ronnie rang off as Daniel walked in from outside. The sleeves of his shirt were rolled up and his hands filthy. He led her over to the central heating thermostat on the wall.

"See? The temperature's been turned right up. Who the hell does that during the hottest summer this century? Then I thought about Maria Grigorenko, so I checked the timer on the boiler. It was set for the heating to come on at one o'clock in the morning. Then I looked at the gas flue outside."

They went out onto the patio , where a pile of dirty rags lay on the ground.

"That lot was blocking it. At one o'clock in the morning, the boiler would have fired up and this place would be full of carbon monoxide. You'd have been a goner."

* * *

Daniel booked seats on the following morning's British Airways flight from Gatwick to Port of Spain. Staying overnight at the flat was asking for trouble, so they checked into a twin room at the cheapest airport hotel.

"How the hell did they find me?" asked Ronnie.

"That's the question of the moment," Daniel said. "These people are far too well informed for my liking. I still can't understand how they knew which plane I was catching a couple of days ago but there's one way they could have found out about you."

"The DNA sample I gave," Ronnie said.

"Yup. Must have matched it to a trace you left in Stone's house."

"But the guy who did the test said the results wouldn't be back till tomorrow at the earliest."

"Maybe the lab speeded them up. You don't know which company did the work, by any chance?"

She shook her head.

"I'll see if I can find out."

He rang Alice.

"It's a good job you didn't go to A&E after your little brush with the black Beamer," she said.

"Why?" Daniel asked.

"Because we picked it up on CCTV. Turned out to have stolen plates. Tracked it all the way to Charing Cross Hospital. On a hunch – not that you'd need to be Hercule Poirot to work this out – I checked out the hospital CCTV. Guess who walked through the door into A&E? Your Ms Bland."

"Fuck."

"She didn't hang around for long. If you'd called me straight away, we might've grabbed her."

"What did Gough say when you told him?"

"I haven't yet. That's the way Tom Edwards wants to play it at the moment. He says Racist Crime have done the legwork on this."

"It's your funeral."

"I can look after myself. What are you up to?"

"Finding out why someone is so anxious to put me in a box. And we're making a fair bit of progress, as a matter of fact."

"If there's a 'we', you're not alone, then."

"I'm with a friend called Veronica Ackerman."

"From the Lipman?"

"You know her?"

"I sat in when Gough interviewed her. She said she barely knew Stone, so how come she's mixed up in all this?"

"Look… We should find out a lot more in a couple of days. And I promise you'll be the first to know."

"I'd better be. Someone's wants you dead and, in case you'd forgotten, it's my job to catch people like that."

"I hadn't. A quick question. How fast do your labs turn DNA tests round?"

"What do you want to know that for?"

"Give me a couple of days and you'll know everything. Promise."

Alice sighed.

"We could get preliminary results back in twenty-four hours but we never do because the lab always double-checks to make sure the evidence will stand up in court. It's usually three, four, even five days, unless they pull their fingers out."

"I don't suppose you know which company does the job."

"I do, as it happens, because the previous lot was so slow we moved the contract to a lab in Basildon. DNA Integrity. They're really fast if we need them to be. They're a subsidiary of Du Long and Freyer."

* * *

"I'm sorry to bother you this late, sir."

"No need to apologise, Alice," said Tom Edwards. "What's happened?"

"Daniel Plowright's been on the phone. He says he'll have a pile of intelligence he can pass on to me in a couple of days."

"And...?"

"He refused to say more at this stage."

"Good job you haven't spoken to Gough, then. Any idea what Plowright might have?"

"No, sir. But he asked about where we get our DNA tests done."

"Why?"

"A whole load of samples taken from the staff at the Lipman are due back in the next couple of days. Daniel says he's working with a friend called Veronica Ackerman, a research scientist there. Commander Gough is desperate to find out who had a cosy dinner with Stone the night before he died. It was almost certainly a woman. I wonder whether it might be her."

CHAPTER THIRTY-THREE

Chapman waited until she got through the interminable airport security queues and into the departure hall before phoning the client. She stood with her back to a shop window full of overpriced sunglasses to make sure no one was eavesdropping.

"You took your time picking up," she said when he answered on the eighth ring.

"Your fuck-ups aren't the only items in my in-tray, Chapman."

"Do you want the good news or the bad news?"

"Get on with it."

"The bad news is your Dr Ackerman is still very much alive."

"How do you know?"

"Because she's on the BA flight to Trinidad that's just taken off from Gatwick."

"Fuck. Must've talked to Stone's brother."

"Yeah."

"I thought you wiped his voicemail message."

"I did," said Chapman, "but he could have rung her again, couldn't he?"

"How do you know she's on the flight?"

"That's the good news. Baz is on the same one. Heard her on the blower talking to that Laura Sellars we've been keeping an eye on. Said she'd be away for a few days visiting a sick uncle or something. And guess who our Veronica's flying with?"

"I'm not a fucking mind reader, Chapman."

"Daniel Plowright."

"Shit. Did he recognise Baz?"

"No way. Baz was well gone by the time Plowright scraped himself up off the deck at London Fields. But my boy's keeping his head down and his shades on, just in case."

"When are you leaving?"

"On the Caribbean Airlines flight in half an hour. I'll get to Port of Spain not long after Baz."

"Can you get someone to unblock the boiler flue? We don't need to get her flatmate mixed up in all this."

"Streets ahead of you there, mate. A couple of my boys went straight round there. But someone got there first. Flue clear and thermostat turned down. Must have been Ackerman and her new boyfriend."

"They're not stupid, these people. Don't underestimate them."

"We won't. And it'll be much easier in Trinidad. It's Baz's home turf. He's already got a couple of guys sniffing around. Out there we don't need no car crash or dodgy boiler. It can be a street robbery that goes wrong and we can kill three birds with one stone … Stone? Geddit?"

* * *

Ronnie didn't wait for the cabin announcement. She switched on her cell phone as soon as the Boeing 777 hit the runway at Trinidad's Piarco International Airport.

There were six missed calls from Todd. She couldn't blame him. The voicemail she left before taking off – in the middle of the night, Colorado time – was one he wouldn't forget in a hurry. She called back and the phone barely rang before he answered.

"Are you serious, darling? I did hear you say a 'complete' cure for cancer, right?"

"You did, Toddy. I thought my voicemail might wake you up."

"It did that alright. Jesus. A cure. I can't believe it."

"And neither will I, until I've seen the contents of this card that Stone sent his brother."

"Where are you now?"

"We've just landed in Port of Spain to pick it up."

"Who's 'we'?"

"I'm with a guy called Daniel Plowright."

"You haven't told me about him before."

"And I can't now. Gotta go. Call you later."

She turned to find an immigration officer standing next to her.

"Dr Ackerman?," he said. "I would like you and your friend to come with me, please."

Ronnie and Daniel were led past the other passengers and out of the plane into a wall of heat and humidity.

"Why are we being given the rock star treatment?" she whispered.

"I don't know but I don't like it."

Inside the terminal, their passports were stamped and then they were led through a side door.

"Good afternoon, Veronica. Welcome to Port of Spain."

Leon Stone was waiting for them

"Leon... How are you? You look fantastic."

Compared with the gaunt figure of a week ago, Leon Stone was a man transformed.

"I'm piling on the weight now," he said, hugging her. "It must be Hasely's AIP drug. Throat cancer was ready to put me in a box till he gave me those injections."

"So you've been on the protocol, too. Like Daniel here."

Leon shook Daniel's hand.

"Good to meet a fellow survivor. We can compare notes later but first let me introduce you to Patrick Lara, who runs Immigration here."

An official in a smart white shirt decorated with epaulettes stepped forward.

"Leon tells me you're concerned about a woman who could be on this flight."

"She might be, though we didn't notice her on the plane," Daniel replied.

"We can check." The officer walked across to a couple of CCTV screens. "I've closed off all but the two Immigration desks you can see on these monitors. If you see anyone familiar, tell me. I'll get my colleagues in customs to pull them aside for a little extra attention."

Leon smiled.

"I told you I had friends in this town."

With only two desks open, it took more than half an hour for all the passengers to go through Immigration. Ronnie and Daniel didn't recognise anyone.

"Mind you, you do get a bit boggle-eyed after the first fifty faces," Daniel said.

"No problem," Leon replied. "We've got an hour before the Caribbean Airlines flight gets in. You can take a look at the passengers on that. Now, are you guys hungry?"

"What I really need to do is brush my teeth," Ronnie said.

Patrick walked towards the door.

"Then come this way. We don't have any dignitaries coming through Piarco today, so our VVIP suite is free."

"VVIP?"

"I can see you haven't spent much time in the eastern Caribbean, Dr Ackerman. Round here we've got Very Important Persons and we've got Very Very Important Persons. Today, you're a VVIP."

"Are you serious?"

"Sure, ma'am. We have a VVIP suite."

The VVIP suite had showers to wash away the grime of a transatlantic flight, with water pressure up to American standards.

Club sandwiches and coffee were waiting for them when they emerged. In between mouthfuls, Ronnie told Leon the whole story. Apart from how she ended up in bed with his brother.

"So if these guys have murdered my brother, this Stephanie Bright lady, three patients on the drug protocol and tried to kill both of you guys, then I'm next in the frame."

"It looks that way, Leon," Ronnie replied. "So what do we do?"

"I've been thinking about that." Leon said. "First off, I'm guessing they'll find out where I live. I'd love you to stay at my home... I've got a beautiful pool and a great view over the Gulf of Paria... But that wouldn't be too smart, which is why I've been keeping my head down In Laventille since you called me. But now you guys are here, why don't we leave town? There's a little place down the coast, owned by a very good friend of mine. Monique will have rooms for us, for sure. Then we can sit down and make a plan."

"We can't plan anything until we see what's on the SD card Hasely sent you," Daniel said. "Have you got it with you, Leon?"

"All in good time." Leon responded with a broad smile. "You're in the Caribbean now."

CHAPTER THIRTY-FOUR

By the time they arrived back at the CCTV screens for the Caribbean Airlines flight, Daniel felt weary. Not for long. There she was. Third in the queue. Ms Bland.

"That's her," he said, clenching his fist. "That's who tried to mow me down on the M4. Ronnie, do you recognise her? Is she the woman who killed Stephanie?"

"I'm not sure... Maybe. The profile's similar but I'd need to hear her voice."

The woman walked away and Patrick Lara flashed up a CCTV image of Baggage Reclaim. Ms Bland stood by the carousel, talking on her mobile.

"I'd love to get my hands on her phone and find out who she's talking to," Daniel said.

Patrick smiled at him.

"I think I might be able to help you there."

Five minutes later, they were in an unlit room with a large two-way mirror covering one wall. On the other side of the glass was the green channel of the customs hall.

"Don't talk too loud in here, people," Patrick said. "The glass isn't completely soundproof."

A customs officer stopped Ms Bland as she walked through and led her over to a table near the mirror.

"Would you mind if I opened your bag, ma'am? It's just routine."

"What's the problem, officer? I'm in a hurry."

Ronnie grabbed Daniel's arm.

"That's Chapman," she whispered. "That's her voice. That's definitely her."

The officer went through the entire contents of Ms Bland's army surplus kit bag. Daniel videoed her through the glass.

"Where are you staying, ma'am?"

"The Hilton."

Leon snapped a picture of his own.

"I'll get one of my guys to keep an eye on her there," he said. "Billy'll be at the Hilton before she gets out of Piarco."

Two female officers appeared behind Chapman.

"Would you please accompany my colleagues."

"What the hell's all this about?" Chapman asked. "You should know I used to be a police officer in the British Army."

"They'll be as quick as they can, ma'am … No, please leave your phone and your wallet here. They'll be quite safe. Please come this way."

Patrick led Ronnie and Daniel into the customs hall the moment the coast was clear.

"Three minutes max, people."

Daniel picked up Ms Bland's mobile phone and pressed a key. The security lock hadn't kicked in since her last call. It was a burner. No contacts in the address book, no apps downloaded and only a handful of recently dialled numbers. He photographed the whole list.

Ronnie went through the wallet and passport.

"She's travelling under the name of Siobhan Anderson. Here's her Computercom business card."

"Photograph everything, Ron."

"I'm on it."

Daniel felt the precious time flying by.

"Time's up, guys," said Patrick, looking at his watch. "We need to get back next door."

"No time for a quick look through her bag?" Daniel pleaded.

"No way." Patrick glanced at Ronnie. "And please put the passport back on the corner of the suitcase, ma'am. That's how she left it."

They returned to the mirror room, as a fuming Ms Bland was brought back to her luggage.

"How dare you search a former police officer like that."

"Be thankful it wasn't an intimate search, ma'am," said one of the officers.

Chapman zipped her bag closed.

"I've never had to pull my damn trousers down for any customs officer anywhere in the world. You have not heard the last of this. Where's your toilet?"

"Over there, ma'am."

She grabbed her belongings and stomped off.

* * *

Gemma Chapman glared at herself in the toilet mirror. Her mobile rang. It was Baz.

"Welcome to TnT. I'm in Arrivals, and—"

"Shut up, Baz, and listen. I've just been strip-searched by fucking customs."

"Shit. I had no problems."

"Well, I did. They said it was routine but that's bollocks. They made a beeline for me. Christ knows why. Leave the airport right now. I'll spend a couple of hours in a shopping mall or whatever. Meet you in the Hilton bar at seven."

"Sure."

"Where are Plowright and the girl?"

"Bit of a problem there. Must have been at the front of the queue cos I didn't see 'em in Immigration. But my mate Frankie was outside and he didn't see 'em, either."

"Did he know what they look like?"

"Course he did. I took a couple of snaps at Gatwick for him. But there was no sign by the time I came through."

"Shit. Where the fuck have they gone?"

"I dunno but we'll find 'em. Stay cool, Gem. This is the Caribbean."

* * *

"Can we get out of a side entrance or something?" Daniel asked. "Just in case there's a reception committee waiting for us outside."

"I've been thinking about that," Patrick said. "Come this way."

He led them through a series of corridors into the open air – and a tropical downpour.

"This is the first rain we've seen in two months," Daniel said. "I never thought I'd be so pleased to get drenched."

He looked up and allowed the warm rain to soak his face.

"I didn't reckon on a Brit coming all the way to TnT to see a little rain," Leon said, laughing. "Come and meet Peewee and Goldie. They'll be around all the time you're here."

They walked across the puddles to a black Range Rover with tinted windows. Two very large men dressed in smart suits stepped out. Peewee leaned down to pick up Ronnie's carry-on. His jacket fell open and Daniel glimpsed a shoulder holster.

"Okay, let's go see Monique," Leon said. "She runs the Bay Motel, about an hour south on the other side of San Fernando."

Daniel waited until they passed the last high-rise in Port of Spain before ringing Alice's mobile. The call was too important to risk the signal dropping out. It went straight to voicemail. He looked at the time. It was nearly midnight in London. There was no harm in trying her direct line at the Met.

"Alice Mahoney speaking."

"Hi, Alice Mahoney speaking. Daniel Plowright speaking. You're burning the midnight oil."

"We all are. The word's come down from on high. Every single lead must be checked straight away. Whatever it takes, whatever it costs. Pity I don't qualify for overtime any more. Why are you phoning so late?"

"It's not late for me. I'm in Trinidad."

"Trinidad? What the hell are you doing there?"

"It's a long story—"

"I'm pissed off with your long stories, Daniel. What the bloody hell is going on?"

"Ronnie and I are here to collect information from Hasely Stone's brother. And Ms Bland, who tried to run me down on the M4 the other day, has just flown in. And we've just found out that she killed both Stone and Stephanie Bright."

"Fuck. Is this a wind-up? If so, I'm not in the mood."

"Never been more serious in my life. With a little help, we managed to look at her mobile. Can you check a few numbers for me? From her recently dialled calls list?"

"So now you want me to break the Data Protection Act, do you?"

"That's about the size of it."

The silence down the other end of the phone seemed to go on forever.

"This is the last time – absolutely the last – I help you on this, unless and until you tell me what's happening. Understand? And I want to know everything. No keeping titbits back for your fucking exclusive."

"You're a star. I'll send the numbers now."

Fifty minutes later, the car came to a halt outside a shabby, single-storey building next to a deserted beach. The rain had stopped. The sun hovered near the horizon, its deep orange rays creating long shadows across the sand. A home-painted driftwood sign proclaimed they were outside the Bay Motel.

A large woman, dressed in a bright green dress and matching headscarf, came out and hugged Leon like a brother.

"Can you book these folks in, Monique? And have you got a room for me tonight?"

"Sure. I've got a room for you any time, darlin'."

"I'll be back in a while."

Goldie drove Leon off in the Range Rover, leaving Peewee to guard Daniel and Ronnie. They sat drinking Carib beers on the veranda, whilst the big orange tiddlywink disappeared below the horizon.

"We do owe it to ourselves, don't we?" Daniel said, smiling.

"You bet we do. Was that another of Susie's expressions, along with 'life is not a dress rehearsal'?"

"Nope, that one's all my own work."

* * *

Alice stared down at the list and typed in the first number, talking to herself

"Untraceable mobile. Probably a burner … Another burner … Another … A landline… There'll be a name attached to that … Fuck. No, there must be some mistake…"

She checked the final number on the list. Another landline. The same name. There was no mistake.

"Jesus Christ."

CHAPTER THIRTY-FIVE

Daniel woke from a doze to the sound of the Range Rover pulling up.

Leon stepped out, waving a white envelope.

"A friend down the road was looking after this for me," he said.

Daniel could guess what it contained.

"Is there anywhere in Trinidad you don't have friends?" he asked.

"I sure hope not," Leon replied, with a grin.

Ronnie took out the SD card, along with a handwritten note.

'Now come on, little bro. No copying, no peeking! H.'

She put the card into her laptop, as Leon's mobile phone bleeped with a message.

"My man Billy's found your Ms Bland at the Hilton. Along with her friends. He managed to take some pictures. Take a look."

Daniel took the mobile, stared at it for a moment or two and then laughed.

"Got you!"

He showed the others the screengrab of the man with the earring at the London Fields protest. The same man was sitting next to Ms Bland at the poolside bar in the Hilton, no question.

"Black Diamond. That's what I call him. I reckon he must be the guy who tried to kill me at the demo. Of all the gin joints in all the towns in all the world, he walks into mine."

"His name is Barrington Williams," Leon replied. "He flew in on your flight."

"How did I miss him? Not to worry. I'll ring Alice with his name once we've taken a look at the SD card. She can check him out."

"First off, a little housekeeping," Ronnie said.

She copied the whole card onto her computer, took a couple of clean SD cards out of a new packet, made two more copies and handed them to the others.

"Keep these safe."

Finally, she opened up the first of Hasely Stone's files. Daniel felt his heart pumping; five people died for the information they were about to see.

There were six files altogether. Stone 1 through to Stone 6. Ronnie tapped the first – a video file – and Hasely Stone's face stared out from the screen.

"Good morning, Veronica. It's 5.30 a.m. on Friday, June the eighteenth. I'm keeping my voice down a little because you're still asleep upstairs. Quite a night, wasn't it? I hope you enjoyed our evening.'

Daniel glanced at Ronnie. She was bright red.

'Now, this might seem a bit melodramatic – paranoid, even – but what I said to you last night about not trusting anyone else at the hospital ... well, that wasn't just the splendid wine talking.'

Leon grinned.

"Hasely always did like good wine – and good company," he said.

'So what's all this about? Three years ago, I decided to tackle cancer using an entirely new approach. You'll see from the other files on this card that it succeeded far beyond anything I could ever have imagined. I found a way, with a little help from Stephanie Bright, of reversing the process by which healthy cells turn cancerous.'

Ronnie gasped.

'You heard that right, Veronica. We haven't just killed cancer cells. We've turned them back into healthy tissue. Sounds extraordinary but it's true. And get this... It works for every kind of cancer we tried it on. We called it the Adoptive Immunotherapy Protocol, for reasons that'll become obvious. Results on mice in the lab were so promising that we decided to check toxicity levels in human patients. We put four through a very limited Phase 0 trial.

'The results blew us away. Within three weeks, we had spectacular reductions in disease in all patients – far better than we'd got from our work with our furry friends in the lab. Still, I guess you gotta be lucky sometime, Veronica. Then we upped the dose a little – not too much. After two months, every patient was completely cancer free. We monitored them for another six with regular MRI scans and blood tests. Still nothing. This regimen makes all existing cancer treatments look like an aspirin.'

"Jesus, was I lucky," Daniel said.

"Shut up and listen," Ronnie snapped.

'I'm not sure I'd want to say this in public, Veronica, but we'd pretty much stumbled across this thing so, to begin with, we stayed quiet. Instead, we made plans to conduct a Phase 1 trial in around fifty patients.

'But two things blindsided me. First, I had a conversation with someone that I found … disconcerting. I won't say who, because, if I'm wrong, I'd be destroying a hard-won reputation. But that little chat showed me how a quick, cheap and complete cure for cancer could be very bad news indeed for some people.'

"I can't imagine which multinational drug corporation he's talking about," Daniel said.

'Second, I got terrible news back home about my kid brother, Leon. He was diagnosed with stage three squamous cell carcinoma of the oesophagus. If the AI-Protocol worked for those first four patients, I had to give it to him. I got the chances he never had and now it was payback time. I bet you're watching this now, bro. Don't you ever forget that I always knew I owed you.'

Daniel glanced to his left. Leon's eyes were glistening.

'That's the reason I went to TnT for a sabbatical. But it also solved another problem. Look, I need a cup of coffee. Then I'll pick up.'

The screen froze as Stone stopped recording. Ronnie tapped Stone 2 and he re-appeared at his desk, taking a noisy slurp from a mug.

'Going back home not only meant I could treat Leon. I could also try out the protocol on a whole cohort of patients and make sure the first four weren't a flash in the pan. I hooked up with a clinic in Laventille run by an old friend of mine called Sister Augustine. Leon can put you in touch with her. We treated thirty cancer patients, mostly stage four, and the results were just as spectacular as in London. None of the patients were told they were on a new drug regimen, of course. Not even my own kid brother.'

"The old fox," Leon said, the diamond in his front tooth glinting as he smiled.

'I realise this is a bit of an unorthodox way of running, in effect, a small Phase 1 trial—'

"You can say that again," Ronnie said.

'—but it was the perfect solution. Now, all this would rattle the cages of those people on the ethics committee at St Agatha's, so I'm trusting you not to reveal the existence of the Laventille trial to anyone, Veronica. Not that I have any regrets. I just didn't have time to go through the hoops before treating Leon. And if I gave him the chance of life, why not do the same for others? Hell, I went to school with a few of 'em and they'd all be dead without it.'

"He's got a point," Daniel said.

'Anyway, the sooner I spread the word about the Al-Protocol, the better, so I came back from TnT early and today the world will find out all about my baby. Everyone thinks the press conference at two o'clock this afternoon is about the peerage, but that's a smokescreen. I'll be telling the world about the protocol.

'So why all this cloak-and-dagger stuff? Because I think there's a chance – just a chance – that I might not be around for that press conference today. So I'm sending Leon this data card for you, Veronica. It contains everything you need to know about the Protocol and, if I don't make it, I want you to tell the world about its contents. He's getting it by way of good old-fashioned snail mail. I know I could send it to you in a heartbeat electronically but, if someone is ruthless and powerful enough to stop a medical breakthrough like this – and I hope to God I'm wrong – who says they couldn't block these files if I did that? So I'm asking you to be very careful before you put any of this material up online.'

Ronnie clutched Daniel's hand.

'I'm sorry to impose this responsibility on you without asking your permission first but when you read the files on these four patients, plus all the others from

Sister Augustine, I believe you'll think it's a risk worth taking.'

Daniel's mobile vibrated.

"It's me," Alice said.

"Hi, Alice. Have I got a story to tell you. Hasely Stone—"

"Never mind Hasely fucking Stone. What the hell is going on, Daniel? And I don't want any more 'you'll know in good time' bullshit."

"Whoa there. What's brought this on?"

"Most of the numbers on your Ms Bland's phone are untraceable burners but two are landlines. They both belong to one person. They're the home number and office direct line of Quentin Plover, Chief of Staff at Ten Downing Street. Heard of him?"

For a moment, Daniel thought he was hearing things.

"Jesus Christ. Are you sure, Alice?"

"Of course I'm fucking sure. What do you take me for?"

"Sorry… Stupid question."

"So give. The whole lot. Right now."

"I'll call you back in five minutes. Let me talk to—"

"Tell me now. Or you're on your own."

"Just give me a couple—"

"Have it your way."

The line went dead.

The others were staring at him.

"What's up?" Leon asked. "You look as though you've seen a ghost, man."

"Those numbers I got from Chapman's mobile... Two of them belonged to Quentin Plover."

"Who?"

"Chief of Staff at Number Ten. The guy who runs Downing Street. You talked to him after Hasely's funeral, remember?"

"The red-haired guy?"

"That's him. So what's this Chapman woman doing, ringing him? At his office and his home?"

"Then this Plover guy—"

"Must be mixed up in your brother's death. But how? Why? I can think of why a drug company like Du Long and Freyer might want to kill the man who discovered a cure for cancer, but I can't think why the Prime Minister's Chief of Staff would."

"I can," Ronnie said, staring at her screen. "Look at this."

CHAPTER THIRTY-SIX

Ronnie scrolled back up to the top of the next file on the card, *Stone 3*, and pulled up two chairs so the others could read it over her shoulder.

"Here's why this Plover guy is up to his pretty little neck in all this. Read it."

10 DOWNING STREET
LONDON SW1A 2AA

OFFICIAL – SENSITIVE - RECIPIENTS ONLY

THE PROJECTED IMPACT OF A UNIVERSAL
CURE FOR CANCER ON THE UK's
DEMOGRAPHY, PUBLIC SERVICES,
INFRASTRUCTURE AND ECONOMY

This paper is written at the request of the Prime

Minister's Office by Professor Hasely Stone, Director of the Lipman Cancer Research Institute, St Agatha's University Hospital, London

ABSTRACT

Cancer kills more people and instils greater fear than any other medical condition. Now a team at the Lipman Institute believe it has found a cure – the Adoptive Immunotherapy Protocol. It is an entirely new way of harnessing the body's own immune system to fight cancer. The AIP doesn't kill off cancer cells. It changes them back into healthy tissue. After very positive results in the laboratory using mice, we trialled it on a small cohort of human patients with different forms of the disease. It worked, to startling effect, in all of them. Assuming early research bears fruit, the AIP will save millions of lives across the world.

This paper looks at the effects the AIP will have when it is rolled out across this country. Because of it, 170,000 cancer patients who would have died will survive every year. Crucially, most of them will be old and economically unproductive. This will have a massive negative impact on the NHS, social care, housing, pensions and the wider British economy unless HM Government acts now to deal with it.

SUMMARY OF FINDINGS

• When the AI-Protocol is rolled out across the UK, **three million extra people will survive over the next two decades who would have died**. That is equal to the populations of Liverpool, Newcastle, Nottingham and

Sheffield combined.

• **The impact of the AI-Protocol will be greater here** than almost any other western European country. That is because we have some of the lowest long-term cancer survival rates in the industrialised world, largely due to late diagnosis.

• **Well over half of those cancer survivors will be above retirement age.** Cancer is predominantly an old person's disease.

• **Treating these extra patients will bankrupt the NHS** unless urgent action is taken by HM Government. We will spend far less on expensive cancer drugs but those savings will be dwarfed by the cost of extra treatments for age-related conditions such as heart by-passes and hip replacements.

• **The present model of social care will collapse** as millions more people require help over time. In particular, the numbers of patients with dementia needing care home places will escalate.

• However, most of the cancer survivors will continue to live in their own homes for longer, **creating an even bigger housing** crisis than at present. Without a significant building programme, house prices will rise so steeply that only the top earners will be able to buy their own home. That will impose even more pressure on social housing, when many priced out of the housing market turn to it for help.

• **Pensions – state and private - will be impossible to sustain in their present form**. If we work on the basis the life expectancy of a quarter of pensioners will increase by another 14 years, pension schemes would have liabilities around 25% higher within a decade. The private pensions industry will quickly go under, as every actuarial projection upon which it is presently based will be obsolete.

• City analysts will spot the implications of all this very quickly, so HM Government should prepare for **an immediate selling of equities, a stock market plunge and a run on the Pound**, similar to that seen when financial markets reacted to the Truss Government's mini budget of 2022.

• Overall, **the British economy will be severely damaged**, dragged down by the addition of hundreds of thousands, and then millions, of economically inactive people. This will reduce HM Government's ability to pay for the increased pensions, social care and health services these extra people will need.

• **It is perfectly possible for HM Government to prepare for the negative impacts of the AI-Protocol but the author strongly advises that this planning is put in place now.**

• **If it fails to do so, the effects on our economy, health service and entire social fabric could be nothing short of catastrophic.**

"That's the gist of it," Ronnie said. "there's another thirty-seven pages that I've skim-read. You can read 'em later but you get the idea."

"I'm not sure I do," Leon said. "Is Hasely seriously saying this protocol of his is a bad idea?"

"No way," she replied. "In the conclusion, Hasely bends over backwards to make it clear that the protocol is good news ... of course it is. But it's the biggest medical breakthrough for generations and will have monumental consequences – for the health service, pensions, the economy. They'll all be damaged when millions more unproductive older people continue to live on in the coming years. It's down to the politicians to sort the mess out."

"And it's down to us," Daniel said.

CHAPTER THIRTY-SEVEN

Gemma Chapman picked up her burner and speed-dialled. She hoped the call would go to voicemail. No such luck.

"So?" Plover snapped, picking up after the third ring.

"We've lost them."

"What? How can you lose them? Baz was on the same fucking plane. You are a complete fuckwit, Chapman, and your oppos are no better."

"Just a minute—"

"What happened to all that it'll-be-easy-when-we-get-to-Trinidad crap?"

"You ought to learn a few manners, Plover. We're doing our best, for Christ's sake. Baz had a guy in Arrivals all afternoon, waiting for them to come out. Not a sign. Must have left by a back door or something. And … there's something else you need to know."

"What else have you fucked up?"

"Nothing, but I got the third degree from customs at Piarco. Strip-search, the lot."

"They didn't find anything, did they?"

"Nothing to find but there's no way I was chosen at random."

"Why you?"

"Dunno, but I don't like it."

"You'd better find them soon, hadn't you?"

* * *

"So Hasely Stone made the greatest medical breakthrough in a hundred years and signed his own death warrant in the process," Daniel said, unable to take his eyes off the screen.

"Maybe, but let's see what other goodies are here before we jump to any conclusions," Ronnie replied.

Stone 4 was a draft press release, headed 'Dramatic Cancer Breakthrough by St Agatha's Research Team' and scheduled for 14.00 hours on the day Hasely Stone was found dead. *Stone 5* contained the files of the four patients on the protocol.

Stone 6 was a draft paper for the British Journal of Cancer. Ronnie skim-read it.

"Apart from a very small dose of Tamoxadrene to kick-start the process, the rest of the drugs in the regimen are all out of patent, so rolling it out will cost peanuts."

"He always was a clever sonofabitch," Leon said as he wiped his eyes. "He got the whole damn thing planned out. They might have got him but he made damn sure they didn't get his protocol."

"But apart from Plover who are 'they'?" Ronnie asked.

"He won't be acting alone," Daniel said. "He doesn't take a shit without Stephen Truman knowing about it."

"Hang on," Leon said. "Are you sure the British Government – the British Government – would kill to stop the country going bankrupt?"

"'Fraid so, Leon," Daniel replied. "Truman and Co need a cure for cancer like a hole in the head. Hasely's paper showed that."

"Well, I'm not sure I buy it. That stuff might go down in some parts of the world but we're talking about the United Kingdom here."

"Look, Leon, even the British Government takes calculated decisions it knows – knows for sure – will result in people dying. It takes them all the time."

"Like how?"

"Like how the last government stopped grossly overweight people getting on heart bypass waiting lists. They knew patients would die but went ahead with the policy anyway to save a measly seventy million quid."

"Okay, but the folks who took that decision didn't know exactly who was going to die. These guys do. They're taking 'em out one by one."

"Then how else do you explain how the phone numbers of Quentin Plover, the guy who runs the Number Ten machine, are on the mobile phone of the woman who killed your brother and Stephanie Bright? And she's now sitting in the Hilton bar with the guy who almost certainly tried to kill me ... What do you think, Ron?"

"I guess so," she said, still scrolling through the documents. "But five minutes ago, we were all convinced Paul Eriksson and Du Long and Freyer were the brains behind all this. Maybe they're involved as well. What about the way all the patient files were wiped? From a new computer system installed by DLF. Or what about my DNA results? That's how those guys must've cottoned onto me. And who owns the testing company? DLF again."

"Fair point," Daniel replied. "But it wasn't Paul Eriksson's phone numbers on Chapman's mobile. It was Quentin Plover's. And if he's involved, where does that leave the Prime Minister?"

"Hasely didn't name the person he talked to about the protocol, remember," Ronnie said.

"No, but we know Truman's chief of staff must be involved. There's no other plausible explanation as to why a killer would be calling Plover at his office. God, even at home."

"Still doesn't make his boss guilty."

"Okay, Ron. Let's assume for a second Truman isn't involved. What about this as a scenario? Plover could be in the Cabinet after the next election if he gets his safe seat. Maybe he asked Hasely to write the paper for Number Ten."

"I can buy that. People have killed for lot less."

"They sure have in Laventille," Leon said. "London, too, I reckon."

"Phew, at last we can agree on something," Daniel said. "So what the hell do we do now?"

CHAPTER THIRTY-EIGHT

Gemma Chapman put down her empty glass. She'd never been much of a drinker but that rum punch had slipped down a treat. Might even order another after she called Plover. For once, she was rather looking forward to it.

"Me again. Got a bit of good news."

"You know it's the middle of the fucking night here? And speak up. I can hardly hear you."

"I'll have to move." She walked onto the terrace by the pool. "There's this guy nursing a beer in the bar who's a bit too interested in our conversation for my liking."

"What do you want?"

"Baz's best mate just called. Reckons he knows where Leon Stone's gone to ground."

"Where?"

"This Laventille place, where he was born. Stone was hanging around there all day yesterday. Bit low rent for him these days but Baz's mate'll put his shirt on Stone staying nearby. We know he's not at his gaff."

"You do have someone keeping an eye in case he goes back home?"

"What do you take me for?"

"I'm not going to answer that question, Chapman. You won't like the answer. Can you get down to Laventille tonight?"

"Not a good idea."

"Why, for fuck's sake?"

"Baz's mate says we'll draw too much attention to ourselves now it's dark. But we'll get there first thing. We'll find 'em."

"You better had."

* * *

"We need a plan of action," Daniel said.

"Simple." Ronnie replied. "We've got all this information. We publish it."

"But it's not that bloody simple, is it, Ron? Bad enough when we thought we had to contend with a multinational drug company. Now we know we're up against a much more powerful adversary."

"So the sooner we put this up online for everyone to see, the better. There won't be any point in these thugs going after us then."

"If – if – we can post the stuff up there. And if – if – we can keep it there long enough for people to read it. But the British Government's tentacles reach a lot further than any drug company's. From now on, we need to work on the assumption that MI5, MI6 and GCHQ could all be used to stop us. If we stick this stuff up online, they could pinpoint where we uploaded it from, find us before anyone gets a chance to read it and take it down. What do you think, Leon?"

His phone warbled before he could answer. It was Billy at the Hilton.

"Chapman's just called Plover again," Leon said, when he finished the call. "Billy boy is worried he might have been rumbled. He's getting out of there."

"Maybe we should be getting out of here," Daniel said. "If Chapman and Williams are onto us, the security services may not be far behind. The last thing we should be doing is just shoving this stuff up online."

"You got another plan?" Leon asked.

"How about this? We could fly back to London straight away and I'll get Star News to run this as a world exclusive. God, this story is up there with 9/11 and—"

"And you can already see yourself picking up a fucking Pulitzer, can't you?" Ronnie said, glaring.

"It's got nothing to do with that."

"It has, too, Daniel Plowright. I reckon our lives are worth a tiny bit more than a damn Pulitzer."

"Cool it," Leon said. "These guys are already breathing down our necks. Bickering ain't gonna help us come up with a plan."

"But I know someone who could," Ronnie said. "Todd."

"No way," Daniel said. "We can't involve anyone else in this."

"But Todd would be perfect."

"Who's Todd?" Leon asked.

"Sorry, Leon. I guess you'd call him the nearest thing I've got to a brother, or even a father. Helped me through some real tough times. Todd's been a real computer fiend since he was a kid. Almost hacked into the Pentagon when he was fifteen. Would've done if his father hadn't caught him. Moved to Colorado last year to work on digital tumour modelling."

"So how can he help us from there?" Daniel asked.

"Because if anyone knows how to get this stuff online and cover our tracks, it's him."

"But if Hasely is right, we can't risk sending this stuff to him."

"We don't have to. Todd'll be here like a shot if I ask him."

"Why don't we go to him?" Leon said. "Then we put a little daylight between us and these guys."

"As soon as we book a flight, our names will be flagged up on the passenger list." Daniel said.

"Only if we use our own passports, but I can fix that. How would you like new TnT passports with US visas?"

"You're putting us on, Leon," Ronnie said, grinning.

"I keep telling you guys, I've got a lot of friends round here. One of them happens to work in the passport office and another at the US Embassy. Shouldn't take more than twenty-four hours to get 'em. I'll get me a fresh one, too, since I don't reckon US Immigration would be too crazy about letting me in with my … history."

"We'd be much safer flying back to London and getting Star News to run the story," Daniel said.

"And what if this Plover guy gets to your bosses?" Ronnie replied. "You're always saying they're right up the ass of the government. Todd's a much better bet."

Daniel held his hands up.

"Okay. Call him."

"Great. I'll put him on speaker so we can all talk."

Todd picked up straight away.

"What on earth is going on, my darling? Are you alright?"

"I'm good. I'm here in Trinidad on speaker with my friend Daniel Plowright and Hasely Stone's brother, Leon."

"Hi there. Good to talk to you. What's up?

"Toddy, we need your help."

"Shoot."

Todd stopped her dead as soon as Ronnie told him about the government connection.

"Don't talk on this line any more. This is what I want you to do. Switch all your phones and tablets to airplane mode, disable the Wi-Fi on any laptops, and then turn all your devices off. All of them, you hear? Only switch them back on in a real emergency. Then get out of there. Is there somewhere else you can go?"

"Sure," Leon said.

"Right. Pick up a few no-contract cell phones as soon as you can. Can you get them at this time of night, Leon?"

"No problem."

"Great. Get four or five and call me back on one of them. Have a pen and paper handy. Most important, get out of there right now. Got it?"

"But Toddy—"

"No questions, my darling. Do it."

CHAPTER THIRTY-NINE

"Where are we going, Leon?" Ronnie asked, as the Range Rover sped along and startled a slumbering herd of goats.

"To Sister Augustine's clinic in Laventille. She'll be surprised to see us so late, but I can't find her number without turning my cell back on. San Fernando's just ahead. There's a bunch of places there to buy phones."

They stopped at a crowded night market full of ramshackle stalls, illuminated by feeble strip lights. A street vendor selling fruit blasted out reggae from one side of the road, clashing with the rap played by his competitor opposite.

"Stay here," Leon shouted, above the din. "Peewee'll take care of you."

He disappeared with Goldie.

Daniel stared out the window.

"A penny for your thoughts," Ronnie said, nudging him. "Isn't that what you Brits say?"

"We don't need a penny, Ron. We need a fucking miracle."

Leon came back with four handsets. Ronnie called Todd on one of them as soon as they drove away from the noise. He gave her the number of a new burner he had bought and told her to call him straight back on that, using a different phone.

"Hi, Toddy. We're on speaker again."

"You got plenty of credit on this cell, Leon?"

"Fifty dollars US."

"Great. Now, did you switch off all your cell phones, laptops and tablets like I told you?"

"You bet. Airplane mode on, all powered down."

"Great. And never – ever – try to pick up your voicemail messages remotely using another phone. If someone's monitoring you, they'll start tracking you as soon as you punch in your PIN code. Got it? By the way, switch off that burner you just used and get rid of it. Don't just take out the SIM. Destroy the card and the handset."

"Understood."

"Okay. Now, I've been thinking about your little predicament and I reckon it's too risky for you guys to send me these files electronically. Professor Stone was right about that. I'd better come to you."

"Leon reckons we're safer getting off the island and coming to you. He can get us TnT passports with American visas."

"Wow. How quick?"

"Twenty-four hours, tops," Leon said.

"Impressive. How the hell can you do that? No. Don't tell me now. How many will be travelling?"

"All three of us," Ronnie said.

"Use three separate routes, message your itineraries to this phone and don't call unless there's a real emergency. Instead, circulate a message to everyone every two hours to confirm you're safe. Your initials with 'M' after it will be fine … 'RM', 'DM', 'LM'. I'll reply to say I've received it with 'TM'. If you do have to speak, be very careful what you say. If they're listening in on calls, they'll be searching for key words. And leave a copy of the SD card behind with someone you trust, Leon. I'll need their details in case this whole shebang goes down the tubes. Good luck."

"Thanks, Toddy."

* * *

Ronnie was shaken awake as the Range Rover bounced over a pothole. They were back in Port of Spain, by the looks of it.

Peewee drew up outside a long, single-storey building in a down-at-heel part of town.

"Wait here, guys," Leon said. He went to a door at the far end and a dim fluorescent glow shone out when it opened. After a furtive conversation on the doorstep, he was back. "Come and meet Sister Augustine. I'll introduce you guys and then I've got stuff to do downtown. You can tell her everything, although she seems to know most of it, from what she told me."

At the doorway stood a plump black woman in her fifties with a beaming smile.

"Welcome to St Saviour's Clinic, people. It's Daniel and Veronica, isn't it?"

"Please call me Ronnie. Everyone does."

"Ronnie … Makes you sound like a boy, but Ronnie it is … Leon, you leave these good people with me. I'll look after 'em."

Her front door opened straight into a sitting room with an ancient TV flickering in the corner. There was an old couch and an easy chair, plus a threadbare rug on the floor. A sideboard stood along one wall, with a wooden cross and a picture of the Sacred Heart hanging above it.

"Are you folks hungry?"

"I'm not quite sure where I am with food," Daniel said, yawning. "It's gone three in the morning, British time. Middle of the night for us."

"What about something to drink, then?"

"A cup of tea?"

"I think you need more of a nightcap than that, young man. In my sideboard I happen to have a bottle of the finest Angostura rum money can buy."

Ronnie laughed.

"You're the first nun I've ever come across who drinks rum, Sister."

"Oh, I'm not a nun, young lady. I like to think I'm a devout kinda woman, and I did think about taking the vows once, but I wasn't cut out for all that discipline. So I became a nursing sister, instead of a religious one. And I most certainly am a rum drinker." She opened the sideboard door, pulled out a square bottle and uncorked it with a loud 'pop'. "Angostura 1919. Smells like honey, tastes like nectar and it's distilled right round the corner from here."

"A small one, please," Ronnie said.

"Young lady, we don't do 'small' in this part of the world. Not when it comes to rum."

Sister Augustine poured out three very generous measures.

"You just got one decision. On the rocks or straight?"

"Straight, please," Daniel replied.

"On the rocks for me," Ronnie said.

"I'm with you, honey. Some folks reckon it's sacrilegious but I like a cube or two. Now you tell me this ain't the best rum you've ever tasted."

It was, and Ronnie really could smell the honey.

"Right, you folks better tell me what you're doing here, though ever since I heard about Hasely, I reckoned it was only a matter of time before someone came calling."

By the end of the story, Sister Augustine looked worried.

"Now, if these people got on your tail so easy, I reckon I should make myself scarce for a week or two."

"Can you do that?" Ronnie asked.

"Sure. I'll hop over to Tobago. That's where I come from. There ain't no way these guys'll find me there." She walked over to the picture of the Sacred Heart and took it down. "And before I go, I got something for you."

Hidden behind the backboard was an SD card. She handed it to Ronnie.

"Here are the records of every one of the thirty patients from here that Hasely put on the protocol. Don't talk to me about how long it took to scan 'em in. The clinic's scanner is fit for the museum. But when I heard about Hasely's death, I didn't buy all that race hate stuff for a second. Somehow I knew his murder had something to do with the protocol and these records would come in handy. You hold onto this and I'll take the hard copies of the files with me."

"Can I give you something in return?"

"Sure. Exchange is no robbery. That was my ward sister's favourite phrase when I worked at St Agatha's."

"You were at Aggies?"

"Sure. That's where I first met Hasely."

Ronnie handed her the envelope containing the original card Stone had sent to his brother.

"I reckon it's time you guys got some rest," Sister Augustine said. "You'll have to sleep next door on the cots in the clinic. I hope they'll be comfortable. You guys married?"

They shook their heads.

"Then no funny business, Okay?" she said, with a wink.

CHAPTER FORTY

"Twenty Dunhill International, please. And a box of matches."

Alice hadn't smoked for five years but couldn't wait to light up the moment she left the corner shop at the end of her road. That buzz you get when you draw in your first lungful? Jesus, did she need it now.

She'd called Daniel back three times last night but he didn't pick up. Leaving a voicemail was not a great idea. Anyone could be listening in.

Alice was running out of time – and choices. Now she had to leave a voicemail if he didn't pick up.

"Daniel, it's me. Look, I'm sorry for hanging up on you yesterday but please, please call me. That list of telephone numbers you gave me? I can't stay quiet about it. You know that, don't you? Anyway, when you're involved with people this high up the food chain, you need protecting.

"I can help you, even if you are on the other side of the world, but we need to talk. So fucking well phone me. Please. Your arse is on the line now. So is mine."

* * *

Daniel looked at his watch. 7a.m. Not bad for the first morning after a transatlantic flight. He crept past a fast-asleep Ronnie and found Leon chatting over breakfast with a girl wearing exquisitely braided hair.

"Get much sleep, Leon?"

"Only an hour on the couch. Still, I'll have plenty of time to rest when we get away from here. But we need the new passports for that, which is where Amy comes in."

Half an hour later, Amy had cut off a sleepy Ronnie's long black curls and turned her remaining bob peroxide blond. Then she gave Daniel a haircut short enough for the Marines.

She was taking Leon's photograph when his burner rang. He walked outside, frowning, with the phone pressed to his ear.

"That call was from Billy," Leon said, when he returned. "He's following our friends from the hotel. Looks as though they're coming our way. Peewee'll put the car round the corner and keep watch outside. Goldie'll look after us here. Sister Augustine, put a sign on the door saying you're closed because of … a family bereavement. Yeah, that's good. All blinds down. Doors locked. Phones on silent. Let's move."

As the last bolt was pushed home on the front door, Leon's mobile vibrated with a message from Peewee. He held it up to show the others.

'Chapman, Barrington Williams + another coming towards you.'

Daniel clutched Ronnie's hand. He was dying for a pee. Too bad.

First, a knock on the clinic door at one end of the building, followed by another. Then the sound of footsteps, stopping every few seconds. They must be looking through each window in turn, Daniel guessed. The footsteps stopped right outside Sister Augustine's front door. Despite the note, they hammered on it once, twice, three times.

At last, they heard the sound of footsteps walking away. Leon's phone vibrated. Another message from Peewee.

'Sit tight. 2 go round back.'

After five minutes, a third.

'Gone.'

"But they'll be back," Leon said. "We can't hang around here. This is Chapman's first morning in this town and where does she pitch up?"

"Can't we hide out somewhere else till we fly out?" Daniel asked.

"For sure. But I think it's time we played it clever, and put some real distance between us and these guys. I'm going to call Patrick Lara at Piarco. If he can help us, I'll need your UK and US passports."

Two minutes later, Leon hung up on Patrick, put away his burner phone and pulled out his personal mobile. Despite Todd's instructions never to use it, he switched it on.

CHAPTER FORTY-ONE

Plover saw the names flash up on his screen, smiled with satisfaction and dialled.

"Chapman? Leon Stone has just booked three Business Class seats on this afternoon's five forty BA flight back to Gatwick via St Lucia and three more on a Copa Airlines flight to Panama City leaving nine minutes later."

"Why are they going to Panama?"

"They can't be on both flights, fuckwit. One's got to be a decoy."

"What do you want us to do?"

"Send Baz to Panama, though I'd be amazed if any of them ended up there. You take the London flight. Steer well clear of them but make sure there's a reception committee waiting this end."

"Easy enough."

"One other thing. It looks as though there may be rather more … litter hanging around here than I thought. I'll need someone to sweep it up straight away, before you get back."

* * *

The propellers of the De Havilland Dash 8-300 began to turn before the cabin door was fully closed. Liat Airlines flight LI309 from St Lucia's Hewanorra International Airport to Port of Spain needed to get airborne fast. Three extra passengers boarded at the last minute.

But the captain was more than happy to hold the flight. He could make up the time on the seventy-minute hop to Piarco, no problem. Anyway, TnT Immigration sent a message ahead. These guys were VVIPs. This was the Caribbean.

* * *

Quentin Plover was still working at his desk past midnight. He didn't need much sleep, an attribute he was secretly rather pleased to share with the late Margaret Thatcher. Fifteen minutes ago, his mobile burst into life with the message from Chapman he was expecting.

'Gatwick flight just landed in St Lucia. All 3 in Biz Class.'

Now a second message flashed up.

'Stone, Ackerman, Plowright listed on Liat Airlines flight from Hewanorra, St Lucia, to Piarco, Trinidad. ETA 20.00 hours local time, 01.00 hours BST.'

Plover's natural self-confidence, honed by years at Britain's most exclusive – and expensive – educational institutions, disintegrated in an instant. He grabbed his phone.

"You fucking moron, Chapman."

"What are you talking about?"

"They've just got off the plane in St Lucia."

"What?"

"They bought tickets to London but they got off at the stopover."

"Christ, are you sure?"

"Of course I'm fucking sure. Can you get off?"

"No chance. We're rolling down the runway. If the cabin crew weren't strapped in, I'd get a bollocking for speaking to you."

"You'll get a bollocking back here, you cretin ... Shit."

"What do you want me to do?"

"Check as soon as you can in case any of them are still on board. Don't spook them if they are. When does Baz get into Panama?"

"Another half hour."

"How fast can he get back to Port of Spain?"

"Not till tomorrow afternoon. Only two planes a day."

"That's exactly why they picked Panama fucking City. They won't be in Business. They're on their way back to Trinidad. They've been playing us all along. Christ, what a fucking, fucking, fucking mess."

CHAPTER FORTY-TWO

Daniel checked his watch as Caribbean Airlines flight BW484 landed at Miami right on time. He couldn't help smiling as he imagined the moment Ms Bland and Black Diamond discovered they'd been had. And what about Quentin Plover? Oh, to be a fly on his wall when the man with the foulest mouth in Whitehall found out.

Sister Augustine had shooed them out the clinic, promising to be on the lunchtime ferry to Tobago. Leon gave her twenty thousand US dollars in cash and a burner phone.

"Remember, no credit cards and leave your regular cell phone behind," he warned.

They'd arrived at Piarco early, first to check into BA Business Class and then for the flight to Panama. Daniel soon spotted Chapman talking to Barrington Williams.

"I wonder how they knew we'd be here today? I think someone with very good connections must have told them, don't you?"

Ronnie and Daniel went through security but Leon stayed back to make sure Chapman and Williams followed them. Then he could cancel their Panama tickets; they needed Black Diamond up and away to Central America, not delayed on the ground by three no-shows and able to leave the plane before take-off. On board, Daniel used his burner to video Chapman walking through Business Class to Economy at the back.

Their exit from the plane at St Lucia went without a hitch, once Leon told the crew how he'd just got news of a death in the family. When they returned from their brief stopover, Patrick Lara let them use the VVIP suite overnight.

At 11p.m., Amy arrived and handed Leon three new TnT passports. They laughed when they saw the false name on Ronnie's – Siobhan Anderson.

"I had to call you something," Leon said, laughing.

Then Amy booked three flights for the following morning, using her own credit card. Daniel was bound for Miami at 8.30a.m. Leon for JFK at 8.55a.m. But first away was Ronnie, on an 8.05a.m. charter flight to Houston. She would get to Todd's first, maybe by late afternoon. The two of them could do with a catch-up by themselves.

Before everyone dozed off for a few hours' sleep, Ronnie gave Daniel a hug.

"All that stuff about the Pulitzer … I didn't mean it."

"Forget it, Ron. And you're right about Todd. We need all the help we can get right now."

Miami Immigration was the usual zoo but Daniel remembered the date as he waited in line and wished the stern-looking officer 'Happy July the Fourth'.

He was ravenous, so went for a beer and burger at a better-than-average airport restaurant, so bedecked in the Stars and Stripes you'd have thought the president was dropping by for lunch. He'd thought about ringing

Alice on his new burner but couldn't risk it. The bad guys found out soon enough about their plans to leave Trinidad. Who's to say they weren't already monitoring the phone of his ex?

He logged onto the BBC UK news webslte, just as lunch arrived. The lead headline flashed up.

'New Aggies Tragedy as Hospital Chief Found Dead.'

Daniel forced himself to read on.

'The body of the chief executive at St Agatha's University Hospital in London, Paul Eriksson, was discovered in a car at the exclusive Chelsea Harbour complex early today. The Metropolitan Police said they were not looking for anyone else in connection with the death.

'It's the third tragedy to hit the leading London teaching hospital in recent weeks. Nobel Prize-winning scientist Professor Hasely Stone, who ran its world-leading Lipman Cancer Research Institute, was bludgeoned to death in a racist attack two weeks ago. Then his deputy, Dr Stephanie Bright, was killed in a fire at the hospital on Monday.

'Health Secretary and Deputy Prime Minister Dr Gerry Crewton sent his condolences to Mr Eriksson's family. He praised the chief executive's 'courage' for pressing ahead with the Government's controversial hospital franchising scheme at St Agatha's. The death an 'absolute tragedy' and a terrible loss to the NHS, he added.

'Meanwhile, Scotland Yard today named two people they wish to interview in connection with the murder of Professor Stone. American researcher Dr Veronica Ackerman and Star TV News reporter Daniel Plowright are believed to have flown to Trinidad together last Friday.'

Daniel's lunch went untouched.

* * *

Alice had never seen the Dog and Trumpet so quiet. Mind you, she never drank here at this hour on a Sunday evening. The location was Tom Edwards' idea. He was late.

She stared down at the ice cubes melting in her Scotch, losing track of time.

"You were miles away."

He stood over her.

"Got a lot on my plate, sir."

"I think we can skip the formalities tonight, Alice. It's 'Tom' on the weekends."

"Of course. Thanks so much for seeing me at short notice. Can I get you a drink?"

"No thanks. Got to be quick. Wife's outside in the car and I'm driving back to Surrey." He sat down. "Now, what's so important that it can't wait till tomorrow?"

"The names of two persons of interest to the Hasely Stone murder investigation were released today."

"I heard that on the lunchtime news."

"Then you'll know one of them is my contact, Daniel Plowright."

"And?"

"He's … a bit more than a contact. We lived together. We were getting married but split up last year."

"I didn't know that."

"I try to keep my head down when it comes to my private life. But I'm not sure I can, now that Daniel's been named. Commander Gough will view it as a clear conflict of interest, so I'll have to tell him first thing in the morning. Should've done it today but I wanted to speak to you first. And, if I tell him about my relationship with Daniel, I've got to tell him about the London Fields attack and the link to Stone's murder, haven't I?"

"I think I might have that drink after all."

Edwards returned with a half pint of bitter for himself and another Scotch for Alice.

"Let's work this through. The minute you tell Gough, he'll take the greatest pleasure in turfing you off the team, and that …" He took a swig of beer. "… would be a pity. How many people at the Yard know about your previous relationship?"

"In the force, only three close friends. And I've already spoken to them today. They won't talk."

"Then … I don't think you should, either. Not at the moment. You've already proved invaluable to this investigation, and to me. Pulling you off it would be completely counter-productive."

"But Commander Gough is bound to find out sooner or later."

"Let's cross that bridge when we come to it."

"As long as you're sure."

"I am. You've told me and you will, of course, let me know if anything changes, won't you?

"And I mean anything."

CHAPTER FORTY-THREE

The setting sun was turning the snow-covered peaks the colour of marmalade as Ronnie's bus reached the sign on the edge of town. 'Enstone – Jewel of the Rockies'.

What a place for a research facility. Todd said there was a rush of applicants every time a vacancy came up at the Cobbett Institute of Oncology. No surprise there.

Ronnie looked at her watch as she pressed his intercom. Six o'clock precisely.

"Toddy, it's me."

"Come right up, my darling."

He stood in the open doorway of his apartment, the setting sun backlighting that familiar shock of bleached fair hair.

"You look great, apart from the new hairstyle," he said, giving her an enormous hug. "I'm not crazy about that."

"I needed it for the passport."

"I'll get used to it. Wanna beer or something to eat?"

"Do you have green tea?"

"Sure. Always knew you'd come calling one day. In fact, I thought you might ring ahead."

"You told us not to, remember?"

"When was the last time you did anything you were told, Veronica Ackerman? Did you know Scotland Yard have issued an APB on you and your friend, Daniel?"

"We thought that might happen."

"And there's something else."

Ronnie burst into tears when he told her about Paul Eriksson.

"I can't stand any more of this, Toddy. I just can't."

"Hey, hey, relax," he said, hugging her.

"How can I? These people won't stop till they've killed … oh my God … Laura. I've got to warn Laura."

"Who's Laura?"

"Stone's PA. Been there a million years. God, why didn't I think of her before? She's the one person left in the institute who knows the protocol exists. I've got to call her."

She rummaged in her purse and pulled out her phone.

"Is that your personal cell?" Todd asked.

"Yes."

He grabbed her hand

"You can't call Laura on that."

"But her number's on it."

"I've got a better idea. Come with me."

He took her into the kitchen, opened the door of the oven and took out the racks. Then he hung two sheets of cooking foil over the front.

"Okay. Take your cell phone and lean as far into the oven as you can with it."

"Why?"

"To block the signal. It'll be a lot safer switching it on in there. Call out Laura's number and I'll write it down. Then switch off again before you come out."

She poked her head inside and Todd wrapped the foil around her.

"Was all that necessary?" Ronnie asked, when she reappeared.

"Can't say for certain but it wasn't worth taking the risk."

It was past 2.30a.m. London time when she got through to Laura.

"Veronica? Is that really you? Where are you?"

"I can't tell you on this line but—"

"What's happening, Veronica? Mr Eriksson's been found dead and people at the institute like that nasty Jason MacGregor man are saying you must be involved somehow and …"

She broke down.

"Laura. Laura. Stop. Stop crying for a moment … That's better. Now Laura, listen. You may be in the most terrible danger and—"

"I know."

"What do you mean, you 'know'?"

"It's the protocol, isn't it?"

"Yes, but how do you know about that?"

"I don't, apart from the fact that it exists. But I worked it out. When Professor Stone was killed and his file was wiped from the IT system, I didn't connect the two events. But then the files of Daniel and the other patients on the protocol disappeared too. Maurice Sutcliffe told me he tried to find them for you. Daniel's with you, I suppose?"

"He will be soon."

"Then Stephanie was killed. But it was only when Rosanna Kings rang to say she's found her husband's file – and told me her terrible news – that it started to click. So I called Maria Grigorenko's number and spoke to her daughter. Poor woman. The police took another look at that boiler, by the way. It was tampered with."

"Laura, Daniel and I had absolutely nothing to do with any of this. You must believe me."

"Of course I do, but I don't understand why all these people have been killed. What's so important about the protocol?"

"I haven't got time to tell you tonight, Laura. All you need to know right now is that you must get away from your apartment."

"I've been thinking exactly the same thing but where do I go? I was about to ring the police—"

"No, don't do that, Laura. Do not – repeat, do not – go to the police. Is there anywhere else you can go?"

"Well, I suppose I could go to—"

"Don't tell me, not on this line. Look, as soon as we've finished talking, I want you to switch your phone to airplane mode and turn it off."

"Why on earth do you want me—"

"Second, pack a bag and leave. You won't be back for a few days. And don't take your iPad, laptop or phone with you. They can trace you if you use them. Then get out of there. Don't use your own car."

"No problem, I can get an Uber."

"Definitely not an Uber, Laura. They'll send the invoice to your inbox, with details of your journey. Can you hail a cab at this time of night?"

"On the main road coming back from town. It's only five minutes' walk."

"Great. Make sure the cab's not followed. If it is, you'll have to go to the police. Otherwise, almost anywhere else is safer. Stop at an ATM, take out as much money as you can and go stay somewhere safe for the night. A small hotel, maybe. Do not use a credit card. Pay cash.

"Tomorrow, go to your bank and get as much money out of your account as possible. Then buy a couple of no-contract cell phones. You mustn't give the phone store your details, so go somewhere small, Okay?"

"Why do I—"

"Trust me, Laura. Now, grab a pen and I'll give you the number of another phone to call me on tomorrow. Don't call this one under any circumstances."

Laura finally hung up.

"Lucky you called her when you did," Todd said. "More green tea, darling?"

"I'm good for now, thanks."

Todd uncapped another beer.

"This guy Daniel … You guys an item?"

"Not exactly. We've decided to take it a little easy till all this is over."

"What's he like?"

She smiled.

"He's great company. I'm never bored. He's funny and he's kind. He knows a lot about a lot of stuff, even if he can be a bit cynical. Typical reporter, I guess. And he's a little guy."

"Little?"

"He's three inches shorter than me."

"No kidding."

"And you'll like him."

"Can't wait to meet him. Right. We'd better see what's on this precious SD card of yours."

CHAPTER FORTY-FOUR

Daniel spotted a familiar figure the moment he walked out of Arrivals at Denver International Airport.

"How was your flight, Leon?"

"Pretty good. Did Immigration ask you what a pearly white guy was doing with a TnT passport?"

"I told them my mother was born in Port of Spain. They were cool."

He told Leon about Eriksson's death.

"No way this could have been suicide?"

"What do you think? Eriksson must have found out too much. And to make things worse, Ronnie and I are now on the 'Most Wanted' list."

"I know what that feels like."

Hiring a car was out of the question. That would require a credit card and driving licence. Leon grabbed a taxi.

"You know it's a hundred miles up to Enstone, sir?" the driver said.

"No problem," he replied, flourishing a wad of cash to prove he could pay the fare.

"I keep meaning to ask you, Leon," Daniel said, settling in the back of the cab. "Where did you make all your money?"

He smiled.

"That's a very personal question, young man."

"Well, I was a very young journalist when I discovered there's absolutely no question too personal to ask, as long as you look someone straight between the eyes and make it sound perfectly reasonable."

"Well, let's just say that in my previous line of business I used to sink rum punches with the old commissioner of police for all the wrong reasons. He's now in jail. These days I sink rum punches with the new commissioner. For all the right reasons.'

* * *

Todd was just like Daniel expected. A warm and genuine smile, stylish, and living in an apartment so clean you could eat your dinner off the floor. He cooked his guests pasta carbonara, rustled up a green salad and opened a bottle of red Zinfandel. Ronnie stuck to green tea.

"There's good news and bad news, I reckon," Todd said, his mouth full.

"I need cheering up," Daniel replied. "Let's start with the good news."

"Okay, I've looked at the files and there's no problem me getting this stuff up online. I can use the dark web. You've used it, Daniel?"

"Once or twice, when I've been following up stories about the seedier side of life. But I'm no expert. And I'm not sure many people would want to log on to it. They'll be suspicious, won't they?"

"Don't worry. You only need a few people to access it for the genie to get out of the bottle. And there's no way to trace anything you post back to your IP address. At least, not in a hurry. Even the British Government couldn't find you or take your files down any time soon."

"Great," Ronnie said, giving him a hug. "So what's the bad news?"

Todd hesitated.

"I'm not sure putting all this stuff online is the best way to achieve what you want."

"What are you talking about, Toddy?" she said, letting him go. "These people are trying to kill us to stop this information getting out."

"For sure, my darling, but it doesn't mean they'll leave you alone if you do publish it. That'll really piss 'em, won't it? They'll still want to hunt you down to make sure you don't reveal anything else you might have. They'll still want to silence you for good."

"So what's the alternative?" Daniel asked.

"Let's consider for a moment what you guys want to achieve. You want to publish the protocol and also nail the bad guys, right?"

The others nodded.

"If you post this material up online, you'd sure get the protocol out there but it'll make nailing the bad guys a damn sight harder."

"How do you work that one out?" Ronnie asked.

"Well, for a start, you don't know who the bad guys are right now, do you? Not for sure."

"We know Quentin Plover has to be one of them," Daniel said.

"But is he running the show or is he answerable to his boss?"

"I'm still not sure the Prime Minister's behind all this," Leon said. "Right now, all we know is that my brother wrote the Prime Minister's Office a paper."

"There you go," Todd said.

"So what do we do?" Daniel asked.

"We need a plan a lot smarter than just putting a bunch of files up on the internet and hoping for the best." Todd gulped down his last inch of his wine and looked round with a smile of satisfaction. "And I think I might have one. Coffee, anyone?"

* * *

Chapman went to the toilet and turned on her phone the minute the plane reached British airspace. Might as well get it over with.

"Sorry, Plover. They're not on the flight."

"How could you be so fucking stupid? Where's Baz?"

"Just messaged. He's still stuck in Panama but he's got people looking all over Port of Spain. Not a fucking sign. He don't reckon they're still in TnT."

"Neither do I. Just before Veronica Ackerman flew out from Britain, she made a call to a Professor Todd Hogan. Used to work with her at Harvard. Now lives in Colorado. Seems he's some kind of father figure to her."

"So what?"

"Shut up and listen. Before Ackerman's phone went dark, she made one last call from Trinidad, once again to Hogan. If she and Plowright have gone anywhere, I reckon Colorado's their most likely destination."

"How could they have flown out without their names being flagged up?"

"I don't fucking know. Maybe they didn't fly. Maybe Leon Stone helped them. He's got lots of friends in the drugs game … Could lay his hands on a fast boat easily enough. Trinidad's only ten miles off the coast of South America."

"So what do you want Baz to do?"

"Leave his friends sniffing around Port of Spain and send him to Colorado to check Hogan out. I'll message you his address."

CHAPTER FORTY-FIVE

"Right, these guys have got two big problems," Todd said, coming in from the kitchen with coffee. "Number one. They don't know where you are. Number two. Even if they found you, they can't kill you till they've got all the copies of the SD card. And you've got plenty of those.

"If you play it right, you might make life so tricky for 'em that they'll decide not to kill you after all. At least, not straight away."

"How come?" Ronnie asked.

"Because you haven't only got the files on the card that'll embarrass them. You've got a load of other stuff they don't know about yet. You've got your eyewitness testimony of Chapman killing Stephanie Bright. Plus her admitting she killed Leon's brother. And you now know three patients on the protocol were murdered, even though their deaths were made to look anything but."

"I wouldn't bet on them leaving us alone just because of that, Toddy."

"I would. At least until they're certain they've swept up all the dirt you've got. And there's one bit of evidence they'll be very anxious to get hold of, as soon as they know about it."

"What's that?" asked Daniel.

"The photo you took of the recent numbers on Chapman's cell phone. That directly links the Prime Minister's top aide to this whole shebang. So, yup, they would love to kill you guys, but they can't risk it happening anytime soon."

"But I can't access that. I'd have to switch my mobile on."

"I reckon it should be safe enough, as long as you shield your phone in the oven, like I did with Ronnie's. And I could hard-wire it into my laptop instead of using Wi-Fi."

"Great," said Daniel. "If we can lift photos off our phones, we've a load more. What about the screengrabs of Chapman and Barrington Williams at the London Fields demo? Then there are the shots Billy took of them plotting round the bar at the Hilton. Plus the video I snuck yesterday of Chapman boarding the BA flight at Piarco. It shows these scumbags were in all the wrong places at all the wrong times."

"Exactly. And once they find out about all that, they may lighten up a little. They might even be prepared to cut a deal."

"A deal?" Ronnie said. "These people don't want to deal with us, Toddy. They want to kill us."

"Of course they do, but they can't risk killing you until they've got all the copies of the card back. And when they find out you've got a load of other material that'll dump them even deeper in the shit, killing you gets even riskier. They'll certainly want to negotiate with you to find out what you've got. And when they do, you'll be able to answer the biggest question of all. Who is behind all this?"

"How do we do that?" Ronnie asked.

"You go back to London and you call up Plover. You tell him you've got Hasely's SD card with a bunch of incriminating files on it, plus a whole heap of other stuff as well. All pointing directly at him. Then you say you want to cut a deal. What's he gonna say?"

"Well, he's an arrogant bastard, so he'll start with the usual derision, denials and threats," Daniel said.

"But eventually he'll have to talk turkey because it's the only way he'll find out what you've got. Then you tell him you don't want to deal with him. You want to deal with your Prime Minister."

"What if he says there's no one else involved?" Ronnie asked.

"That's exactly what he'll say but you tell him that's bullshit. You tell him if you don't get to speak to his boss next time you call, you'll go public with the contents of the card and all the rest of the stuff you've got."

"Brilliant," Daniel said. "If Truman knows nothing about this, Plover will be terrified of him finding out. Even an operator like him won't be able to hide it."

"But if Truman is involved, he'll be on the line next time," said Todd. "You record all the calls, go tell the world what you've discovered and, hey, save a few million lives into the bargain by publishing the protocol. I'd call that a good day's work, wouldn't you?"

"But these guys are smart," Ronnie said. "If we offer them the card in return for leaving us alone, they'll think we're trying to double-cross them."

"Which is why you won't be doing that. You're going to sell it to them."

"What, blackmail them? Blackmail is a criminal offence, in case you'd forgotten, Toddy."

"Absolutely, and you need to establish credibility with these assholes. The way to do that is to stoop down to their level. Takes a thief to catch a thief, I'd say."

"Sounds damn risky to me."

"Sure it is, Ron darling, but it's also damn risky going round the rest of your life with a bunch of killers on your tail."

"And what if they try to double-cross us?"

"They probably will, so it's wise to take out a little insurance, like Hasely did. And I can give you that. I can post these files up online the moment Plover or Truman or whoever double-crosses you. By the end of all this you should be able to publish the protocol, get these assholes off your backs, nail Mr Big and give Daniel a great scoop for his TV show. Neat, eh?"

"Neat?" Daniel said, beaming. "It's bloody brilliant, mate – if it works."

"I think it will. But these guys won't spook easy, so you've got to find a way of making them blink first. Can you pull me up a public transportation map of London?"

CHAPTER FORTY-SIX

Chapman arrived home in Camden with a thumping headache and severe jetlag. At least she'd got good news from Baz on the train back from Gatwick. Should shut Plover up for a while. She dialled him.

"Found them yet?"

"No, but Baz struck lucky in Panama. There's a direct flight to Denver and he's just taken off on it. Only six hours."

"Make sure he doesn't fuck up again."

"He didn't fuck up last time. Neither did I. Shit happens. That's all."

"So you don't think it's a fuck-up when they con one of you into flying to the arse end of Central America and the other back to London? Well, it's certainly not a ringing endorsement of your competence, is it?

"By the way, I've got another job for you. Plowright's ex. You'll definitely need to keep an eye on her."

"Who is she?"

"Detective Superintendent Alice Mahoney of Scotland Yard's Racist Crime Command, no less."

"Shit."

"Quite. I've already got an initial download of the traffic to and from her mobile and Daniel Plowright called her not long after he landed in Trinidad. She rang him back once. Keeps trying, though he's not picking up. I don't think she's calling to give him restaurant recommendations."

* * *

Daniel crept past Todd, fast asleep on the couch, and made his way to the bathroom. He was about to open the door when the toilet flushed and Ronnie came out.

Ten minutes later, they were together on the terrace outside, drinking steaming cups of tea and gazing at the mountains through the crisp atmosphere. God really had got His paintbrush out this morning. A coral-pink emulsion coated the eastern sky as the sun began to pick out the white tops of the Rockies.

"I didn't sleep much," he whispered.

"Me neither. My body clock's all over the place."

"It wasn't just the jet lag. It's this bloody phone call. Couldn't get it out of my head. I'd better make it."

"Good luck."

Daniel went into the kitchen, closed the door and dialled.

"Alastair Plowright speaking."

"Dad, it's me."

He knew his father would react in one of two ways. The most likely response would be to give him a rocket for not calling, worrying his Mum to death and dragging the family's good name through the mud. To Daniel's surprise, his Dad chose the second.

"Thank God. Are you alright?"

"Not bad, all things considered."

"Where are you? Police right across the world are looking for you."

"Look, Dad, listen to me very carefully. I can only stay on the phone for a short time and I can't tell you much, but I badly need you to do something for me. And I need you to trust me."

Daniel wanted something only his father could arrange in a hurry; an offshore bank account. If they were to look credible, an ordinary account at a high street bank wouldn't cut it. He gave the briefest of details about his predicament and explained what he needed. Then he waited. The silence went on for ever.

"Right, Daniel. Let me get this straight. You're in trouble. You can't tell me why in detail – I understand that – but you say you've done nothing wrong."

"Nothing, Dad."

"No weasel words here. Can you assure me you've committed no crime and you've done nothing, and I mean absolutely nothing, your mother and I would be ashamed of?"

"I promise."

"And this friend of yours … Veronica. She's done nothing wrong, either, even though several people have been killed because of information the two of you now possess?"

"Correct."

"And you want me to set up an offshore account so you can trap the people responsible."

"I hope to God no one's listening in on this call."

Another agonising silence.

"The only way I could set up an account in anything under a week would be to put it in my name. That would implicate me in your plans, so I ask you again. Have you done anything illegal or wrong?"

"No, Dad. I wouldn't dream of getting you involved if I had, however much trouble I was in."

"Right. I'll get one set up by close of business tomorrow in somewhere respectable. Singapore, probably. How do I get the details to you?"

"I'll call you. Dad, you're a complete star."

"I won't be telling your mother about this. She would only worry even more than she is at the moment. Don't let me down, that's all."

Daniel hung up. His father's reaction had been remarkable. He'd staked his entire reputation, built up over forty years in the City, on a judgement call. That his youngest son was telling the truth.

"I love your Dad already," Ronnie said, after he gave her the news. "Let's wake the others."

They didn't need to. Leon, his body clock two hours ahead of Colorado time, was already up and Todd was soon disturbed by all the comings and goings.

"Right, Leon, call Sister Augustine," Todd said, over a hurried breakfast. "She'll need to bring her copy of Hasely's card to London for this to work."

"No problem. There's a Gatwick flight from Piarco later today."

Then they needed to buy tickets for their own flights. Todd had an idea.

"I'll get the travel office at the Cobbett Institute to do it. I'll say three very good friends of mine won a bundle of cash in Vegas. They'll buy it."

He left to buy the tickets.

Now it was time for Daniel to put his professional skills to good use. He wrote a press release, headlined 'Six Murdered in Bid to Conceal Revolutionary Cancer Cure', and added a timeline that set out the grisly sequence of events.

Ronnie's burner rang. It was Laura. She put Daniel on the line.

"We need somewhere to stay, Laura. Big enough for five people. Somewhere near the centre of town but not too close."

"I've got the perfect place. I rang my best friend from school to see if I could stay with her for a few days. Told her I had a water leak in my flat. She was only too pleased because, first thing tomorrow, she's taking her children sailing in Croatia for a week. I'm house sitting for her. She lives in south London. Norwood. There's plenty of room for everyone."

"Perfect … Next, go to the hairdressers and treat yourself to a completely different hairstyle. And change colour."

"Are you sure that's necessary?"

"'Fraid so, Laura. You'll be a lot safer with a new look. Finally, please be in Terminal Five Arrivals at Heathrow tomorrow to check the coast is clear. We're on BA0218, due to arrive at eleven-thirty-five. I'll phone you before we come through. You got all that?"

"Yes. Except I've realised there's someone else at the hospital you need to warn."

"Who?"

"Angela Stone."

"Fuck. Why didn't we think of her before? Any idea how much she knows about the protocol?"

"No. But even if she doesn't know anything, won't these terrible people assume she does?"

"Too right. Have you got her number?"

"I'll message you with it."

Todd returned with the tickets. He'd also been to the mall, and handed Daniel a shopping bag containing two battery-powered portable wireless hard drives, a plug-in earpiece microphone and a small toolkit.

The phone call with Angela Stone was difficult. She was convinced the BUP had killed her husband, even though Daniel tried to persuade her otherwise. After ten minutes, Todd gestured for him to hang up.

"Angela, I've got to go. I'll call you back in one minute."

"That call lasted too long," Todd said, switching the phone off and dropping it into the trash.

"She wasn't buying any of it," Daniel said.

He called her on a second mobile, but it was only after Todd made him switch to a third that Angela Stone accepted she might be in danger. She agreed to pull the boys out of school for a few days and stay with a friend.

"Don't tell me where, Angela, not on this line." Daniel said. "Get out as soon as you can and leave your car and usual mobile at home. Tablets and laptops, too. And don't let the boys take any devices with them. Even their game consoles.

"Buy a new mobile as soon as you can and message me, so I've got a number for you. Use cash at all times.

No credit cards. We've got a plan we hope will sort all this out. We'll know in a few days if it's worked. Till I call you, stay under the radar."

"I've decided to do the same," Todd said, after Daniel rang off. "I'm going to get away and lie low."

"Do you think they'll follow us here?"

"No idea but, once I've dropped you guys at the airport, I'll grab a few things from here and head out west to Utah. A friend in Moab'll put me up."

Todd loaded Daniel's press release and timeline onto a website he'd created on the dark web overnight. It already contained the rest of their evidence.

"Stone's video files needed a little editing," he told Ronnie. "I took out everything about the thirty patients in Trinidad. And I thought your dinner with Hasely the night before should hit the cutting room floor as well, darling."

"Thanks, Toddy," Ronnie said, blowing him a kiss.

"You've thought of everything," Daniel said. "How much sleep did you get?"

"Only a couple of hours but I'm a night owl. Now listen up. Record every phone call Ronnie makes to the bad guys and upload them to the website as you go. In fact, shoot videos of her making the calls, if you can. People love moving pictures."

Next, Todd and Ronnie compiled a list of everybody who was anybody in the world of oncology in case he needed to activate their 'insurance policy'. Daniel added the email address of every MP from the House of Commons directory and details of a handful of journalists he could trust with the story.

"I didn't know the words 'trust' and 'journalist' belonged in the same sentence," Ronnie said.

"I was out in Syria with a couple of these guys. You soon find who you can depend on in a war zone. And there's one other person who might be able to help us if this all goes to rat shit, even if she is pissed off with me right now."

"Alice?"

"Yup. I'll put her contact details on the list."

Todd copied the entire contents of the website onto three new SD cards and gave one to each of them.

"If you pull this off, you won't need the dark web. You can put it up online for everyone to see from the get-go."

Finally, he created a new email account – 'ai.protocol.com', with the password 'HaselyStone'.

"AOL might seem a little retro but someone's already taken 'ai.protocol@gmail.com'," he said, smiling. "I checked."

They were ready.

"Remember, as soon as you land, you must message me every two hours between eight in the morning and midnight, London time. If you don't, I'll wait another two hours for another message. If I don't get that, I'll push the button on your insurance policy. I'll message you guys from Moab, too. You can't be too careful. How long do you think it'll all take?"

"Well, Ronnie should be making the first call tomorrow evening, London time," Daniel replied. "The sooner we let Plover know we're around, the better. If she spooks him good and proper, we should be close to making a deal by, say, Friday night at the latest.

Might slip a day but this plan of yours will fly by Saturday evening. Or crash and burn."

"Okay. You're as ready as you'll ever be. Go get your stuff. Wheels roll in fifteen.

CHAPTER FORTY-SEVEN

They decided to sit separately on the plane and Daniel's luck was in. The seat next to him was empty. No one could look over his shoulder, either, because he chose the back row. Perfect.

He took out the iPad he bought in Denver Duty Free and began the first draft of the report he hoped Star News would soon transmit. First, he calculated how many words he could use. A half-hour *News at Ten* bulletin on ITV ran for twenty-four minutes and fifteen seconds, excluding programme titles and ad breaks. Even if the editor-in-chief, Francesca Cross, gave over the whole bulletin to the story – and he would be very disappointed if she didn't – they would still have to carry a two-minute summary of the day's other headlines.

That left twenty-two minutes, fifteen seconds for his report. People talk at about one hundred and eighty words a minute, so Daniel calculated he had around four thousand words to play with. Not long for the story of the century. But that's telly for you.

After three hours' solid work, the script was in good shape and down to time. He sank a large Bourbon with ice and was out for the count until the plane hit the runway in London.

"Good morning, ladies and gentlemen. First officer speaking. Welcome to Heathrow. It's 11.33 in the morning. I hope you had a comfortable night and could get some sleep. Please keep your seatbelts fastened until the plane comes to a complete halt and the seatbelt light is switched off."

Daniel pulled up his eye mask and allowed his eyes to adjust to the light. Then he switched on his burner phone. Straight away he was concerned. There were two messages from Sister Augustine and three from Laura. None from Todd. He was more anal about messaging than any of them.

He rang Todd's number. Voicemail. He must be Okay. He must be.

Then Daniel's journalistic instincts kicked in. He Googled 'Enstone, Colorado' and 'news' and clicked 'www.SummitCountyNews.com'. A chill went through him.

'I-70 closed by jack-knifed truck after suicide'.

He forced himself to read on.

'Two lanes of the I-70 west were closed late Monday for three hours after a man jumped off the Frisco Overpass. A truck jack-knifed when the driver tried to swerve out of the way but the jumper suffered critical injuries. No one else was hurt.

'He was pronounced DOR at the scene and taken to St Anthony Medical Centre in Frisco. He has not been formally identified but he's understood to be a computer analyst from Enstone.'

CHAPTER FORTY-EIGHT

Daniel walked down the concourse, his mind spinning. He didn't need to wait for the computer analyst to be named.

First reaction? Mind-numbing shock. That quickly gave way to another. Rising panic.

He never panicked. He didn't panic that dreadful day on the road to Aleppo. He didn't panic when he was diagnosed with cancer. He was panicking now. With Todd gone, they had no Plan B. They were completely on their own. He forced the air deep into his lungs to slow his racing pulse. Back in control.

Daniel decided not to tell the others until they were all together at the safe house. Ronnie would go to pieces and he couldn't look after her right now. He had to collect Sister Augustine, who was already waiting at Gatwick, so he played 'Mr Red Eye' to stop having to talk too much.

Ronnie asked why Todd hadn't messaged and he played it down. She bought it but he spotted a frown flicker across Leon's forehead.

They split up to go through Immigration. Daniel and Ronnie's faces were all over social media, with sightings from Yellowknife in Canada's far north to the South Island of New Zealand. But officials at Heathrow were on the lookout for an American woman with long, dark hair, not a blond Trinidadian. Daniel's beard had grown so fast that even his best friends would need a second glance. A pair of cowboy boots he bought in Denver Airport helped, too. They increased his height by nearly two inches.

Laura waited for them in Arrivals, transformed by a new chestnut brown cut.

"It's rather growing on me," she said. "I might keep it when this is over."

On the bus to Gatwick, Daniel logged back on to the Summit County News website; Todd's name was public. He hoped Ronnie wouldn't find out before he could break it to her, though he hadn't got the slightest clue how to do it. By the end of the journey, he was still no closer to finding the right words.

Sister Augustine was at the rendezvous point in the South Terminal with a beaming smile. Daniel led her to the motorcycle bays in short stay parking, using a very circuitous route.

The first time he checked Susie over, he missed it. Anyone with an untrained eye would assume the chrome-plated nut was there to fix the crash bar to the chassis. Then he realised this nut wasn't screwed onto a bolt.

"So that's what you look like, is it?" Daniel said, prising the tracker off.

"What are you going to do with it?" Sister Augustine asked.

"Well, my first instinct is to throw it into the back seat of the first convertible passing by. That would send somebody off on a wild goose chase. But I'm not sure that's such a great idea. If I leave it …" he leaned down and slipped it underneath a crash barrier "…there, they'll think the bike hasn't been moved."

"How did they know your motorcycle was here in the first place?"

"All these car parks have cameras that read vehicle registrations."

"Won't those cameras pick us up when we leave?"

"Yes, and so would the automatic number plate recognition cameras on the main roads. But not with this."

Daniel held up the small toolkit Todd had bought him on their last morning together.

"Keep watch, Sister Augustine."

He unscrewed the Bullet's number plate and wandered down the line of motorbikes until he found what he was looking for – another Enfield with plates the same size. The switch took less than five minutes.

"Let's hope the owner's gone off on a nice long holiday."

* * *

"How the hell did Todd Hogan end up in bits on a fucking Interstate?"

Plover screamed so loudly that Chapman had to hold the phone away from her ear.

"Look, shit happens, right? Baz waited outside his flat for half an hour to check the coast was clear before he went in. Plowright and the girl were definitely there, by the way. Baz found a notepad from the Bay Motel, Trinidad."

"I'm not interested in a fucking notepad."

"Just saying. Anyway, Baz was searching the place when Hogan crept in all quiet. Then the tosser picks up a kitchen knife and starts playing the tough guy. He was no match for Baz, of course. Slipped over in the punch-up. Blade straight between the ribs. Must've hit an artery or something. Bled out in no time."

"You couldn't fucking make it up."

"Baz had to clear up the mess and then had to get rid. So he waited till dark and threw him on the motorway. Made a hell of a bang, he said, but they'll never be able to piece together enough bits of him to know what killed him."

"Priceless. Absolutely fucking priceless."

"There's one other thing."

"What?"

"This Todd Hogan knew exactly who Baz was. 'Hello, Barrington', he said."

"How the hell did he know that?"

"Search me, but they're clever, these people."

"Just worked that out, have you?" barked Plover. "What a complete fuckwit you are." Silence. "Well, aren't you going to say something?"

"As a matter of fact, I am. I'm going to tell you a story, Mr Plover, and—"

"I haven't got time for your fucking stories Chap—"

"And you're going to listen. I had a captain once when I was a Red Cap. He had a bit of a complex. Didn't like any of the female Red Caps much but he hated me, 'cos I got so much time off boxing for the army. Whenever I came back to Colchester, he'd give me all the crap shifts. Christmas, New Year, Bank

Holidays. The whole nine yards. Said it made up for the 'cushy' life I led most of the time.

"But worst of all was the way he talked down to me. I was a twat, a fuckwit, a moron. A cunt if he was in a really bad mood. One Sunday night I came back from winning a boxing tournament in Germany and found this arsehole had put me on weekend nights for the next six weeks. When I complained, I got the usual lip, but this time he decided to do it in front of the whole unit."

"Spare me the lecture, Chap—"

"Do you know what happened to that cunt? Two nights later they found him outside a pub in Harwich. Whacked with a claw hammer. Nasty head injury. Brain damage. Permanent. Never found out who did it. Invalided out of the army a few months later. Never worked again. Sound familiar, that? Someone whacked with a claw hammer? So sod you and your posh school and your posh university and your even posher job. I'm not your fucking skivvy and neither are my boys. And we don't expect to be treated like that.

"Get the message, Mr Plover?"

CHAPTER FORTY-NINE

"I killed him, Daniel," sobbed Ronnie. "Just as much as if I'd pushed him off that overpass, I killed him."

"You've said that about twenty times now, Ron. I understand why, but it's crap."

"But I did kill him. I did. I got him into this mess."

"Todd wanted to help. Wild horses wouldn't have stopped him."

Daniel walked into the kitchen of the house in Norwood, ran the cold tap and splashed his face. Somehow, he had to get Ronnie's brain into a different gear, because they'd all agreed. She had to be the negotiator.

Quentin Plover made deals with people like Daniel all the time but a thirty-something female American oncologist was way outside his 'Westminster Village' comfort zone. He wouldn't find Ronnie anything like as easy to read. Her different accent, turn of phrase, way of thinking would all tilt him off balance.

Daniel filled a glass with water and brought it back for her.

"Think about it this way, Ron. What's the first emotion everyone feels when someone dies? Grief? No. Grief comes second. The first is guilt. I feel it. You feel it. The Archangel-bloody-Gabriel probably feels it."

"So?"

"So you didn't kill Todd. Those bastards did. But you feel as though you did."

"But—"

"No 'buts', Ron. Listen to me. What would Todd want you to do? Would he want you to go on crying like this with the clock ticking? No. He'd want you to help catch the people responsible for his death. So the one good thing you can do for that lovely guy is to pull yourself together – I know, you're not supposed to say that but, for once, it's bloody true – and make that call."

The sobs began to recede.

"Okay, but first I've got to call his fiancé in Connecticut. Gerard has got to know it wasn't suicide."

"You can't say—"

"I'll be careful what I say but I've got to talk to him, Daniel. I got the love of his life killed and he's sitting there thinking God knows what. He's got to know Toddy didn't kill himself."

After the call, she was calmer, more resilient. Determined, even.

"Give me that asshole's number."

Ronnie picked up a burner phone, switched it to speakerphone and dialled Plover's home number. Daniel picked up the other and started videoing. The call went straight to voicemail.

"Good evening, Mr Plover. My name is Dr Veronica Ackerman. I think you know who I am. I'm calling you from London at seven o'clock on Tuesday evening. I've got something you want very much, so we need to meet. I'll call you back at ten tomorrow morning. Make sure you take the call and have a laptop or iPad available so you can go online when we talk."

CHAPTER FIFTY

Ronnie knew she mustn't be there too early. Standing around in public wouldn't be smart. Not when you're Britain's most wanted woman.

She took the long way round, through London's Olympic Park. The giant Amish Kapoor Orbit sculpture, the tallest structure there, looked forlorn as the summer rain lashed it. Two months ago, Ronnie accepted her flatmate's dare to slide down the giant helter-skelter spiralling around its red girders. She reached the ground with her insides feeling like they'd been spun in a tumble dryer. Not so different from today, then.

Ronnie arrived on platform two of Stratford station with eight minutes to spare. Just about right. The train was already waiting, so she stepped on board and looked up and down the carriage. Only a handful of passengers. None paid her the slightest attention.

She took out her personal cell phone, switched it on, checked the ringer was turned up to full volume and deactivated airplane mode for the first time in almost a week.

As she waited for the signal to appear, her burner phone vibrated with the message from Daniel she was expecting.

'Outside at RV point. Remember, he's more scared of you than you are of him! Go for it. Dx'

Daniel had been her lifeline since she found out about Todd. He kept her busy, going over the phone call to Plover time and again. Then he was up before dawn, switching Susie's licence plate once more, checking the route and making sure Laura, Leon and Sister Augustine were clear on what they had to do.

Ronnie plugged a microphone earpiece into the burner. No way could she use speakerphone for a call like this. She pressed 'record' then glanced at her personal mobile. Phew. Signal at last. It was so long since she turned it on that she'd worried it wouldn't connect, though there was no reason it shouldn't.

Time to call him.

"Good morning, Mr Plover."

"Dr Ackerman."

"Shall we get down to business? You and I are going to make a deal."

"A deal? I did hear that right, didn't I? In case you've forgotten, Dr Ackerman, you're wanted by the police for the murder of Professor Hasely Stone."

They'd talked about this. Plover was pretty certain to go on the offensive right away. She mustn't get rattled.

"I'm not wanted for murder, Mr Plover. I'm wanted by the police for questioning in connection with his murder. A very different matter. If I talk to them – and whether I do very much depends on you – I'll have quite a story to tell. A story I don't think you'll want seeing the light of day. Seven people have been murdered because of you."

"I haven't the faintest idea what you're talking about."

"Oh, I think you do but, before you say another word, I'd like you to log on to an AOL email account, please. You do have separate access to the internet as instructed, I hope? Please log on to this address … 'ai.protocol@aol.com'. And yes, since you're wondering, we do know all about the Adoptive Immunotherapy Protocol. The password is 'HaselyStone', by the way. Cap H, cap S, no spaces."

Silence on the line for ten seconds.

"And what am I supposed to be looking at here?" asked Plover.

"If you look in 'Drafts', you'll see an email there with two folders attached. This is only a fragment of the evidence we've compiled about you and your people but it'll do as an appetiser. In folder one you'll find the picture of your friend Ms Chapman, or do you prefer Siobhan Anderson? We took it at the London Fields protest when Daniel Plowright was attacked."

"I can't see what any of this has to do with me—"

"Chapman's friend, Barrington Williams, was there, too. We've got a picture of him, see? You'd already started killing by then, of course. You'd murdered Heather Spink and made it look like a car crash. Then you killed Hasely Stone and tried to blame it on the BUP. There was Harry Kings' supposed suicide. Maria Grigorenko and the gas boiler. Am I going too fast for you?"

"I haven't the slightest fucking idea what this is all about, but—"

"Then Chapman killed poor Stephanie Bright. I was in the room when she did that. Ask her what Stephanie's last words were before she crushed her cervical vertebrae. What were they now? Oh yes. 'Tell those bastards I never want to hear from them again'. That was it. Check it out with her. I'm sure she'll call you on that cell phone of hers soon. She calls you a lot, doesn't she?"

A pause. A long pause.

"I don't know anyone called Chapman," he said finally, in a low voice.

"Oh, I think you do, Mr Plover but, to refresh your memory, please open folder two. In there is a photo of Chapman at Customs when she flew into Port of Spain. You'll see pictures of a business card and passport she used in a different name. Siobhan Anderson. She used that name when she wiped the information from all those patient files in the computer system at Aggies, and the backups in Leicester. But you'll know about those, too, won't you?"

"How many times do I have to tell you? I haven't—"

"You really are a piece of work, aren't you, Mr Plover? Open up the final picture file and you'll see a photo of the recently dialled numbers on Chapman's cell phone, taken whilst she was searched by Customs at Piarco. We were able to take a look at it. You don't need to know how. Recognise the last two numbers, Mr Plover?"

Ronnie thought the silence would never end.

"What do you want?"

"I told you. I want to make a deal, Mr Plover."

"What sort of deal?"

"You'll find out when I call at midday tomorrow. Shall I call your home number or would another be more convenient for you?"

"The home number is ... alright."

"Good. I'll let it ring three times, hang up and call back. Make sure you pick up. And if you try to trace this call or double-cross us in any way, there will be repercussions you won't like. Goodbye."

Ronnie's hands were shaking so much she needed both thumbs to hang up. Then she stopped recording, dropped her personal cell phone into a trashcan, opened the train door and stepped out onto the platform.

The 10.05a.m. service from Stratford to Richmond upon Thames was about to depart.

CHAPTER FIFTY-ONE

It took a lot for someone to get under Quentin Plover's skin but this woman had done that, all right.

Then his screen flashed into life. *10.06 hours … Station Street, London E15 1DE.*

He couldn't resist a bit of a smirk. After the last round of phone franchises were negotiated, quite a few people in the business owed him favours. He was calling them in now – to track Ronnie and Daniel's mobiles if they ever switched them on.

Plover punched *E15 1DE* into the postcode finder already open on his laptop and called Chapman.

"Ackerman's in London. Stratford Station."

"Stratford East or Stratford International?"

"How the fuck do I know? Here's the postcode … echo-one-five-one-delta-echo. Got it?"

"Yeah."

"Get someone from your lot over there. It can't be you. She knows what you look like."

"Shit. How?"

"I'll tell you later. Who can you send?"

"No one. They're all on a job up north."

"Fuck. Where are you?"

"At home in Camden."

"Then you'll have to go but keep your fucking distance."

"No probs. How come she knows what I look like?"

"I said 'I'll tell you later'. Follow her. And look out for the others. She must be here with Plowright. Leon Stone may be with them, too. He's disappeared off the face of the fucking earth. And never phone me using this mobile again."

"It's a burner."

"And Ackerman knows you've been calling me on it. Ring me back on another phone when you're on your way."

Quentin Plover was never unnerved. That's what made him one of the best tacticians in Whitehall. But he was feeling very jumpy now. How the hell did Ackerman know all that?

He didn't have time to think about it, because another postcode flashed up. *E9 5LH*. Hackney Wick Station. Then a third. *E9 5SB*. Homerton Station.

Plover brought up a map of the London rail network and followed the Mildmay overground line westwards. Stratford, Hackney Wick, Homerton, Hackney Central, Dalston Kingsland, Canonbury, Highbury and Islington, Caledonian Road and Barnsbury, Camden Road.

"Camden Road," he said out loud in triumph and redialled. "Chapman?"

"I thought you said don't use this phone any more. I was about to chuck it."

"Don't go to Stratford. She's on a train …The Mildmay Line from Stratford to Richmond. She's reached Homerton. How far are you from Camden Road Station?"

"Three minutes. It goes right past our place."

"Hang on, she's moved again … Hackney Central. Get to Camden Road and wait for her there."

CHAPTER FIFTY-TWO

"I got to him big time," Ronnie said, as she hugged a rain-soaked Daniel sitting on Susie outside Stratford station. "He blanked me until he saw the photo of Chapman's phone with his home and office numbers on it. That really spooked him."

Daniel beamed.

"Well done. Here … put these waterproofs on or you'll get drenched. Then let's go and meet Leon at Canonbury. The train's due there at 10.18 but I think he'll make sure it's a little late today."

* * *

Plover punched *N1 4RH* into the postcode finder. Her train was just outside Canonbury Station. It was still there when Chapman rang five minutes later.

"I'm at Camden Road Overground," she said. "This is my new burner. Call me on this from now on."

"When's the next train back to Stratford due?"

"Hang on … one due in a minute."

"Get on it. Her fucking train's been stuck outside Canonbury for the best part of five minutes … Yup, it's still there. See if you can get to Highbury and Islington before she does. It's only two stops. She could get off there and go into town on the Victoria Line. If she does, follow her. If not, get on the train and find her."

* * *

A familiar figure was already waiting when Daniel and Ronnie pulled up outside Canonbury Station.

"Everything all right, Leon?"

"No problem. Folks weren't too happy when I pulled the emergency handle but they were very understanding when I told them I'd left my insulin at home. A guy was about to phone for an ambulance but then I found it in my pocket after all."

He winked, shaking a bottle of aspirins he'd borrowed from the bathroom cabinet that morning.

"You don't take insulin in tablet form," Ronnie said. "Acid in the stomach would break it down before it got to the liver."

"Good job this guy wasn't a doctor, then," Leon replied, laughing.

"Off you go, you two," Daniel said. "There's a train every fifteen minutes to Norwood Junction from here. You might even see Laura on it. She'll be arriving at Highbury and Islington about now. God, those poor passengers must be so pissed off. Two different people pulling the alarm on one train has got to be some sort of record."

* * *

Chapman speed-dialled her new burner as she walked through the train for one final check.

"She's not on the train, Plover."

"Are you sure?"

"Course I'm fucking sure. There's only four carriages and there's hardly anybody left this near to Richmond. She's definitely not here, unless she's turned into a Sikh with an orange turban or a fat black woman ... hang on a sec ... I'll call you back."

* * *

"Plover? It's me. I've got her phone ... started ringing in a rubbish bin. I answered it but the line went dead ... no, Ackerman's not on the train, I told you that ... there's no point in swearing at me."

Even Ronnie managed a watery smile when Sister Augustine replayed her covert video to the others after they were all back in the Norwood safe house. Their plan had worked perfectly. Leon and Laura delayed the train long enough for Chapman to get on board. Sister Augustine attracted her attention by ringing Ronnie's phone at the right moment. And filming her phone call to Plover was a real bonus.

"Of course, we had nothing to lose," Daniel said. "If they hadn't taken the bait, all we'd have wasted is few hours riding the London Overground.

"But we had luck on our side today. Another day, we won't be so lucky."

CHAPTER FIFTY-THREE

Gough burst out of his office and over to Alice's desk, looking like the cat who'd got the cream.

"Plowright's back in the country. ANPR picked his motorbike up ten minutes ago. He's heading north up the M23. Mobile units are looking for him now."

"Great, sir," is what Alice heard herself reply. 'Fuck' is what she really meant.

"Car's standing by. If we blue-light it south of the river now, there's a chance we can be in on the arrest."

Double fuck. Daniel was the last person she wanted to meet, with Gough in tow.

"Wouldn't it be better to monitor events from here, sir?" she said.

"No, it bloody well wouldn't. I want to be in on this one."

Alice let Melanie Booth sit next to Gough in the back of the police car. She needed time to work out how to play it when she came face to face with Daniel.

"They've found him, sir," Booth said, a mobile pressed to her ear. "Male riding an Enfield motorcycle … Pillion passenger, probably female. Heading north east along Gipsy Road, Norwood. Mobile unit has fallen in behind and waiting for back-up before pulling them over. If they continue their present course towards Dulwich Village, they'll be at the Calton Avenue traffic lights in six minutes."

"How far are we from there?"

"Five."

"Tell them to wait till then. I'll make the arrest myself … I'm enjoying this."

Alice wasn't. Why the hell did she take Edwards' advice? If she'd ignored it and had gone to Gough the moment Daniel was named as a 'person of interest' four long days ago, she wouldn't be sitting here in the front seat of a police car, wanting the world to swallow her up.

It was all right for Edwards; he was two years off retirement, an inflation-linked pension guaranteed and a lucrative career in consultancy waiting for him. Meanwhile, she could kiss good-bye to her promotion, for sure. A demotion might even be on the cards. Plus the bollocking of the century.

"Suspects still on the move towards Dulwich village, sir," Booth said. "Mobile units now in front and behind, plus a motorcycle unit standing by Calton Avenue in case Plowright tries to make a run for it."

They arrived at the intersection as two unmarked police cars, lights flashing, came round the corner on the road ahead. Between them was the Enfield motorbike.

Uniformed officers swarmed around the rider and passenger the moment they were brought to a stop. Gough strode forward, Booth in tow. Alice hung back, her heart pumping. Things could get very messy very fast.

They did, the minute the bikers removed their crash helmets.

"Who the fuck is this?" Gough yelled.

* * *

For once, Ronnie was rather looking forward to her next call with Quentin Plover. She'd couldn't wait to wipe the smirk off his face.

"Pity it's not a Zoom call, or we could watch," she said to Daniel, who was getting ready to video her.

"Let's not get cocky, Dr Ackerman. We're not home and dry yet."

Plover picked up immediately.

"Dr Ackerman. I'm glad you phoned because I've been having a think about how this woman – Chapman, did you say she was called? – could have ended up with my numbers on her phone, and—"

"Shall we cut the crap? Please log on to the AOL address again and you'll find another email waiting for you in 'Drafts', with a video file attached. Play it."

Ronnie imagined Plover's face turning ever more purple as he watched Sister Augustine's video of Chapman on the train.

"Rather profitable, yesterday's exercise, don't you think? We wanted to see if you would try to double-cross us. We're disappointed you did, of course, but getting such a beautiful picture of Chapman calling you on the phone, and mentioning you by name, more than makes up for it."

"Who's 'we'?"

"You'll find out soon enough. If you decide to co-operate."

"And what is it you want from me?"

"From you? We don't want anything from you, Mr Plover. Not now. I told you not to trace my call and what's the first thing you did? No, we've dealt with the monkey for long enough. It's time to deal with the organ grinder."

"I'm sorry?"

"You're out of the picture, Mr Plover. Tell the Prime Minister we'll only deal with him from now on, because—"

"You can't bring Stephen Truman into this."

"He's your boss. He gives the orders."

"I'm sorry, Dr Ackerman, but you've got it completely wrong if you think the Prime Minister knows anything about this. Stephen Truman knows nothing. Nothing, you understand. Nothing."

"Oh, I think he does, and—"

"I tell you, he doesn't. He fucking doesn't."

"Are you seriously expecting me to believe the man who runs this country, who you answer to, is completely ignorant of what you've been doing?"

"Yes, yes. I promise you. You must believe me. You must."

"My, my, you're a dark horse, aren't you, Mr Plover? I'll phone your office later with further instructions. Make sure you're available to take the call."

CHAPTER FIFTY-FOUR

Daniel chose his parking spot, just outside the Ministry of Defence, with care. Ever since the Provisional IRA drove a van down Whitehall in the early nineties and fired off three home-made mortars, the lights at both ends had been set to prevent traffic jams building up. He and Ronnie would get down to Parliament Square on Susie in a couple of minutes.

What happened after that was much less predictable.

"Okay to call him, Ron?"

"Yup. Ready to video?"

Daniel nodded.

"There's nobody much about, so I reckon you can risk using speakerphone."

Plover answered straight away.

"Dr Ackerman. What can I do for you this time?"

"Well, we thought you should see a little of what you're buying. Please take a stroll across Westminster Bridge to the white lion statue outside the old County Hall building. Wait there and you'll receive a package. Do it now."

"Now? I can't just walk out of my office like that. I'm about to start a meeting with the Cabinet Secretary."

"I'd postpone it, if I were you. If you don't collect the package, its contents will be sent to all your friends – and enemies – in time for tomorrow's front pages."

Ronnie rang off without giving Plover a chance to reply.

"He'll be there," she said.

"He'd be mad not to. I'll message the others."

Laura was already stationed by the imposing wrought-iron gates at the end of Downing Street, ready to spot their quarry if he came out through the famous black door. Sister Augustine stood a few yards further up, outside the Cabinet Office at 70 Whitehall. That was a much more discreet way to go in and out of Number Ten.

Daniel drummed his fingers, waiting for a message back from his 'spies' on the ground. The next few minutes were critical, because they weren't just delivering a package. They were delivering a statement of intent – that they were in charge, not Plover. They needed him to do their bidding, not the other way round. But if they failed to hand over what they'd just promised, their credibility would crumble.

The White Lion of County Hall stood two thirds of the way across Westminster Bridge but Daniel and Ronnie didn't have the slightest intention of handing over the package there.

If Plover double crossed them again and the police blocked off both ends of the bridge, they would be sitting ducks. Instead, they planned to make the switch before he reached it. That needed luck and timing.

Their phones pinged simultaneously with a message from Sister Augustine. Their target was on the move. Within seconds, so were they.

Plover's red hair was easy to spot as they weaved in and out of the sparse Whitehall traffic. He was walking fast over the pedestrian crossing next to Parliament Square and then disappeared round the corner towards the bridge.

The lights changed and Daniel turned left to follow – straight into a solid wall of cars and buses. Not even a push bike could get through the jam, let alone a hefty motorbike with two adults. Plover was already outside Westminster Tube station, just a hundred yards from the bridge. They'd never reach him in time.

Unless … The road was rammed but the pavement wasn't. Daniel revved up the bike and rode up onto it, zig-zagging his way through startled pedestrians.

"That's far enough, Mr Plover," Ronnie shouted as they reached him. She tossed him a brown Jiffy bag, bound up with parcel tape. He fumbled the catch and it fell on the floor. "You'll never make the cricket team."

They turned onto Victoria Embankment and were gone.

* * *

"Daniel, it's Alice … again. Look, I know you're back in the fucking country. That bike at Gatwick you switched plates with? Stopped earlier today in Dulwich.

"If you haven't called me by first thing tomorrow, I'm speaking to Gough. I'll be in for an even bigger bollocking after this morning's fiasco but now he knows you're here, I've got no choice.

"Things have got very … complicated this end. The longer I stay quiet, the deeper shit I'm in, because I can't expect Tom Edwards to watch my back any more. Not when he finds out I've kept him in the dark about that list of phone numbers you gave me.

"So now you've got a deadline, Daniel. Call me by nine o'clock tomorrow morning or I'm telling Gough everything."

* * *

"Hello again, Mr Plover."

"Dr Ackerman … Perhaps you'll tell me what that song and dance outside Westminster Tube proved."

"It proves we don't trust you. What would have happened if we'd met you in the middle of the bridge and you'd decided to double cross us again by telling the cops?"

"I won't even dignify that taunt with a reply. Anyway, I've looked at your SD card. And what do you think it proves?"

"Quite a lot, I'd say. It's only part of the story, of course, but it's a bit like a jigsaw, isn't it? Add in all the other evidence we've got – the picture files, the video of Chapman on the train phoning you, my eyewitness evidence of the moment she killed Stephanie Bright – and I think we've got quite a tale to tell, don't you?"

"And what do you want?" he said, finally.

"How many times do I have to tell you? We want to make a deal."

"What kind of deal?" he snapped.

A bit early to fly off the handle, Ronnie thought.

"Calm down, Mr Plover. We've got something you want very badly. The other copies of Hasely Stone's SD card. And you can have them. You'll also get all the other evidence we've accumulated that I'm certain the police would love to get their hands on. What do we want in return? A guarantee you'll get off our backs for ever, plus a lot of money."

"And what do you mean by 'a lot' of money?"

"At this stage, let's just say there are five of us and, if you want us to keep quiet, we don't come cheap."

"So you're resorting to blackmail now, are you?"

"I'd prefer to call it a fair exchange, but we'll leave the detailed negotiations till we meet."

"And what makes you think I'm prepared to meet you?"

She could hear a definite quiver in his voice by now.

"Because you've got no choice, Mr Plover. We both know that."

"And how do you know I'll stick to my guarantee the second you return this material?"

"We'll talk about that tomorrow but I think you'll find it's not in your interests to double-cross us. Now or at any time in the future. I'll meet you for coffee at ten thirty."

"That's completely out of the question. I've got Cabinet."

Daniel chose the time for that very reason. To knock Plover off balance.

"Then you'd better get a sick note, Mr Plover. You and I are meeting at ten thirty tomorrow in the lounge of a central London hotel, or not at all. At ten, you'll get a message on your cell phone with the exact location. Be around the West One area and you'll make it in good time. Don't show up and the party really will be over."

Ronnie hung up before he could answer. Then she realised. Plover didn't actually promise he would be there.

CHAPTER FIFTY-FIVE

Ronnie had only been there five minutes but she was already climbing the walls. And what elegant walls they were.

The five-star Landmark Hotel, with its famous ground floor atrium adorned by magnificent forty-foot palms, was the perfect location for the meeting. There were two ways to escape.

Daniel had thought about the Grosvenor House. It had two entrances but one faced Park Lane; far too open for a surreptitious getaway. So did the Savoy, but the Strand exit opened onto a cul-de-sac; too risky if things went wrong.

The Landmark was ideal. The main lobby opened onto the busy Marylebone Road, along from Aggies. The rear faced the splendid red-brick Victorian façade of Marylebone Station. You could disappear into the Tube there or a maze of nearby side streets.

Ronnie wandered around, as if she were taking in the opulent surroundings. In fact, she was following Daniel's instructions. Check out the two exit routes, the strength of her phone signal and whether she was being tailed.

She sat down at a low table in one of two wingback chairs and, for the first time in a week, switched on her personal laptop. Then she positioned the screen so the built-in camera captured her face, before minimising the image. The screen soon slipped into 'sleep' mode.

Ronnie ordered green tea from the waiter, trying to convey an impression of calm, even though her heart felt as if it were about to burst out of her chest. And her pulse … It wasn't this fast when she made that first call to Plover.

She went across to examine an impressive display of white lilies on a marble pedestal. When she returned, she sat in the other chair. Ready at last.

At ten o'clock precisely, two middle-aged women took one of the empty tables across from her. Laura wore sunglasses and sat with her back to Ronnie, in case Plover recognised her. Sister Augustine faced the other way and would film a wide shot of the meeting on her phone, screened by her companion.

They assumed Plover would send in someone to scout the place out as soon as Daniel messaged him with the location. No one seemed to fit the bill so far. Certainly not the four badly dressed American pensioners three tables away drinking tea. Or the group of yummy mummies across the atrium, braying in loud, upper-class voices.

Then a tiny thirty-something businesswoman, with long, jet-black hair, sat down at the table next to the Americans. She ordered a pot of coffee and began typing away on a tablet, apparently oblivious of everyone around her. She could be a Plover plant.

But a tall fair-haired man joined her. Just flown in, judging by the flight tag round the handle of his carry-on. They were soon engrossed in a business meeting with brochures and spreadsheets.

Ronnie gazed at the table in front of her for the thousandth time. Everything was just so. A silver strainer for the tea and tiny pastries – culinary works of art – arranged on an old-fashioned paper doily. The last thing she wanted to do was eat any but she couldn't leave them all. That would make her look far too nervous.

Maybe she could sneak a couple into her purse. Nope, not a good idea. It would make a real mess of the portable wireless hard drive, already sitting in there all snug. It would record every moment of the meeting with Plover that her laptop's camera and microphone was ready to capture. Laura's purse contained a duplicate, in case of a foul-up.

The drives! Ronnie had forgotten to link her laptop to them. She slipped into the other chair and, without changing the elevation of the screen, found their wireless signals and connected them.

She moved back, telling herself – yet again – to take deep breaths and keep calm. Daniel had practised with her for hours, as he would before any big TV interview. His final instructions were imprinted on her memory. 'If you feel unhappy about anything, walk away'. He would be outside the back entrance on Susie within a minute of her pressing speed dial.

Ronnie looked at her watch. It was time.

Her phone vibrated with the message from Leon she was expecting. He was in a taxi out front, keeping watch for Plover.

It was her cue to wake up the laptop, tap the 'record' icon and minimise it before her guest arrived. Only then did she read the message.

'C not PI'.

It made no sense. She read it again. Weird.

"Good morning, Dr Ackerman."

Ronnie looked up. Dr Gerry Crewton was standing over her and smiling, as though this was just a routine meeting during another busy day for him as Deputy Prime Minister.

CHAPTER FIFTY-SIX

"I thought you'd be surprised to see me," he said, settling into the wingback chair next to Ronnie.

"You could say that."

The ever-attentive waiter interrupted them. Crewton ordered a pot of black coffee.

"You weren't exactly what I expected," he said. "I barely recognised you with your new hairstyle. That's how you got back into the country, I presume."

"That and a fresh passport."

"The UK Border Agency clearly needs to pull its socks up."

"Mr Plover unavoidably detained, was he?"

"In a manner of speaking. I'm afraid Quentin hasn't acquitted himself terribly well over the last couple of days, has he? No, let's be frank. I can be frank with you, can't I?"

"Of course. We must try to trust each other."

"Well, you people have rather run rings round him, haven't you? I thought it was time I got this business sorted out, once and for all. Without any more … slip ups. By the way, don't take that as a sign of weakness on my part, Dr Ackerman. It's not."

The waiter brought the coffee.

"By the way, please call me Gerry."

"I'd rather not, if you don't mind. This is a business meeting and I'd like to conduct it in a business-like manner."

"As you wish."

"So, shall we get down to business, Dr Crewton?" He nodded. "What you have done is unspeakable. Leon Stone will never forgive you for what you did to his brother and I'll always despise you for what happened to Todd Hogan. But we're realists. You want something, we want something. You want every single copy of Hasely Stone's SD card—"

"And what is it that you want, Dr Ackerman?"

"Exactly what I told Mr Plover on the phone. We want to live long and happy lives, preferably in a little comfort. Sounds like the makings of a deal to me. But, first off, shall I go over what's for sale?"

She leaned across and tapped a key on her laptop. It burst into life. A list of folders appeared and she opened the top one.

"This is the copy I made of Professor Stone's SD card, straight onto here. You already have the original and you'll get the other two copies, along with this laptop, of course."

She clicked open a second folder.

"And here's the complete set of all the picture and video files we have of Chapman, Williams and so on. I guess Mr Plover has shown you these already?"

Crewton nodded, as he took a large bite out of a mille-feuille cream slice. How could anyone eat pastries at a time like this?

"How do I know you haven't kept copies?" he asked.

"You don't, but would I be here today if we wanted to publish this material? I don't think so. We could have posted it online from anywhere. But we realised – and I have to admit I was the last to come to terms with this idea – that if we didn't come to … an accommodation with you, we'd be forever looking over our shoulders. We can't be on the run all our lives, so we have to make a deal with you, however unsavoury it is. You must decide whether you want to make a deal with us."

"None of this stuff is conclusive."

"No individual piece of evidence may be a smoking gun but, as I said to Mr Plover yesterday, it's a bit like a jigsaw, isn't it? When you put all the pieces together, you soon get the picture."

"So what do you want in return for all this … evidence, as you call it?"

They'd spent hours talking about this. Ask for too little and they wouldn't be taken seriously; too much and they would appear naïve. Ronnie looked at Crewton straight between the eyes.

"There are five of us, so let's say five million each. Pounds Sterling. I'll leave you to do the math."

She waited for a reaction in his face. Not a flicker. This guy was impressive.

"And who is the 'us' you talk about, Dr Ackerman?"

"I suppose you have to know sooner or later. Then you'll see how difficult it'll be to keep the lid on all this unless we can come to a mutually beneficial arrangement. There's myself and Daniel Plowright, of course, plus Hasely Stone's brother and his PA, Laura Sellars. Then there's someone – you don't need to know their name – who helped Professor Stone carry out his Trinidad trial. You know about that, I presume?" He nodded, his mouth full of pastry. "So, you see, I'm not alone."

"And where do you think I'm going to get twenty-five million pounds from?"

"Governments can usually find the money if they have a pet project or two."

"You're sadly mistaken, Dr Ackerman. My colleagues in government know nothing about this. None of them. And, before we go any further, you need to set my mind at rest on a couple of things."

"Go on."

"First, why the hell should I trust you?"

"Because if we go public after you've paid us five million each to keep quiet, we'll have a lot of questions to answer, won't we? Blackmail is still a crime in this country, apart from the fact none of us are thinking of declaring our cut for tax purposes."

"Then answer me this. Why are you prepared to trust me? What's to stop me asking the detectives, who guard me twenty-four hours a day, to arrest you for blackmail right now? They're out in reception."

"Because that would be very silly, wouldn't it? You'd have me but you wouldn't have my four associates. And they'll make sure all this material is in the capable hands of the media by the end of the day.

"Think about it this way. The word 'trust' might not be on the tip of anyone's tongue right now, but we have everything to lose and nothing to gain by double-crossing each other. We want to sleep easy in our beds, not fretting about whether someone will blow our heads off tonight. And I'm sure you don't want to lie awake, wondering if tomorrow will be the day when the newspapers and TV will be full of AI-Protocol stories and your part in Hasely Stone's murder."

"You've got no proof linking me to Hasely's—"

"Let's stop playing games, Dr Crewton. The very fact you're sitting opposite me here when you should be at a meeting of the British Cabinet puts that one to bed." He looked away. "This way, you get the files and never hear from us again. We get the twenty-five mill and never hear from you. I'll undertake not to pursue any research into adoptive immunotherapy. That goes without saying. Then we all go off abroad some place where we'll be out of your hair, leaving you to continue your glittering political career. Okay, so it's not fool-proof collateral of our good intentions, or yours, but it's the best any of us are going to get."

The moment Gerry Crewton glanced down to pick up his coffee cup, Ronnie knew she had him.

"Twenty-five million is out of the question."

She looked away, determined not react too quickly.

"Twenty-five mill split five ways, don't forget."

"I can't lay my hands on that sort of money."

"Dr Crewton, I hate to put it in such blunt terms, but you haven't got a lot of choice. Either the money is transferred within the hour or I walk out of here and we take our chances with your gorillas. Daniel Plowright is ready to press the button on an email – with attachments, of course – that tells the whole story. It'll go to every MP and all major media outlets, not to mention everybody who's anybody in the world of oncology.

"And in case you think you might be able to silence us later, you should know all five of us will be keeping in very close contact. If anyone touches so much as one hair on any of our heads, we could still make life very uncomfortable for you. With or without the evidence on that card."

"No one will believe you."

"Maybe. Maybe not. But there would be one hell of a fuss and you'd have a lot of questions to answer, wouldn't you? Better to let sleeping dogs lie, I'd say."

"Five million is the most I could go to."

"Don't be ridiculous, Dr Crewton. A million each won't take us very far, will it? Look, if we don't conclude this soon, my bank in the Far East will close for the day and then it all becomes more complicated."

"My absolute limit is ten."

Ronnie took a sip from her teacup to give her time to think.

"Let's cut the crap, Dr Crewton. I want twenty-five million from you. You want to pay me ten. We could go on like this forever or we could go straight down the middle at seventeen and a half and get this deal wrapped up now. It's still three and a half mill for each of us. What do you say?"

He'll never go for this, she thought. He may be desperate but he's not seventeen and a half mill desperate.

"Give me your bank details," he said, after an agonising pause.

Ronnie handed him a slip of paper, trying to stop her hand from trembling.

"As soon as I get word the money's hit our account, you'll get the other copies of the card and this laptop. We both stay here till then. Agreed?"

Crewton nodded and speed dialled a number.

"It's me ... Seventeen and a half ... Just pay it, Plover. Here are the bank details."

Crewton finished the call and leaned across to pick up the computer. Ronnie put out her hand.

"Not so fast, Dr Crewton. You don't touch this until I get confirmation the money has been transferred."

She detected it immediately. Beneath his pungent aftershave was the tell-tale trace of strong liquor. It didn't come from an evening's heavy drinking. She knew that for sure. Her freshman year chemistry professor was a functioning alcoholic, if such a thing exists. After a few classes with him in a small seminar room, Ronnie could spot the difference between the stale odour you get from sweating out last night's drinking session and the cleaner smell of strong liquor drunk in the morning. Crewton had already been drinking today.

Then she remembered the last time she saw him close up, in Stone's garden after the funeral; how anxiety flitted across his face when he had an empty glass in his hand. The sign of a guy with a real drink problem. She had an idea.

"Dr Crewton, I know it's a little early but would you like a drink? I could do with one. You might even say there's something to celebrate, in a weird kind of way."

His face relaxed straight away.

"Sounds like a very good idea." He hailed a passing waiter. "I'd like a glass of red Rioja, please. Do you have a Gran Reserva?"

"Only by the bottle, sir—"

"Let's have a bottle," said Ronnie. "I'm sure we could do it justice."

They sat in silence until the waiter returned and uncorked the wine. Crewton made a great play of tasting it before downing half his glass in two gulps. He soon refilled it.

"Dr Crewton, answer me one question, could you? Why do all this? Why sabotage the protocol?"

"I thought you of all people would understand but you don't, do you?"

"I don't think so."

"The protocol would have been a total disaster for this country."

"But this is the greatest medical breakthrough since penicillin and—"

"Come on, Dr Ackerman. You've read the paper he wrote. You know what the repercussions would be of exposing this country, our economy, the NHS, to this pestilence … You're shocked, aren't you? I can see it in your face. Me calling it a 'pestilence'. Well, that's what it would have become."

"But what about all those patients who'll die without it?"

"What about all those other patients who are already dying because they don't reach the top of the NHS waiting list in time to be treated? Or the thousands more who aren't even put on a damn waiting list because our creaking bloody health service can't afford the dozens of new pioneering treatments being devised by clever people like you every year? It's no longer a question of whether we can save people's lives, but whose lives we choose to save. In government, my job is about making hard choices and they get harder and harder with every new, eye-wateringly expensive, medical breakthrough."

"But the AI-Protocol wouldn't be expensive," Ronnie said.

"Don't be so naïve, Dr Ackerman. It would bankrupt the NHS in the blink of an eye." Crewton's pupils were beginning to dilate. Just a little. She stayed silent. "Someone lives, someone dies because of the decisions people like me have to make every day. The NHS is on its fucking knees and we can't afford life for everybody."

He poured himself another glass of wine. Ronnie glanced at the businesswoman, who had spotted the Deputy Prime Minister's prodigious alcohol consumption at this time of day.

"And that's only the start. A plunge in the stock market, a run on the Pound. The City going into free fall as soon as it discovers we'll have all these extra unproductive mouths to feed and house each year. The pensions industry wrecked. Is that what you want? Is it?"

"I'm not a politician, Dr Crewton."

"Lucky you. I am."

"But even if you are right, couldn't you have gotten the professor to delay the announcement for a while?"

"Don't you think I tried? I didn't ask Hasely to forget the bloody protocol. Just leave it a year or so, at least until we could work out the best way to deal with it. But would he? Would he hell? The 'Big-I-Am' wanted his 'Big Idea', as he called it, out there. Now. Sod the consequences. Sod what it would mean for this country. I told him it would be a complete catastrophe but he wouldn't have it. Then I said, 'if you think there's no problem, go away and find out what would happen if this thing does see the light of day'. That's how he came to write his bloody paper. I got him to do it."

"What did the Prime Minister say when he read it?"

"Truman?" snorted Crewton. "I didn't show it to him. He wouldn't have the guts to do anything about it. We'll get shot of him after the next election and then we can really get down to sorting out this bloody country." He took another gulp. "And the irony of it all is that I saw it coming years ago, long before Hasely. I realised how close he was after he discovered Tamoxadrene."

He poured the last inch from the bottle into his glass. Ronnie's was still half full.

"Getting him to write that paper ... probably my biggest mistake of all. When he saw how his fucking discovery could transform the world, he really could see his name up in lights. I thought maybe a peerage might help him to see sense. That he'd keep quiet for a while. At least until we'd sorted out some of the economic implications. Then I found out he was planning a fucking press conference."

"Who told you? Paul Eriksson?"

"Eriksson?" sneered Crewton. "Eriksson knew nothing about any of this. He'd have tried to get Du

Long and Freyer in on the act, so Hasely was manic about him not finding out. If only Eriksson had kept his damn nose out, he'd still be alive today. A pity. He was the best thing that happened to that hospital in years."

This was going better than Ronnie could have hoped.

"So who told you about the press conference?"

"Stephanie Bright, of course. We needed someone to keep an eye on Hasely, and she was perfect. Told Quentin everything."

"So why did she have to die?"

"Look, no one would have had to die if the 'Big-I-Am' had shut up about his 'Big Idea' for a year or two. But would he do that? Oh, no. I've known him for nearly thirty years and he's always been the bloody same."

Crewton's eyes were beginning to glaze over.

"It gets to you after a while. On my first day at Imperial, my tutor said I was one of the most impressive candidates he'd ever interviewed. Then this guy from Trinidad flies in. Within a few weeks, he was the only student anyone was talking about. At Cambridge – I should never have gone there for my PhD after I found out he'd been accepted – all they could say was how delighted they were that he chose them over MIT. Angela fell for him in no time."

Ronnie stayed still. By now, Crewton was almost talking to himself.

"We were so good together, me and Angela. Then Hasely took her away from me. He always had to be one step ahead. Even taking her. One of the reasons I went into politics was to get out from under his shadow and then along he comes with his fucking protocol, ready to do it again. Well, not this time, Hasely."

Whatever fragment of sympathy Ronnie might have felt for Crewton's predicament evaporated in a moment. It all came down to this man's ego. Now she just wanted out of here. To her relief, her phone vibrated with a message.

'£17.5m arrived in account. Good luck. Alastair P.'

"The money's there, Dr Crewton. Wait here, please."

She walked across to Laura, who'd received the same message and was retrieving the SD cards out of her purse.

"Everything Okay?"

"I guess so. As long as you don't mind drinking red wine before midday with a narcissistic killer. Is Leon waiting for you out front?"

"He messaged a minute ago."

"See you guys later."

She went back to her seat as Crewton was settling the bill. In cash.

Laura and Sister Augustine walked past as Ronnie handed over the two SD cards.

"Was that Laura Sellars glaring at me?" Crewton asked, slotting the first card into the laptop to check it.

"Yes."

"Thought so. I don't think she ever liked me much."

"She certainly doesn't now. Can you blame her?"

"You must understand I never wanted any of this."

Ronnie had taken about as much of Crewton's self-pity as she could bear but was saved from any more by his mobile ringing.

"Hold on … I'm sorry, I've got to take this."

Crewton put the second card in the slot as he walked away with the laptop towards the back of the atrium, cradling the phone in his shoulder. Ronnie took another sip of her wine. Ugh. Who drinks red wine at this time of day?

"Dr Ackerman?"

Two men were standing over her.

"Dr Veronica Ackerman? My name is Chief Inspector Nathan Benton from the Homicide and Serious Crime Command at Scotland Yard. I'm arresting you on suspicion of murder, blackmail and illegal entry into this country. You do not have to say anything but it may harm your defence if you do not mention when questioned something which you later rely on in court. Anything you do say may be given in evidence. I think it would be better for all concerned if we don't put the handcuffs on until we're outside. Agreed? Come with me please."

She'd been played. Just like they played Gemma Chapman in Trinidad, Barrington Williams in Panama and Quentin Plover in London. That's why the bastard was so willing to make a deal.

Ronnie and the police officers walked towards the Landmark's rear entrance. Crewton was waiting.

"Did you seriously think you would get away with this? You are a very stupid woman."

"Fuck you, you murdering bastard."

"I haven't the slightest idea what you're talking about," he replied, with a smirk. "Take her away, Chief Inspector."

A third cop, this one in uniform, appeared with a pair of handcuffs. As he pulled Ronnie's hands in front of her and snapped them in place, she remembered what Daniel said. 'Another day, we won't be so lucky'.

'Another day' had arrived.

CHAPTER FIFTY-SEVEN

Daniel knew it was all over the moment the unmarked white van skidded in front of him outside the Landmark's back entrance.

"Armed police. Get off the bike. Slowly."

Two officers in full SWAT gear were pointing submachine guns at his temples. German Heckler and Kochs. Standard Metropolitan Police issue.

Laura, Leon and Sister Augustine were led, in handcuffs, down Melcombe Place and put in the back of the van, its blue light flashing away on the dashboard.

"Daniel Plowright. I am Chief Inspector Nathan Benton from the Homicide and Serious Crime Command at Scotland Yard. I'm arresting you on suspicion of murder, blackmail and illegal entry into this country. You do not ..."

Daniel felt the blood drain from his face. A familiar figure stood in the hotel portico. Gerry Crewton didn't try to hide his satisfaction as Ronnie was frog-marched out of the hotel.

"What's Crewton doing here?" Daniel whispered to her, as they were bundled into the van.

"He's behind all this. The Prime Minister knows nothing about it."

"Fuck."

A policeman sat beside them, cradling a Glock pistol in his right hand. Daniel stared at the image of a small bird tattooed near the base of the man's index finger; a pathetic attempt to block out the gravity of their predicament. He remembered Alice telling him how the Met relaxed the rules on visible tattoos a few years back. Fuck her.

Daniel's plan was too clever by half. What on earth was he doing, sending both Laura and Sister Augustine into the hotel? To get a good shot of Ronnie's meeting, of course. Perfect for his news package. At least, it would have been.

And why leave Leon a sitting duck out front, just to pick up the others? If he was back in Norwood, at least he would be free to do something. Too late now.

Bloody stupid, too, asking for money. It seemed perfect to make them look credible. Now they would all come across as grubby crooks, including Dad. He'd just become an accessory to blackmail. After all Daniel's promises.

And who arrested them? Homicide and Serious Crime. The lot Alice was assigned to.

"Thanks Alice, for letting me down – again," Daniel said out loud.

No one was listening.

* * *

Ronnie gazed out of the steamed-up window as the van drove across the south side of Trafalgar Square and down onto the Embankment by the Thames.

Her mind spun through the events of the last hour. Something didn't add up. Even with the alcohol talking, Crewton said far more than he needed. In fact, sealing the deal couldn't have been easier. Too easy.

When he walked into Landmark, he must have known he would be destroyed if the details of his meeting with Ronnie ever became public. That's exactly what would happen when she and the others came to be interviewed by the cops. Yet he tipped them off.

In fact, shouldn't it have crossed his mind she might be recording the meeting in some way? The Internet was full of gadgets to record stuff in secret – pens, watches, key rings. Crewton made no attempt to check if she was carrying anything like that.

But there was an easy way out of this mess. Ronnie tapped the shoulder of the uniformed officer in the front passenger seat.

"Excuse me. There's something you need to know. We have evidence that Dr Crewton, who I met at the hotel this morning, is involved in a plot that has led to the murders of seven people. We can turn this evidence over to you right now."

"Shut the fuck up."

Ronnie didn't need to see the cop's face to understand in a flash what had happened. The voice was unmistakable.

But Gemma Chapman turned around anyway. Her ugly smile, along with the pistol she held in her right hand, left no room for doubt.

CHAPTER FIFTY-EIGHT

"What are you going to do with us?" Daniel asked.

His question broke the dumbfounded silence as the van reached the approach to Tower Bridge.

"Oh, I don't think it'll take long for you to work that one out," Chapman replied. "You lot thought you were so clever, sending us on a wild goose chase. But all five of you in one location? Not very bright, was it?"

"You don't know how many of us there are," Ronnie said.

"True enough. I suppose one or two others might crawl out the woodwork. Your father, for instance, Mr Plowright."

"Dad's not part of this. He set up the bank account, that's all."

"Maybe. We'll find out soon enough. I find inflicting punishment ... unpleasant, but Baz here rather enjoys it."

Daniel looked in the rear-view mirror, reflecting the eyes of the uniformed driver. They widened into a sinister smile and he could see they belonged to Barrington Williams.

He tried to calculate the odds. They weren't good. As well as Chapman and Williams in front, there was a uniformed thug at the back pointing a pistol at Leon,

Laura and Sister Augustine. Plus the guy with the tattoo next to him. A white BMW travelled behind with four more goons.

There must be something he could do. The famous photo of Mordecai Vanunu's hand came into his head. The Israeli technician, jailed in the 1980s for revealing details of his country's nuclear weapons programme to The Sunday Times, was still a hero to investigative journalists like Daniel. He wrote details about his abduction by the Israelis on the palm of his hand and pressed it up against the window of the van taking him to court in Jerusalem.

But Daniel didn't have anything to write with. He wasn't even sitting next to a window. The van sped under the north pylon of Tower Bridge.

"You don't think you'll get away with this, do you?"

"Oh yes, Mr Plowright, I think we will. You will tell us precisely what we need to know or Baz will make sure the end of Dr Ackerman's life is so prolonged you will end up begging to tell me. The choice is yours. Painless co-operation or painful resistan—"

The van jerked to the left and smashed into railings that separated the road running across the bridge from the pavement. A maroon transit had clipped the offside front wing and now blocked the way in front. A black saloon screamed to a halt in the outside lane, as alarmed passers-by scattered in all directions. There were loud bangs as tyres were shot out and shouts of 'armed police, armed police'.

Chapman raised her pistol but dropped it immediately. Gun muzzles were pointing at them from all directions. It was a textbook execution of what the Metropolitan Police call a 'hard stop'.

"You little darling!" Daniel shouted. "You absolute little darling!"

CHAPTER FIFTY-NINE

Ronnie and the others were bundled out of the van and police officers – the real deal, this time – removed their handcuffs.

Daniel was in a world of his own.

"I thought you'd let me down," he mumbled. "I really thought you'd let me down."

"Hello, Daniel."

Across the road stood a small woman with long, black hair. He ran across and lifted her off her feet.

"Steady on," she said, laughing. "I'm on duty."

Ronnie knew she'd seen her somewhere before. Then it clicked. It was the businesswoman in the Landmark.

"You're a star," Daniel said. "Thank God you believed me."

"Thank God you turned onto Tower Bridge. I wouldn't have fancied a 'hard stop' along the Whitechapel Road. There are no railings sealing off the pavement there. Anyway, I wasn't certain I did believe you but I had to check it out, so I popped into the Landmark for coffee this morning. The moment they arrested Ronnie, I knew. That guy's never set foot inside Homicide and Serious Crime in his life."

"What's with the black hair?"

"Couldn't risk Ronnie recognising me. I sat in on her interview, remember? And we were both at the funeral."

Daniel beamed as a bemused Ronnie walked across.

"What the hell is going on?"

"Dr Veronica Ackerman … meet Detective Superintendent Alice Mahoney."

"Only 'temporary superintendent' at the moment."

"I don't get any of this," Ronnie said.

"You will," Alice replied. "Right now, I need all five of you to make yourselves scarce. Get across the bridge as fast as possible but don't run. You can pick up a cab in Tooley Street."

"What will you tell them at the Yard?"

"I'll say I lost you in the confusion. I'll be in so much shit when this is over, an extra bucketload won't make much difference. Can you get your award-winning report ready for the ten o'clock?"

"I'll say. Unless they're charged in the meantime."

"Not a chance."

Alice smiled at Ronnie.

"Look after him better than I did, will you? He's a lovely man. Now go on, all of you. And switch on that bloody mobile of yours, Daniel … By the way, you might want this." She slipped him a phone. "Let's say a helpful tourist happened to be videoing on the bridge as this lot were arrested, shall we?"

CHAPTER SIXTY

Daniel managed to hail a cab in no time, despite the rain.

"The Landmark, please, and then on to Star News in Gray's Inn Road."

"Why are we going back to the hotel?" Leon asked.

"To pick up Susie. She's bound to have a ticket by now. I don't want them towing her away."

"Now, Daniel Plowright," Ronnie said. "Perhaps you can tell us all what the hell just happened."

"I think I know," Laura said, smiling. "You told Alice about our plan, in case it all went wrong."

"And a bloody good thing I did," Daniel replied.

"Why didn't you tell us?" Ronnie said, her eyes blazing.

"For a start, because I wasn't sure she'd do anything. I half expected her to get us all arrested. When we got picked up by that lot, I thought she had, and that she didn't have the guts to be there. And all the time she was sat drinking coffee in the bloody atrium."

"But you could have told me."

"No I couldn't, Ron. You were the last person I could tell. You had to play it for real. If you had any idea there may be another way out, how convincing would you have been in there? I thought about telling

318

the others but that didn't seem fair. Anyway, everyone had to play their part."

"I'm still damn furious," Ronnie said.

"Me too, but I'll get over it," Leon said. "I've been in a few tight spots in my time but I wasn't too sure how we'd get out of that one."

"Now I've got to ring my editor-in-chief," Daniel said. "We've got a news package to prepare."

"I suppose you rang her yesterday as well," Ronnie said.

"I did, as a matter of fact."

Francesca Cross picked up immediately.

"Quentin Plover didn't meet Ronnie," Daniel said. "Gerry Crewton did."

"You are joking?"

"Never been more serious in my life, Francesca. We've got him bang to rights."

"For the murders?"

"For everything. He admitted to everything."

"Why the hell did he do that?"

"Because he thought we'd all be safely tucked up in the hands of his gorillas by now. I'll tell you the rest when we get to the office."

"Don't go anywhere near Gray's Inn Road."

"What are you talking about?"

"I mean it. I didn't think for one minute you'd pull this off. And I won't be convinced, by the way, till you show me what you've got. But if you want to lead tonight's *News at Ten*, the office is the last place you should go."

"Why?"

"Because the Star Corp suits on the seventh floor will pull it."

"They won't be able to, not after we've shown them our evidence."

"Come on, Daniel. The bunch of wimps they've brought in to emasculate the legal department will crawl over every syllable until way after Crewton is charged and then it will all be 'sub judice'."

"So what do we do?"

"Come up to my place in Hampstead. In case you pulled off this ludicrous plan, I put together a team on standby. Shall we say forty-five minutes?"

"Get the coffee on."

After Daniel ended the call, he remembered his promise to Alice; he took out his regular mobile and switched it on. The screen lit up with dozens of messages. But the name on one of them leapt out. He opened it.

'Daniel. Paul Eriksson here. This will sound crazy but your life is in GRAVE danger. I have discovered that three of the four patients on the drug trial you were on have been KILLED. You are the ONLY one left. Call me ASAP.'

* * *

Daniel gazed at the raindrops trickling down Francesca Cross's dining room window, obscuring the view of Hampstead Heath beyond.

"Eriksson messaged me the evening he was found dead. It must have been the last thing he did. If only I'd called him."

Ronnie clutched his hand.

"Come on. You were the one telling me not to feel guilty about Todd. What could you have done for Eriksson?"

Francesca came in from the kitchen with coffee.

"I can understand why you're feeling terrible, Daniel, but we've got work to do. Rob Richardson and Mark Lowe have set up edit suites upstairs and are ready to cut."

"Good choices, both."

"I brought a drive from the office with all the possible library footage we might need and the crew's due here any minute to record interviews and pieces to camera. It's Jon Foote on camera and Will Jeffes on sound."

"Perfect."

"Roger's coming up to legal it. He's the one lawyer left in our place with a backbone. And I've asked Ed and Victoria from the multimedia team to join us. They can get everything ready to go live on the website whilst we're stitching your report together. We'll take it into Gray's Inn Road at the last minute."

"I admire your balls, Francesca, but what reason can you possibly give for not telling the Star Corp suits?"

"I'll say this is a story of extraordinary significance concerning the highest level of government and people were told on a need-to-know basis. The suits'll go ballistic, of course, and probably sack me on the spot but that's enough about my employment prospects. What have you got? I need to see everything. And you'd better not be giving this topspin."

The covert footage of Crewton in the Landmark impressed Francesca the most. The built-in camera and microphone on Ronnie's laptop captured every moment of the meeting. And she loved Alice's footage of the arrests on the bridge. A great finale to the story.

"Right, everyone. Phones off. We mustn't be distracted until we've cracked this. It'll be tight but the fact you've already written a draft script makes all the difference, Daniel. We'll get there."

* * *

Daniel walked into the dining room at 8.45 pm, just as Ronnie hung up the call with Todd's fiancé.

"Gerard's still in a terrible state, of course, but he was really grateful I called him," she said.

"He deserved to know before it was splashed all over the airwaves," Daniel replied.

"How's it all going?"

"We've just finished. I can't believe we've cut a twenty-two-minute package so fast."

"Gerard's going to watch online when it goes out live."

"If it goes out live. Between Gerry Crewton and the Star Corp suits on the seventh floor, I'll believe it when I   see   it."

CHAPTER SIXTY-ONE

Daniel's heart beat out of his chest as Francesca shooed everyone across Star News reception and into the glass-sided newsroom.

"Watch the faces of Justin Hillman and the rest of the news desk pondlife when she tells them," he whispered to Ronnie.

Francesca took charge, telling a bewildered Hillman tonight's bulletin would be scrapped and replaced by Daniel's exclusive report.

"There's no time for long explanations if we're going to get this on air. Part one is twelve minutes fifteen. You'll need to write a two-minute rip-and-read of the other main headlines for the end. That'll take it up to fourteen minutes fifteen.

"Part two is ten minutes dead. We'll play both parts in live. Get transmission control to sort that out, will you? Any of the Star Corp suits still up on the seventh floor?"

Three heads on the news desk shook in unison.

"Good. I certainly don't have time to explain everything to them. And don't call them. That's an order. Next, get onto the Westminster office. They'll need to line up the first rent-a-gob MPs they can find. If we stay on air after ten-thirty – and my betting is that we will – they'll need to have watched the package and be ready on College Green for an instant reaction. Finally, get me the ITV Director of Programmes on the line. I'll speak to him in a minute but I've got one more call to make first … Daniel, Ronnie. Come with me. Jon and Will, film this, will you?"

They followed Francesca across a newsroom full of astonished faces and into her office. She closed the door, dialled a number and switched on speakerphone.

"Gerry … Crewton speaking."

"Good evening, Dr Crewton. This is Francesca Cross, the editor-in-chief of Star News. Dr Crewton, this phone call is being recorded. On tonight's *News at Ten,* we are running a special report featuring covert footage of a conversation that took place earlier today between you and Dr Veronica Ackerman of St Agatha's University Hospital. In it, you admit to your part in a plot to kill Professor Hasely Stone and several others. Do you or Mr Plover, who is also implicated, have any comment?"

A long pause.

"Dr Crewton?"

"No … No comment at this stage."

"And does that go for Mr Plover, too?"

"Y–yes."

Francesca walked out of the office and got up onto a chair.

"Good evening, everyone. Standing up here isn't very dignified but I hope you can all see and hear me. I know you must be wondering what Daniel Plowright is doing here when half the police forces across the world are searching for him. Daniel has been working on perhaps the most important story this news organisation has ever covered since it was founded in the nineteen-fifties.

"Tonight, we're scrapping our usual news bulletin – apologies to everyone who's been working hard on it all day – and replacing it with a special report. I don't have time to tell you more now. You'll see it in a few minutes, in any case. But please be ready to pick up the phones. It'll be all hands to the pump as soon as we TX, I promise you."

The newsroom descended into an excited hubbub as Leon, the perfect gentleman, helped Francesca down. She marched over to the news desk.

"Gerry Crewton and Quentin Plover have given us a 'no comment'. Make that the lead on the rip-and-read at the end of part one.

"Ed and Victoria … The website can go live. Nothing's going to stop this story now. I'd better talk to the Director of Programmes."

Four minutes later, the title music struck up, interspersed by the chimes of Big Ben.

'This is ITV's Star News at Ten. Tonight, a world exclusive … The deadly conspiracy at the heart of the British government to stop the world learning about a cure for cancer … The Deputy Prime Minister confesses to his part in a plot to murder the man who discovered that cure … Dr Gerry Crewton, secretly filmed at a luxury London hotel admits to treachery … And the dramatic arrests on London's Tower Bridge earlier today. Good evening. My name is Daniel Plowright.'

At first one telephone rang. Then a handful. Soon every phone was ringing off the hook.

The end of part one was met with a crescendo of applause and cheers from every journalist in the room, apart the three on the news desk. Daniel's colleagues rushed across to congratulate him but Francesca stepped in.

"No time for pats on the back, Daniel. Get into make-up and take Ronnie with you. The Director of Programmes has been on the phone. We're going open-ended. You two are on for an extended interview after the ten thirty ad break."

Daniel groaned.

"What's open-ended mean?" Ronnie asked.

"It means we stay on air with no definite finish to the programme. It only happens with massive stories, like the death of the Queen. Come on. Let's get some slap on. You look a wreck."

"Thanks. You don't look so good yourself."

* * *

Ronnie came out of the studio with Daniel after an intense thirty-minute interview. She felt drained. Francesca was waiting by the studio door.

"Well done, you two. Brilliant stuff. The suits on the seventh floor aren't happy, of course. They're a tiny bit annoyed I didn't mention it to them earlier. I think I'll be looking for another job after this. So might you, Ronnie, because—"

Her phone started ringing.

"Francesca Cross … Hello … Yes, I'll pass you over to her."

"Ronnie Ackerman speaking."

"Good evening, Dr Ackerman. This is Commander Adam Gough. I think we'd better have a little chat, don't you? Shall we say ten o'clock tomorrow morning at Charing Cross Police Station? Bring any travel documents you have. And a solicitor. You'll need one."

CHAPTER SIXTY-TWO

Star News went off air at 1a.m. The story had gone global, with the Gray's Inn Road press office fielding calls from news organisations across the world.

But the volume of media inquiries was swamped by calls from desperate people, pleading for more information about the AI-Protocol for themselves and their loved ones. Hard-bitten news journalists came off shift with tears in their eyes.

Leaving the Star News Centre was out of the question; the building was besieged by rival media teams. Then Francesca had a brainwave. The penthouse suite at the top of the building, used by Star Corp executives over from the States, slept four but could accommodate five.

Ronnie volunteered to take the couch; she figured she wouldn't be getting much sleep tonight. The moment she switched off the light, she felt very alone. By tomorrow night, she could be in jail, awaiting deportation. Then she heard a door open.

"Veronica."

"Laura?"

"I need to talk to you."

"What is it?"

"There's something I need to tell you."

Ronnie switched on the table lamp next to her.

"What's on your mind?"

"It's something I said … Something I'm not proud of. If I hadn't said it, you certainly wouldn't be in the mess you're in now."

"What are you talking about, Laura? Sit down. Tell me all about it."

She perched on the edge of the couch and swallowed.

"When I was interviewed by the police, I told them you had a migraine that day – the day before Professor Stone was found dead."

"That's what I told you."

"But I knew it wasn't true. At least, I was pretty certain it wasn't."

"Why?"

"Hasely asked me to book a table for him and Daniel at La Bella Gioconda but then he asked if you were around. Twenty minutes later, he told me to call Daniel back, cancel dinner and reschedule his TV interview for the following morning. I knew what happened. He invited you to dinner instead, didn't he?"

Ronnie nodded.

"But we didn't eat at the restaurant. He decided it would be … better to dine at home."

"Sounds like Hasely. And at the end of the evening, you stayed over, didn't you?"

Ronnie looked away.

"How did you guess?"

"Because the same thing happened to me in my second week at Aggies. He took me to dinner. The Ivy. One of the most fashionable places in London then.

Even when he didn't have a lot of money, Hasely had style." Laura gazed into the mid-distance as tears filled her eyes. "I was smitten from the start. Funny word … smitten. Rather old-fashioned. But I was. And he was smitten with me. Honestly. It was … perfect. That's what it was, for two months. Perfect.

"Then I thought I was pregnant. It was a false alarm but he went into a real panic. That's when I realised everything he told me about leaving Angela was … Well, he was never going to leave her, was he? Not for a medical PA. He broke it off soon afterwards. Next on the scene was the consultant nurse on the oncology ward. Then one of the post-docs. Then a registrar. That went on for six months, the registrar. Nice woman. I tried other relationships when we split up but I think I was still in love with him. Always have been a little, maybe."

"But I still don't understand why—"

"Why I told the police you'd gone home with a migraine when I thought you'd ended up in bed with Hasely? Because I was jealous, I suppose. I wanted to put you on the spot, Veronica. Make life difficult for you. I felt guilty as soon as I'd said it. That's why I couldn't look you in the eye when I met you coming down the corridor outside the interview room."

"I thought that was a bit weird. You didn't think I killed him, did you?"

"Of course not. It didn't even cross my mind you'd discovered his body. I assumed you'd woken up, found he wasn't there and slunk into work late. Like I did, that first time."

Laura began to sob.

"But none of this would have happened if I hadn't told the police the story about the migraine. It stopped you telling them the truth. If you'd been honest with them, you couldn't possibly have gone to Hasely's funeral, so you wouldn't have met Daniel again. The two of you wouldn't have started to investigate. Todd would still be alive. And all because I told the police a story I thought was untrue from the start."

Ronnie handed Laura a tissue and hugged her.

"There's no need to apologise, Laura."

"Why?"

"Think about it. Once Chapman found out I was at the scene, she would have killed me, no question. They blocked the boiler in my apartment as soon as they got the DNA results, didn't they? So my flatmate might have ended up dead as well. And they'd have got Daniel in the end, for sure. Plus you knew the protocol existed. So what would do you think would have happened to you? You didn't risk my life, Laura Sellars. You saved it."

"I suppose … when you put it like that."

"I do put it like that, Laura. What's more, there's no way the protocol would ever have seen the light of day if it hadn't been for all of us."

The perpetual lines across Laura's face relaxed a little.

"No one at the institute knows about any of this. About Hasely and me, I mean."

"And I won't tell anyone."

"Thank you."

"No, thank *you,* Laura. You really did save my life. And I'll be there for you if you ever need someone to talk to. At least, I will if they let me stay in this country after tomorrow. That'll be down to Commander Gough."

CHAPTER SIXTY-THREE

Ronnie shuddered as the cab reached the south side of Trafalgar Square. When she travelled the same route less than 24 hours ago, it was in very different circumstances.

She spotted the reception committee outside the cream-coloured portico of Charing Cross Police Station the moment the taxi turned into Agar Street.

"How did these press people know to be here?" she asked Daniel.

"Because the Yard tipped them off. I would have, too, if I were as pissed off as Gough. Walk through them and look confident."

"I don't feel confident."

"Don't let them see it. And that goes for Gough, too. Remember, Crewton and Co would have got away with murder – literally – if it wasn't for you."

The commander met them in reception.

"Have you arranged for a solicitor, Dr Ackerman?"

"I haven't had time."

"There's a duty solicitor here."

"Is that like a public defender? Am I going on trial?"

"That'll be down to the Crown Prosecution Service. And the Director of Public Prosecutions will certainly get involved. I need to know if you want a duty solicitor present today."

"No … Thank you."

"Then come this way … No, Mr Plowright, please stay here."

Gough led her down a nondescript corridor and through a door marked 'Interview Room 1'. Sergeant Melanie Booth, his sidekick at the previous interrogation, stood behind a table in the middle of the windowless room. She pressed the red button on a recorder and gestured to Ronnie to sit down.

"Right, Dr Ackerman," Gough said. "This is an interview under caution. You do not have to say anything. But it may harm your defence if you do not mention when questioned something which you later rely on in court. Anything you do say may be given in evidence. Do you understand?"

She nodded.

"Dr Ackerman has signified she understands. I'll begin by taking your passports. All of them … Thank you. Now, Dr Ackerman …" Gough locked onto her eyes "… I've been a detective for more years than I care to remember and two things put me in a very bad mood. The first is interviewing suspects who know more about a case than I do. The second is interviewing suspects who lie to me. You fit the bill on both counts."

"I'm sorry—"

"We can come to apologies, such as they are, later. But, given your performance at your last interview, I think it'll save us all a lot of time if I tell you what we already know and you can start from there."

Ronnie swallowed.

"We know you were in the house around the time of Hasely Stone's murder, even though you wiped your fingerprints off everything. And a very good job you made of it. We also know you were in bed with the deceased in the hours leading up to his death because we found a hair on the sheet. The DNA on the follicle matched yours."

"I think I can—"

"Don't even think about lying to me, Dr Ackerman. It was a pubic hair."

Ronnie could feel herself turning red.

"So I don't need any more lies or prevarication from you. It'll be in your interests to tell me the whole story. Right from the start. Do I make myself clear?"

Ronnie reached the point where they were crossing Tower Bridge when there was a knock on the door. Gough stopped the recording and stepped outside. When he returned, he had Daniel in tow.

"Mr Plowright. I need your British and Trinidadian passports, please … Thank you. This interview is now suspended. I would like both of you back here at ten o'clock on Monday morning, along with Leon Stone. Please make sure he brings his passports with him and, in the meantime, do not talk to the press."

"What's happening?" Ronnie asked.

"I've received a message that Quentin Plover has attended his local police station with his solicitor. We need to talk to him, obviously. And I'm sorry to say that, a few minutes ago, the Diplomatic Protection Unit forced entry into Dr Crewton's official residence after hearing a loud noise. They found a body. Dr Crewton appears to have taken his own life."

* * *

They all needed time to recharge their batteries and the house in Norwood was the perfect place.

Nobody felt like eating much but Sister Augustine raised everyone's spirits a little when she produced a bottle of Angostura 1919 rum she'd bought in Piarco Duty Free.

Daniel checked the early editions of the Sunday papers on his iPad. They all led with Crewton's suicide, of course, but it was the angle of the headlines on the inside pages that were most intriguing.

The Sunday Times led page three with 'TRUMAN CRUSHED BY CREWTON's TREACHERY'. The Observer countered with 'CAN TRUMAN SURVIVE?' 'BACKBENCH TALK OF NO CONFIDENCE VOTE' was the Mail on Sunday's take.

At 9.59p.m. precisely, their phones started to ping. An email from 'ai.protocol@aol.com'.

'Hi guys. There's a little gift coming your way at 10p.m. London time, in case it's all gone wrong. Todd.'

Another email popped up as the TV in the corner heralded the start of *Star News at Ten*. But it wasn't only addressed to the five people in the room. It had hundreds of recipients. All the scientists, politicians and journalists on the lists they compiled in Colorado, plus a link to the website Todd created on the dark web.

Todd Hogan had taken out his 'insurance policy' after   all.

CHAPTER SIXTY-FOUR

"Come."

Alice walked into Gough's room at 11a.m. on Sunday morning and breathed an inward sigh of relief. He was alone. If he were about to start formal disciplinary proceedings, there would be another police officer present as a witness.

That comforting reassurance lasted all of five seconds.

"Sit down, Mahoney."

"I'd rather stand, sir."

"I said 'sit down'."

"Sir."

"Yesterday, I conducted an interview under caution with Dr Veronica Ackerman. She had quite a tale to tell. A tale I rather fancy you already knew a lot about before it was splashed all over the TV news on Friday night."

"Some of it, sir. I'm sorry, sir."

"Let's go through it, shall we? How did you discover that whoever whacked Plowright at London Fields wasn't a member of the BUP?" Alice told Gough about the picture of Daniel's attacker captured by the police photographer. "And that wasn't worth mentioning to anyone? Me, for instance?"

"I couldn't be certain, sir. I didn't want to … send your team off on a wild goose chase and—"

"I think it's my job as Senior Investigating Officer to decide what fucking geese to chase."

"Yes sir."

"Then there were two more attempts on Plowright's life. You didn't report those, either, even though you knew by then that they were linked to the Hasely Stone murder."

"I would have come to you at that point, sir, but Daniel said he would give me all the evidence he had if I waited a couple of days."

"And you wanted to walk through the door with your tail up, telling everyone what clever bastards you lot in Racist Crime are."

"It's not the way I would put it, sir."

"Well, I would. Did you talk to any of your colleagues there?"

"I hadn't discovered anything concrete, sir."

"Don't mess me around. Did you tell anyone else?"

"Commander Edwards asked me to keep him up to speed, sir."

"I bloody knew it! I knew it was a mistake bringing a liaison from Racist Crime onto this investigation. And what did Edwards say?"

"He thought you … already had enough on your plate without me … muddying your investigation with speculative information. But I didn't tell him everything, sir. I didn't tell him the two telephone numbers in Chapman's phone belonged to Quentin Plover."

"But you told Plowright, didn't you? You just forgot to tell the SIO of the murder investigation – that's me, by the way – that the bloody Chief of Staff at Number Ten was up to his neck in it."

"I didn't tell Daniel anything else, sir. He'd turned his phone off and I didn't hear from him again until last Thursday—"

"And by that time at least two more people, Paul Eriksson and Todd Hogan, were dead. Deaths that could have been avoided if you'd told your colleagues what you'd discovered."

"We don't know that, sir."

"And when Plowright did ring you on Thursday, what did you do? Did you pick up the phone to tell me two people of interest to this investigation had slipped back into this country and had been in touch? Did you hell. You went for coffee at the Landmark fucking Hotel."

"Commander Edwards didn't know anything about that, sir. Or me calling in the Armed Response Unit on Tower Bridge. It happened too quickly for me to refer up."

"But that won't bother Edwards one little bit, will it? His Command will still get the credit for this collar, not your hard-working colleagues in Homicide and Serious Crime. They've been busting their arses to clear this up whilst you've been in cahoots with your ex-boyfriend. He's a shoo-in for reporter of the year and I'll be awarded twat of the year."

"I'm sorry, sir."

"Get out of my sight, Mahoney. I'm reporting you to Professional Standards. At the very least, this is a failure to carry out lawful orders and very probably gross misconduct into the bargain. Start polishing up your CV."

CHAPTER SIXTY-FIVE

"The pack is back," Daniel said, as the cab turned the corner and Charing Cross Police Station came into view. "Gough's still pissed off, then."

"I reckon he'll want red meat, and that'll be me," Leon said. "I can't see me leaving with you guys today. Not after the problems I had getting into this country last time."

"Come on, Leon, I'm sure you'll be fine."

But Daniel wasn't sure and he could see Ronnie wasn't, either.

Inside, Melanie Booth led them to the same windowless room as before. Adam Gough was there already, sitting alone behind the table with three chairs in front of him. He didn't get up.

"Good morning Dr Ackerman, Mr Plowright, Mr Stone. Sit down. Let's get straight down to business, shall we?"

"I've arranged for a solicitor to represent us," Daniel said. "He should be here within the next few minutes."

"We don't need to wait for him."

"I'm sorry, Commander, but we're not—"

"Do yourself a favour, Mr Plowright. Shut up and sit down." They did as they were told. "First things first. I've totted up how many laws you lot have broken. It's quite a haul. All the way from perverting the course of justice to theft. But … fortunately for you, a decision has been taken – way above my pay grade – to treat you rather more leniently than you deserve.

"Dr Ackerman, you in particular were very close to having the book thrown at you. You of all people should know you don't tamper with forensic evidence."

"I'm sorry, Commander. I promise it won't happen again."

"If I had a pound for every time I'd heard that, I'd be sunning myself on a beach somewhere. On this occasion, I think you might actually mean it."

"I do."

"You're still a very fortunate woman." He threw her American passport across the desk. "You'll need to take it to the Immigration Office in Croydon to get it stamped, since you signed a landing card in a false name with a false passport at Heathrow the other day. They're expecting you. The same goes for you, Mr Stone. You need to do it today because I want you back here at ten thirty tomorrow to complete formal statements. And bring Miss Sellars and Sister Augustine with you. After you've written yours, Mr Stone, the Home Office won't want to see you back in this country for a while, unless you're required to give evidence in court."

"No problem, sir. And I'd be very happy to do that."

"Will I be needed to give evidence?" Ronnie asked.

"The woman who discovered the body of Hasely Stone? I should say so. But the DPP has decided the prosecution won't use evidence from you about everything that happened in the hours leading up to

Professor Stone's murder. In particular, they won't be volunteering any information to the defence about where you slept that night, as long as you admit you were in the house and found the body."

"Thank you, Commander. Thank you so much."

"Don't thank me, Dr Ackerman. Professor Stone wasn't short of influential friends and the powers-that-be have decided his widow has suffered enough. The finer points of her husband's activities during his last few hours won't be part of the prosecution case and splashed all over the tabloids."

"Is there something I'm missing here?" Leon said.

"I'm sure Dr Ackerman can fill you in later on the details of her night with your brother, Mr Stone."

"What will happen to Plover?" a flushed Ronnie asked.

"He'll get life, of course, but don't be surprised if he walks out of an open prison a lot earlier than he deserves. He's talking his head off at the moment."

"They won't let him turn state's evidence and get away with it, will they?"

"We call it 'immunity from prosecution' in this country, Dr Ackerman. But, no. He's in way too deep for that. Chapman's started talking, too."

"What's she saying?" Daniel asked.

"Off the record? And this is off the record, yes?" Daniel nodded. "Gemma Chapman is her real name. She's already admitted killing your brother, Mr Stone. A sad case. Former military police officer, I'm sorry to say. Used to box for the army. In the British Olympic team for London 2012 but got injured. That hit her hard."

Gough slid a photograph across the desk; a woman with long blond hair, warm eyes, a beaming smile and a much thinner face.

"This is Chapman?" Daniel asked.

"Looks like a completely different person, doesn't it? Probably accounts for why our facial recognition software didn't pick her out from the snap you got at London Fields. Anyway, she went off the rails for a while. Left the army and had a daughter, courtesy of a drug dealer in Ipswich who she soon split from. The kid's all she's asking about. Maybe some leverage there."

"So how come she got mixed up with the likes of Plover and Crewton?"

"You can blame Delmar Associates for that, Mr Plowright. They're a security firm. At least, that's how they describe themselves on their website. Based in the City with a number of unsavoury clients. East European oligarchs, mostly. Chapman joined them last year and then Plover hired them a few months ago. We knocked on Delmar's door yesterday with a search warrant. They were in the process of deleting all their files but we found a backup drive full of goodies."

"What about Chapman's oppos?"

"She recruited most of them. Mainly ex-Paras. The one you'll be most interested in is Barrington Williams. Former SAS. Invalided out. But still fit enough to stab you at London Fields, Mr Plowright. He killed Todd Hogan as well, though Chapman says that was an accident. Fell on a kitchen knife in a scuffle, she says. We'll know more when Williams starts talking, which he will if his brief gets him to see sense. Either way, they should be charged tomorrow or the day after."

"Any reason we can't talk to the press now?" Daniel asked.

"I'd rather you didn't but I can't stop you. Just remember this'll soon be 'sub judice'. Dr Ackerman, you need to know our contempt of court laws are rather more draconian than what you're used to in America."

"I've been trying to get in touch with Alice Mahoney but she's not answering her phone," Daniel said.

"That's because I ordered her not to speak to you."

"Why? Is she Okay?"

"Not if I've got anything to do with it. I'll be recommending she's disciplined for gross misconduct. She deliberately kept my team in the dark about what she discovered. Not to mention the unauthorised accessing of telephone records."

"That's really unfair," Ronnie said. "If Alice hadn't traced those phone numbers back to Plover, we'd be dead meat by now. She deserves a medal."

"She deserves to be dismissed from the force. And, if I have my way, she will be."

* * *

Daniel called Francesca Cross immediately they left the interview room.

"Gough says we can give interviews. He's not happy about it, of course, but he knows he can't stop us until Plover and Co are charged. That won't happen till tomorrow at the earliest."

"Great," she replied. "Why don't all five of you do a joint presser here in a couple of hours? That'll keep the Star News brand up there. Should cheer the suits on the seventh floor up a bit. And it'll get the American networks off our backs. Their big anchors have all flown over and they're tearing their hair out for an interview with Ronnie."

CHAPTER SIXTY-SIX

Prime Minister Stephen Truman came out of Number Ten and walked to the lectern.

'Since the shocking news about Gerry Crewton and others emerged on Thursday night, I have been consulting with Cabinet colleagues and the parliamentary party about the implications. I understand charges will be laid shortly.

'Police investigations up to now indicate no other members of this administration were involved in this truly deplorable affair. But the fact remains that this took place on my watch. There are times when politicians have to accept responsibility for events, even when they're not directly to blame. I believe this is one of them. Accordingly, I have decided the only honourable course of action is for me to step down as Prime Minister. No questions at this time. Thank you.'

The five of them watched the statement on Daniel's iPad as a cab took them back to Charing Cross Police Station.

"The whole government will be out next and there'll be a general election before Christmas," he said.

"No chance it'll win under a new leader?" Ronnie asked.

"Not after this. So we won't be handing any more of our great teaching hospitals over to big pharma, thank God. On the downside, they'll have to lift the ban on the BUP, of course. This won't do them any harm at the ballot box."

"So the racists who hated my brother could actually get a sympathy vote out of all this?" Leon said.

"'Fraid so," Daniel replied. "You couldn't make it up, could you?"

* * *

Alice took a deep breath as she walked into Scotland Yard. She was determined not to give Gough the satisfaction of seeing her scared shitless today.

The news that she was out would go round the place like wildfire. By tonight, rivals she'd passed on her meteoric rise up the ladder would be raising a glass in the Dog and Trumpet.

She checked her make-up on the way up in the lift. No mascara. Couldn't trust herself not to cry. Ten years' hard work down the drain.

It wasn't her fault. Most of it wasn't, anyway. More than once, she wanted to tell Gough what she knew. It was Tom Edwards who stopped her.

So she was astonished to find Edwards sitting alongside Gough when she was summoned.

"Remain standing," Gough said. "You're very lucky, DCI Mahoney. My instinct was to pass this over to Professional Standards and I wouldn't have given much for your chances. But Commander Edwards here has … persuaded me there may be another, less confrontational, course of action."

"Sir?"

"You will play no significant part in the prosecution of Quentin Plover and the others. You will need to give a statement, of course, but in it you will describe yourself as a detective chief inspector attached to the Homicide and Serious Crime Command. No mention of Racist Crime. This is my collar, Mahoney." She gulped and nodded. "In return, I won't be requesting a Professional Standards investigation and we'll … overlook the fact that your unauthorised accessing of telephone data was, at the very least, gross professional misconduct and probably illegal."

"Thank you, sir."

"By the way, you can forget 'Detective Superintendent' for the next few months. You remain a DCI. And I'll see to it you're not on the list when the commendations are doled out."

"No, sir. Of course not, sir."

"Neither do I want to see you at the piss-up when this lot eventually go down."

Gough stood up.

"Right. I've got a car outside to take me down to see Mr Plowright and his friends at Charing Cross nick. Clear off, Mahoney."

* * *

"Gough's not taking disciplinary action against Alice," Daniel said, staring at her text on his phone. "Thank God."

"I should think not," said Ronnie. "She saved us."

The door opened. Gough breezed in.

"Good afternoon. I think I've put your friend DCI Mahoney back in her ambitious little box for a while, Mr Plowright."

"Thank you for not throwing the book at her."

"She's told you, then. Don't think I wasn't tempted, but she's seen the error of her ways. And I've got enough on my plate sorting out this lot. Your statements will be ready for you to sign in a few minutes. Then you're free to go."

"Before we do, could you explain a couple of things, commander?"

"As long as it stays within these four walls. Agreed?" Daniel nodded. "What's on your mind?"

"Well, one thing I don't understand is how Stephanie Bright got caught up with these people. Crewton told Ronnie that they needed someone 'to keep an eye on Hasely'. What was the deal there?"

"That was extraordinary foresight on Crewton's part," Gough replied. "He realised how fast Stone's research was progressing and the possible implications of it. So he needed a spy in the camp. He and Bright worked together fifteen years ago, before he went into Parliament. Had a brief affair, apparently. He rang Paul Eriksson to recommend her for a job at the Lipman and she was more than happy to report back to Plover. But Bright discovered an early draft of Stone's press release

351

announcing the protocol and emailed Plover a copy. Stone was terminal after that, and so was she."

"Why did they risk killing Paul Eriksson?"

"Because he knew too much, even if he didn't realise it. Crewton asked him to pass onto Plover any information that came his way, and Eriksson was very conscientious about doing it. That's how they found out about the preliminary DNA results from Du Long and Freyer's lab that linked you to the crime scene, Dr Ackerman."

"We guessed as much," Ronnie said.

"Then Miss Sellars here told him that three patients on Stone's cancer trial had died in a matter of weeks. The moment Eriksson mentioned that to Plover, he was 'dead man walking'."

"You know, I still don't really get why Crewton did all this," Daniel said. "To be honest, he made a fair bit of sense when he talked to you, Ron. The protocol could cause this country real economic problems. But to kill to stop it getting out? Why go that far?"

"Come on," Ronnie said. "You heard him whining on about being in Hasely's shadow. It wasn't just political. It was personal, too."

"Exactly," Gough said. "Plover says Gerry Crewton, far from being Hasely Stone's best friend, hated him. Stone was the more brilliant student. Had much more charisma.

"But there was one place where he didn't play second fiddle. The world of politics. Then his old mate comes up with a discovery that could fatally damage Crewton's ability to run the country before he even walked through the door of Number Ten. He couldn't let that happen. Maybe he thought he might have a chance of getting back with Angela, as well, with her husband out of the way. He hated her being stolen from him. His suicide note was addressed to her."

"So it all came down to the usual," Daniel said. "Sex, jealousy and money."

"Usually does," Gough replied. "The impact of the AI-Protocol on this country was a huge factor, of course, but I doubt if Gerry Crewton would have gone to the lengths he did if someone other than Hasely Stone had discovered it."

There was a knock on the door and Sgt Booth came in with hard copies of their statements.

"Sign these," said Gough. "Then you can all piss off."

* * *

Alice was on her second large Scotch and ice in the D&T when Tom Edwards arrived.

"How on earth did you pull that off, sir?"

"Come on Alice. You're a lot brighter than me. Think about it."

"I just assumed I was finished."

"That's because you're too close to all this. Gough would love to throw the book at you – of course he would – but it would be almost as bad for his career prospects as yours."

"Why?"

"Because it would show he wasn't in control of his own investigation. A senior member of his team hides crucial evidence and the first he knows about it is when an Armed Response Unit catches the buggers in the middle of Tower Bridge? A 'hard stop' he hadn't sanctioned? Doesn't look good."

"So—"

"So if he plays nicely, he can take all the credit for Homicide and Serious Crime. Nobody needs to find out he knew sod all about it until you handed Plover and Chapman to him on a plate. If he doesn't, I made it crystal clear the powers-that-be would find out how far behind the curve he was. Another Scotch?"

* * *

Daniel stopped the cab on the way back to Norwood and bought a couple of bottles of his favourite Lebanese red to go with takeaway pizza.

"At last, we've got something to celebrate," he said. "Well, sort of."

"What's everybody got planned now?" Leon asked.

"They're hoping to hold Todd's funeral in Connecticut at the end of next week," Ronnie said. "That's assuming the county coroner releases his body in time. I'll be there, of course."

"Can I come with you?" asked Daniel.

"I'd like that very much," she said, with a warm smile. "And then Gerard wants me to join him in Enstone, where he's going to scatter Todd's ashes on the slopes. Toddy loved the Rockies more than anywhere."

"Say sorry for me not being there," Leon said, "but I don't reckon Uncle Sam will want me back in the country for a while."

"Don't worry. I'll apologise to him. Any plans, Laura?"

"Well, it's still chaos at the institute—"

"Which won't be moving to Birmingham, you mark my words," Daniel said.

"But we're going into temporary accommodation in Goodge Street next week, so there's plenty to do. And then I thought I might take a holiday,"

"Laura, everyone knows you never take holidays," Ronnie said, giggling. "Where are you going?"

"Well, actually … Leon's invited me to stay with him in Port of Spain and —"

Daniel and Ronnie opened their mouths in unison.

"Life is not a dress rehearsal."

THE END

Printed and bound in the UK by CMP Books, Dorset

**Introducing *Deadly Messages*,
the next Ronnie Ackerman thriller**

CHAPTER ONE

If you're going to make history, dress to kill.

Ronnie Ackerman stood out from her fellow Nobel Prize recipients as they entered the neoclassical splendour of the Stockholm Concert Hall. They were all middle-aged men, wearing regulation white tie and tails. She was dressed in a dazzling maroon evening gown, lent to her by an exclusive Mayfair fashion house.

The Chair of the Nobel Foundation Board stood up.

"Today is a very special day," he said, in meticulous English. "Since 1974, the Statutes of the Nobel Foundation have stipulated that a Prize cannot be awarded posthumously. This year, those statutes have been changed to do precisely that. We believe this is what Alfred Nobel himself would have wanted.

"This year's Nobel Laureate for Physiology or Medicine, Professor Hasely Stone of St Agatha's University Hospital, London, cannot be here today. The discovery for which he is awarded this honour – the most important medical breakthrough in a century, a cure for cancer – led to his death two years ago.

"Professor Stone was murdered in an attempt to stop the world finding out about his momentous discovery and it would still be a secret today were not for the actions of colleagues and friends.

"Already, the lives of hundreds of thousands of patients who have taken part in Phase 3 clinical trials of his Adoptive Immunotherapy Protocol have been saved.

"I now invite Professor Veronica Ackerman, director of the Stone Cancer Research Institute at St Agatha's, to receive this Nobel Prize on his behalf."

Ronnie stood up and approached the Queen. She accepted the diploma, hand-crafted by the finest Swedish calligraphers, and the Nobel medal. Following tradition, she bowed to Her Majesty, the Foundation trustees to her left, the new Nobel Laureates behind her and to the audience, who responded with enthusiastic applause.

Then, in the middle of this most ceremonial of occasions, Ronnie broke all the rules. She walked to a woman standing in the front row with three tall young men. Hasely Stone's widow.

"I'm so pleased you're here, Angela," she said.

"The boys would never have forgiven me if I'd missed it."

"Neither would I. You had to come. And you must have these."

Ronnie handed her the medal and diploma.

Angela shook her head. "They were given to you, for the institute."

"If you decide to donate them to us, they will be displayed in a place of honour. But the hospital believes you and the boys should make that call."

The Chair of the Nobel Foundation appeared at Ronnie's side and escorted Angela Stone and her sons onto the stage, amid more applause.

Ronnie was about to follow them when a man in white tie and tails strode from the side of the hall. Her face lit up.

"Daniel Plowright. What are you doing here? You said your plane was so late you'd never make it."

He kissed her.

"I landed forty-five minutes ago. The British Embassy used its influence to whisk me through Immigration and into a police car. Changing into this garb on the way was a bit of a performance but I got here just before it started."

"I'm so pleased you made it."

"I wouldn't have missed it for the world, my darling. Let's party. You deserve it."

"So do you."

* * *

The check-in agent at Stockholm's Arlanda Airport pursed her lips. It was obvious she wanted to ask Ronnie a question.

"Please could I see your medal, Professor? After ABBA, we Swedes think of the Nobel Prize as our most famous export."

"Of course," Ronnie replied, smiling, and handed it over. "But please be careful. It's made of eighteen-carat gold."

She was thrilled when Angela Stone agreed to the medal and certificate being displayed in the institute that bore her husband's name. She certainly wouldn't have done so, had she known how her husband spent the last night of his life.

Ronnie still harboured bitter regrets about spending that night in Hasely Stone's bed, however many times Daniel mentioned the words 'Me Too'. Of course she'd been the victim of a powerful boss plying her with drink but that didn't stop her feeling like the dumbest Nobel Prize recipient ever.

"You've been upgraded to Business Class for your trip to London," the agent said. "You'll find your fellow Nobel laureate, Professor Chen, is seated just across the aisle."

Ronnie's mobile phone warbled. Daniel.

"Hi. My cab's just arriving at Gray's Inn Road. Tonight's *Star News at Ten* won't fall off air after all."

"It's a shame you couldn't fly back with me. I've just been upgraded."

"I thought you might be. Jack Woodcock's just called. He's on your flight. And he's in Business, too."

"How come? I thought Star's dreary new accountant banned your reporters flying up front."

"Jack wangled an upgrade as well. The Swedes were rather chuffed that we sent a film crew to cover the Nobel ceremony. He's travelling back with your fellow Nobel recipient, Professor Chen. Says he's onto a great story and the prof is key to it. He's cosying up to him on the flight home."

"What's it about?"

"I thought you might be able to wheedle that out of him. He doesn't want to jinx it by telling me anything else."

"I'll ply him with a glass or two of complimentary Champagne at forty thousand feet. That should work."

Ronnie was first on the plane and settled back into her aisle seat. She was half way through her first glass of Charles Heidsieck Brut Réserve when Jack Woodcock came on board.

"Ronnie. I didn't know you were on our flight."

"Call yourself an investigative journalist, Jack?" She smiled at him and Professor Chen, who was just behind. "How are you today, Patrick?"

"Good. My university won't pay for me to sit in the expensive seats very often, so I'm going to enjoy the Business Class experience."

"Same here," replied Ronnie. "This is only the second time I've sat at the front of the bus. And since the last was a short hop in the Caribbean with a multiple murderer sitting a few rows back in Economy, that doesn't really count."

Chen eased himself into the aisle seat across from Ronnie and accepted a glass of bubbly from the ever-attentive cabin staff. So did Jack, sitting next door. Plenty of time to talk to him later.

* * *

"Good afternoon, ladies and gentlemen, boys and girls. First Officer speaking. You may have noticed that the seatbelt signs are now switched off, so feel free to move around the cabin. But please leave the belts loosely fastened when you return to your seats. The flight time to London Heathrow today will be approximately one hour forty minutes. Sunny skies and calm conditions are forecast for our journey, so please sit back, relax and enjoy the flight.

"You might also like to know that we have two celebrities on board today. Professor Veronica Ackerman and Professor Patrick Chen were both presented with the Nobel Prize in Stockholm yesterday. Scandinavian Airlines offers both of them our warmest congratulations."

Applause rippled down the cabin behind Ronnie and she turned to acknowledge it.

At that moment, a young man got up from his seat half way down the plane. He strode up to her row, stopped and turned to face the two passengers across the aisle.

Jack Woodcock never stood a chance.

DIAMOND
CRIME

PASSIONATE ABOUT

CRIME
MYSTERY
THRILLER

BOOKS IT PUBLISHES

diamondbooks.co.uk

DIAMOND
BOOKS

DIAMOND
CRIME

FOLLOW:

Facebook: **@diamondcrimepublishing**
Instagram: **@diamond_crime_publishing**
Twitter: **@diamond_crime**

diamondbooks.co.uk

DIAMOND
BOOKS

Printed in Great Britain
by Amazon